THE
OBTUSE
EXPERIMENT

MALCOLM ROSE

D1634315

adlib... Scholastic Publications Limited

Scholastic Children's Books
Scholastic Publications Ltd,
7-9 Pratt Street, London NW1 0AE

Scholastic Inc.,
730 Broadway, New York, NY 10003, USA

Scholastic Canada Ltd,
123 Newkirk Road, Richmond Hill,
Ontario, Canada L4C 3G5

Ashton Scholastic Pty Ltd,
PO Box 579, Gosford, New South Wales,
Australia

Ashton Scholastic Ltd,
Private Bag 1, Penrose, Auckland,
New Zealand

First published by Scholastic Publications Ltd 1993

ISBN 0 590 55169 8

Printed in England by Clays Ltd, St Ives plc

For the scum of the earth

This isn't a song for your leaders
To hear at their victory parades,
It isn't for the politicians
They can always sing their own praise.

Sometimes they might even glimpse you
As the black Limousine glides past,
Filtered through air-conditioning,
Their vision distorted by bullet-proof glass.

Pity your simple leaders
They can only do simple sums
They equate power with money
And estimate strength in numbers of guns.

Why don't you lie down and die quietly
Instead of persistently staying alive
Cluttering up their statistics
When against all the odds you survive?

You are the wealth of nations
You are the power in the land
You have the power to move mountains
You carry the earth in the palm of your hand.

They only see that you have nothing
They cannot see what you are worth
I sing in praise of the scum of the earth.
There's not much that I can offer
Here's a song for what it's worth
I sing in praise of the salt of the earth.

From the song, *Salt of the Earth*, by Maggie Holland and Jon Moore
© 1988 Rogue Music

acknowledgements

The surnames in this story are not of my own making. I thank my colleagues in analytical chemistry, and mass spectrometry in particular, whose surnames have been purloined and used without permission throughout this novel.

contents

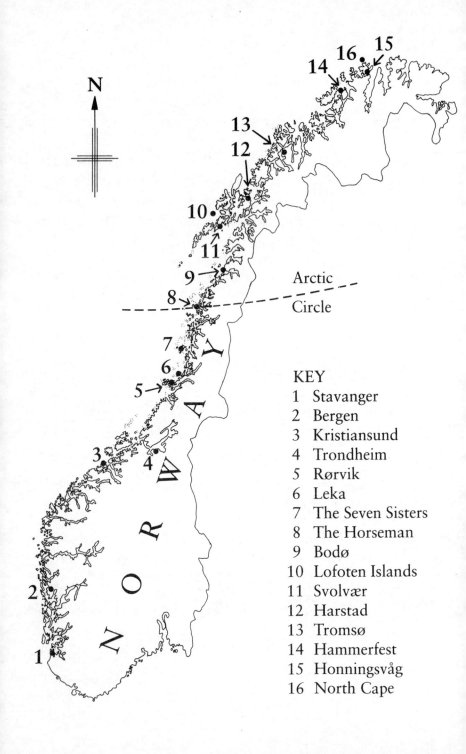

N

Arctic
Circle

NORWAY

KEY
1 Stavanger
2 Bergen
3 Kristiansund
4 Trondheim
5 Rørvik
6 Leka
7 The Seven Sisters
8 The Horseman
9 Bodø
10 Lofoten Islands
11 Svolvær
12 Harstad
13 Tromsø
14 Hammerfest
15 Honningsvåg
16 North Cape

The Embarking

Once, the dockland boasted working building-berths and rows of giant cranes with arms swinging this way and that. In stifling workshops, massive steel plates and bars were heated, cut, bent and drilled. Bolted together, they made strong skeletons from which great ships evolved. But all that activity had ceased a long time ago. No longer did the crowds gather to watch an ocean liner or an oil tanker slither for the first time into the sea. Even so, the quayside was again alive with colour, noise and people. A razzmatazz fit for the old days. There were flags, the local brass band, a host of parents jostling, waiting and waving with mixed feelings, three hundred impatient children in four long queues waiting to embark, the ship itself (the once proud *Queen of the Fjords*), even the Minister for Education (the still proud Mr Sternhell), and a swarm of reporters and photographers.

Suddenly, the brass band stopped its cacophony and, on cue, the clamour of the crowd slowly died away. Among the first line of schoolkids, Gabby turned to her sister, Gail, and muttered, 'Here we go. Sternhell's going to smile and, if he can manage it, talk at the same time.'

The MP's normally sombre face cracked into a sincere smile as he stepped towards the microphone. He thrived, as would any politician, in this situation. Clicking cameras, hundreds of happy children, even more hundreds of grateful parents and voters, and a silence waiting to be filled. It was his day, his time. He had planned everything meticulously. No one suspected anything. He couldn't put a foot wrong. The sun shone and the two rainclouds on the horizon made no move towards the docks. Even a seagull, circling overhead, curious about the hoo-ha and spotting a politician, missed Mr Sternhell's head and did it instead on his right shoe.

In the second queue of children, Alan Splinter cursed. 'Damn!' he said. 'That would've been better than egg on his face.'

Mr Sternhell glanced down momentarily and, undaunted, still confident that nothing could go wrong, took a deep breath.

Gabby grumbled, 'I knew it. A bloody speech.' Gail sighed and carefully put down the large holdall that she was carrying.

'We're here,' Mr Sternhell began, 'to see off all these children on the most important and valuable journey of their lives. And it's no ordinary voyage. They will, courtesy of the Government's new initiative – the OBTUSE programme – see foreign lands in an enlightening, rewarding adventure that, without OBTUSE, they would never have had the opportunity to experience.'

Alan whispered to his neighbour, a boy named Roger, 'Yes. One's tempted to ask what brought on this laudable but highly uncharacteristic fit of generosity, isn't one? Beware of Greeks bearing gift horses.'

'Er, yeah,' Roger replied. 'What's this OBTUSE mean, though?'

'It's what you're on now. Roger Klotts, this is your big

break. To go on the very first Overseas Boat Trip for Unsettled Schoolchildren in England.'

'Oh, I never knew that.'

'What? That you're officially classified as unsettled? One of life's deviants.'

'No,' Roger answered. 'Someone told me it meant mysterious.'

Alan grinned, but not unkindly. 'That's *abstruse*. But you might be right – OBTUSE is mysterious enough. Not a mystery tour, more a mystery why we're being sent on a tour.' All of the humour drained from his face as he added, 'He's got a scheme, has Sternhell. A big fat juicy one, if you ask me. No ordinary voyage! He ain't kidding. There's something nasty in the air.'

'How do you mean?'

'Watch him. He doesn't look at us, the kids. It's like we didn't matter – or maybe he's too ashamed to look us in the eye. He's playing a dirty game and we're pawns on a sticky wicket. I don't like it.'

Mr Sternhell was still revelling in the limelight. 'Now, I don't want to turn this address into a speech, or party political broadcast,' he smiled and paused for laughter, 'but I feel it encumbent upon me to say a few words to our children on how they can reap the richest educative rewards from this trip. For five weeks, they will observe, note, undertake projects, and learn to live together in a new community. After all, learning to live together in our new world order is, in many ways, the most important lesson of all. It requires consideration, discipline, virtue and, of course, adherence to the rules – the law.'

'Yes,' Alan griped. 'We live in virtuous times. And if you don't conform, you've had it. Wouldn't his regime just love to outlaw individuality? It's such a nuisance.'

'Whilst on board, there will be normal lessons as well,' the Education Secretary droned on. 'Conducted by a hand-picked team of teachers.' He waved towards a group of adults who were already on board and forming a line against the rail of the upper deck.

'Hand-picked for the job!' Gabby exclaimed. 'Look like a bunch of dickheads to me.' The boy in front of her giggled. 'Ah,' she said, 'someone agrees. What's your name?' she asked boldly.

'Mike,' he said in a faltering voice. 'Mike Zlatkis.'

'Okay, Mike,' Gabby replied, nudging him. 'Perhaps I'll see you later, on board.'

'Er,' Mike answered awkwardly. 'Maybe.'

'It's a date, then,' Gabby smiled, enjoying the embarrassment that she was causing him.

Sternhell was about to conclude. 'So,' he was saying, 'it is with the greatest of pleasure that I stand down and allow embarkation to continue. To allow these children to embark upon the adventure of a lifetime. And then to allow the *Queen* to set sail for the fjords. To slip anchor from these magnificent docks to a bright new future.'

During the polite applause, Alan commented dryly, 'For "magnificent docks" read "once decent shipyard converted into yuppie housing development".' Then he added, 'For "adventure" read "skulduggery".'

The bustle and brass band music resumed. The *Queen* joined in by sounding her vulgar horn. Like everyone else,

Gabby jumped at the sudden loud boom. 'Boring old fart,' she exclaimed. 'Gives a whole new meaning to the ship's poop.' Then she gave Mike a friendly push in the back. 'Go on,' she said. 'Your turn next.' She hesitated then grinned. 'Not to blow off. To check in.'

The man who checked Mike's identity card sported a tasteful sailor's outfit. He wasn't going anywhere; he was just joining in the spirit of the occasion. He ran Mike's card through a machine and waited for his monitor to respond. 'Ah, Zlatkis, M.,' he said. 'Alphabetically speaking, you're the pits.' He looked up at Mike to see if the humour was well taken. Mike did his best to smile. Actually, he was longing to see what the computer was reporting about him but his view was restricted to the back of the VDU. 'Let me see,' the man said, as he scanned the monitor. 'What's this?' Mike waited rather nervously. 'Mm, can I take a look at your case?' As Mike handed over his bag, the official responded, 'No, not the bag. That splendid-looking case.'

Reluctantly, Mike put it on the counter. The man stood up and tried to open the case. He failed. 'The key please, Mr Zlatkis.' Even more reluctantly, Mike gave him the key. The case opened to reveal a keyboard and small screen. '*Very* nice,' the man said, with real admiration and enthusiasm. 'This will have cost. Best portable computer I've seen. Dual disc drive too.' Mike said nothing at all. 'But,' the official continued, 'you won't be needing it on board. You're on holiday from that sort of thing.'

'But ...' Mike tried to find an excuse to keep his computer. 'It'll be useful in class.'

'Oh, you'll be given a calculator for that. Nothing wrong with calculators. In my day, it was a slide rule and log book – dreadful things. Anyway, this,' he said, closing the case, 'will be kept safe for you till you get back.'

'But,' Mike still protested, 'it's only a PC. What harm can it do?'

'Yeah,' Gabby chipped in. 'Let him take it if he wants to. Why not?'

Gail tapped her sister's shoulder and whispered, 'Don't make trouble, remember.'

The man ignored Gabby and said to Mike, 'We both know what *you* can do with one of these.' He swung the case down behind his desk and out of view. 'No arguments,' he said in a sergeant major's voice. 'You can embark now. Block G is where you've been put, on Deck 3. Go on. You're holding up the queue.'

Mike muttered something angrily then turned and trudged towards the gangway, shaking his head sadly as he went.

'Next,' the man said, apparently forgetting the incident immediately, like a doctor preparing to examine another patient.

Gabby stepped forward with Gail in her shadow. 'Hello, sailor,' Gabby chuckled. 'You can do us together. The Grobb sisters.'

'Ah, yes,' the man said once he'd processed their cards. 'G and G. The Grobb twins, in fact.' He hesitated. 'Hang on. What's this?' His face crinkled as he looked at his monitor.

'What?' Gail asked anxiously, from over Gabby's shoulder.

'Twins with different dates of birth. How come?'

'Ah,' Gabby explained, 'I'm older, by twenty minutes. I arrived at ten to midnight and Gail …'

'Arrived ten minutes after,' the man interrupted. 'Got it! I understand.'

'Bleeding genius,' Gabby muttered.

'Gabby …' her sister warned, quietly.

'Yes, well,' he said, nonplussed by Gabby's retort. 'You can go on now. I think it's someone's idea of a joke to put the Grobbs in cabin G1.'

'Hilarious. Cell Block G, room 1,' Gabby replied smartly.

The sisters picked up their bags and walked away. They had gone only a few steps when the official called after them. 'Miss Grobb – of the Gail variety.'

Gail gasped and turned, holding onto her heavy bag with both hands. The man called, 'We do supply kitchen sinks, you know. You don't have to bring your own.'

It was Gabby who shouted back. 'She's a devil for shoes and frocks is our Gail. Brings the lot. Us girls do have to look our best, sailor.'

The man laughed and shook his head. 'Women! Go on!'

Gail sighed and lugged her holdall away. When out of sight of the man at the desk, she put the bag down and whispered into it. 'Done it! Not long now. We just need to find the cabin, then it'll be over.'

'All right, you lot! Get your bags in your cabins, then all hands up on deck to wave your fond farewells to your beloved parents.'

Gabby put her head round the door of cabin G1 to see a man, in his thirties and halfway dishy, stomping up and down G section, banging on the doors. He didn't look like one of the ship's crew – in jeans, tee-shirt and trainers, he was not smart enough for that – but he did have an unwelcome air of authority. 'Oi,' she called after him. 'Do we *have* to wave to our parents? They're only too pleased to see the back of us and we won't see them in the crowd anyway.'

'It's your duty as daughter and heir to get up to the Sun Deck – as it appears to be called – and wave. Sternhell needs happy smiling faces in the papers tomorrow.'

'Humph. Do I have to listen to you?' Gabby replied. 'Who are you?'

'I'm afraid you do. I'm Mr Beever. I'll do the introductions later, but basically I'm your form teacher. My form being Block G.'

'Cell Block G more like it. Have you seen the size of these cabins?'

Mr Beever laughed. A raucous laugh, quite unlike a teacher's. 'Good name. That's what we'll call it. And my guess is that we call you Gabby Grobb. Right?'

'In one. Fame at last.'

'Well, I cheated. Recognized you from the details in your file.'

'File, eh?'

''Fraid so. I get a file on each of my charges, or inmates. They've given me the scum of the earth, if I'm to believe them.'

'Don't then. Salt of the earth is what we are.'

'Don't be put out. I never believe files. And there'll be a

great big fat one on me somewhere as well, no doubt. Anyway, I'll talk to you about your record in due course. Private counselling, we'll call it. But for now,' he said firmly, 'upstairs with you. Practise your royal handwaving for your mum and dad, and the cameras. Just think, you could be in the *Sun* tomorrow.'

'We don't have to take our clothes off as well, do we?'

'Just get your sister and get waving.' Mr Beever turned away and carried on along the narrow metallic corridor, knocking on doors. There were a couple of lads standing outside cabin G7. Clearly, they had heard Mr Beever's exchange with Gabby because one of them said to him, 'I hate to throw a spanner in the ointment, but Roger and I must be excused, surely. Neither of us has parents out there, eager to get emotional for the cameras and their offspring. Mine are away at a conference and Roger ...'

'I ain't got parents no more.'

'Haven't got parents any more,' Mr Beever corrected. 'But both of you have a duty to be happy, grateful and photogenic.'

'That's the problem. If I'm seen in the *Sun*, I'll be a laughing stock when I get back,' the first boy objected, not entirely seriously.

'Parents at a conference and a morbid fear of the *Sun*,' Mr Beever hesitated, searching through his memory. 'You must be Alan Splinter, young political activist of the learned family fame.' Seeing Alan nod, he continued, 'So what's the problem? Get up there and smile just at the *Guardian* photographer as we set sail into Sternhell's bright new future. And I'll see you later. We'll get on well, you and I.' Turning to

Roger, Mr Beever said, 'And you look like the beefiest of my crew – you can fight a way to the front of the delirious seething masses for Alan and yourself.'

As soon as he had got rid of Alan and Roger, a third boy appeared. He was listening to his personal stereo, slouching down the corridor to some inaudible music, not hearing a word of Mr Beever's shouts. As the boy came past, Mr Beever lifted off one of his headphones and said, 'Dump your bag and get upstairs.'

'Sure,' he answered, probably without even hearing what had been said to him.

'What's that you're listening to?'

'Oh, you won't have heard of them,' he said dreamily.

'Let me listen.' Mr Beever put his ear to the headphones and smiled. 'I approve,' he said. 'It's Blind Noise.'

'Hey, that's impressive for ...' The boy hesitated, realizing that he was about to be rude.

'For someone my age?' Mr Beever laughed. 'I may be ancient but my ears are still in working order. Who are you?'

'Charlton, sir.'

'Bobby Charlton? Charlton Heston?'

Charlton looked puzzled. Clearly he hadn't heard of either. 'Ng, sir. Charlton Ng's the name.'

The teacher hesitated. For a moment, he contemplated a less flippant approach for this particular boy, but he dismissed the idea. He would be doing Charlton a disservice to single him out for special treatment right from the start. 'Ah yes. Charlton Ng,' he replied. 'And I'm Beever. Mr Beever's the name.' He opened to door to cabin G9. 'You're one of the lucky ones. A cabin to yourself. Sling your bag inside and get up to the Sun Deck. And if I were you I'd keep listening to Blind Noise. The whole business will be less painful that way.'

Mr Beever strutted away, singing the song by Blind Noise. Charlton stared after him, first in wonder, then in admiration. For the first time in an age, a smile appeared on Charlton's face.

Actually, it *was* worth being on deck for the big send-off. Because, even to the amateur, it was clear that the captain made a wrong turn and very nearly rammed a jetty as the ship edged its way, painfully slowly and in reverse, out of the dockland. When the stern got closer and closer to the jetty, dock workers on the quay and deck-hands on board ran around in panic but the *Queen* merely touched the jetty rather than actually rammed it.

'Looks like the driver is as big a wally as the teachers,' Gabby commented.

'There's nothing designed to annoy a sailor more than calling the captain a driver,' Alan noted with pleasure. 'Anyway, he's just trying to finish off the destruction of British docks.'

Charlton, a boy of few words normally, came to the defence of the teachers. 'Mr Beever seems okay – at least he does to me.'

'Yeah. Me too,' Roger echoed.

'Why? Because he hasn't let you down yet?' Gabby sneered. 'Give him time.'

The thickly painted metal plates that formed the base of the Sun Deck, and the rails around the deck, visibly shook as the *Queen of the Fjords* wheeled slowly round to face the open sea. Once she was set on course, she sounded her dreadful foghorn twice more in a last farewell to the crowd on dry land.

'At least the driver knows which button operates the horn, even if he's not sure about the steering wheel,' Gabby said. 'If only he can find the choke and accelerator, we can get going.'

The strong vibrations, which seemed to make all of the fittings rattle in resonance, were replaced by a tolerably gentle throbbing. The *Queen* belched smelly grey smoke from her funnel then gathered speed as she approached the gap in the harbour walls that curved out into the sea. Like a kidnapper, she raced to escape through the gap between the arms of the harbour before they closed in a protective embrace, landlocking the port and returning her victims to the safety of mother earth. But the ship slipped away unhindered. No one tried to arrest her. The abduction was a complete success. The young passengers filtered towards the decks at the stern to watch their parents, the fishermen lining the harbour walls, the idle cranes, and then the dock itself receded into the distance. They watched till a sudden cold wind drove them all inside.

Back on the quayside, the members of the brass band had mercifully ceased playing 'Sailing' and were packing up their instruments. Parents had stopped waving and, feeling empty, relieved and slightly anxious, were making their way out of the enclosure. The press had decamped quickly and were hoping that a disaster might happen, or royalty might appear, in the vicinity. Mr Sternhell's chauffeur had positioned the black Limousine conveniently to speed the Minister back to the House for an afternoon debate on the role of the armed services. As he settled himself in the back of the car for a comfortable return journey to London, Sternhell's face bore a self-satisfied smile. Amongst the entire throng that now diffused away from the quay, he alone knew the true destination – or destiny – of the *Queen of the Fjords*.

Beever's Briefing;

Bad Vibrations

'We are gathered here today,' Mr Beever began his mock sermon, 'in this converted lounge that serves as Block G form-room to learn about living on board, the facilities on offer, the schedules for classes, the meal-times, laundry and medical arrangements, details of the cruise, sleeping arrangements, and the meaning of life. In fact, there's ninety minutes so crammed full of facts that you'll forget most of them or die of boredom before I get to half-time. So, instead, we'll use the time to get over some essential info and to get to know one another a little. Because there are twenty-nine of you, I'll split you into smaller manageable groups so you can get to know each other a few at a time. Indeed, some of you have already met – during embarkation or even before that, living in the same area, going to the same school or, in one case, living in the same house. I think you've all seen me but, just in case, I'm Trevor Beever – your form teacher. Governor of Cell Block G, as Gabby over there has christened it.

'So, first, a roll-call on the inmates of Cell Block G. Let's take a couple of rows at a time, knowing that every two rows will become a group later on. Start here,' he said, pointing to Roger. 'You can just shout out your names in turn. Nothing fancy and no cheating – no Donald Ducks – just the name you'd like to be known by and your family name. Okay? Go on.'

'Roger Klotts. Is that what you want?'

'Yes. Nothing too arduous. Just a name. Then it's Alan, isn't it?'

'Yes. Alan Splinter,' he said clearly, for the whole class to hear.

Next it was Mike. 'Zlatkis,' he said. 'Mike Zlatkis.' His voice betrayed someone who was already a little seasick or homesick, or from whom a prized possession had been removed.

An even quieter voice behind him said, 'Ng. Charlton Ng.'

'Squirrell,' the next boy called. 'Graham.'

'You don't shorten it to Gray, do you?' asked Mr Beever, grinning. Graham shook his head. 'Just as well,' Mr Beever said, as everyone in the class except Graham chortled. 'You and I make a fine pair: Beever and Squirrell.' Again the class laughed, apart from Graham who didn't look the jovial type. His face was flabby for a boy of fifteen, with folds of skin under his chin. A frown seemed to be a frequent feature of his face and his thick lips were downturned. The overall appearance was of a dour character who did everything deliberately and precisely. A pernickety miserable bugger, as Gabby would have put it.

In fact it was Gabby's turn to introduce herself next. No one had trouble hearing her. 'Well, you know me, Trev. Grobb number one, Gabby.'

Much quieter, but quickly before Gabby got into trouble, her sister announced herself, 'Gail Grobb.'

Behind her, a boy with a long scar on his left cheek said, 'Peter,' and nothing else.

'Peter what?' Mr Beever queried.

'Peter Fallick, I'm afraid.'

This brought on another fit of giggles, especially from Gabby. Roger turned and whispered to Alan, 'Why's everyone laughing?'

'Because,' Alan whispered back, 'it means he's a prick.'

'Oh,' Roger murmured. 'He looks all right to me.'

'Okay. Settle down,' Mr Beever cried. 'I see that I'm going to have trouble with this first group. Anyway, let's carry on.'

'Toni Junk,' said the girl behind Peter.

'Okay,' Mr Beever interrupted. 'End of the first two rows and we'll call it Group A – or maybe the Splinter Group.' He continued through the other four rows till everyone had given their names. 'Good,' he said, sitting himself on the desk at the front and swinging his legs to and fro. 'Now, fifteen or twenty minutes of important info, followed by an hour in group sessions. Then three members of the crew will arrive to escort the three groups around the ship. I'll join Group A for that. We'll see all the interesting bits, locate quite a few boring bits as well, I dare say, and get a talk on safety. What to do if an iceberg hits us and so on. In other words, generally get our bearings on board. And we'll have a sort of assembly to hear from the Headteacher – Mr Uunk – who'll tell you all about maintaining dignity whilst on board.

'So, the promised information. Behind me on the wall you see a map or, as us sailors call it, a chart. The red dotted line shows our intended course. You can examine it later in groups. As you already know, we're headed for Norway with five ports of call. First, Stavanger. We'll have a tour of the fjords there, and a few trips on land. From there we sail to Norway's second biggest city, Bergen. There'll be another tour of fjords when we make a brief call at Kristiansund. The fourth stop's Trondheim. We'll see quite a lot there. Ancient rock carvings and that sort of thing. One of the overland trips will be to a place called Hell, by the way. Now, if you could see the map clearly from where you are, you'd see that as we sail north from Trondheim, we'll cross a dotted line. Any ideas what it might be?'

Gabby piped up, 'It's where you fold the map when you put it away.'

'Very droll, Gabby. But wrong. This line is curved. That's a hint.'

'The Arctic Circle,' said a quiet voice behind Gail. It was Peter.

'Spot on. Across the Arctic Circle, a long slog up the coast to our last port of call, Hammerfest. Famous for being the most northerly town in the world and dark from mid-November to mid-January. When we're there, it'll be light all the time, called the midnight sun. I hear a rumour that we might also pop up to North Cape – weather permitting.

'So what do you do as we cruise around? Sit with your feet up? Play table tennis? Congregate on the stairs between decks making nuisances of yourselves? Well, a bit of all those, no doubt, but also some work.' Mr Beever paused for groans. 'But given that we're into the second half of the summer term, your timetable is not exactly strenuous – even for you lot. Here it is. Take a copy and pass the rest round. It's self-explanatory, I think, so I don't have to go on about it. You'll find the other classrooms in due course. They're converted rest rooms and the like. There's also a library on board, you'll be glad to know, and I'm sure that much of your so-called free time will be spent in there working on your chosen projects.' More groans. 'Yes, there are lots of topics for you to pick from, like "Rock carving", "Northern lights", "Norwegian geology", "Stave churches", and "Midnight sun". There's nothing, as far as I know, on Norwegian saunas and nude bathing, so hard luck.'

Mr Beever hesitated as he collected his thoughts. 'The meal-times are shown on your timetable too. The food will be great – assuming that you like fish. There's a shop where you can buy extras: chocolate, and toothbrushes to minimize the damage of the chocolate. As a special offer, the duty-free shop will remain closed throughout the tour.

'What else?' He paused. 'Yes. The free periods – when you're not in the library – can be used for recreation. There's a TV room so you can keep up with the soaps and the news. More importantly, there's a surprisingly good music room and a small but reasonable gym. The games room has darts, table tennis, snooker and the like. Snooker must be fun in rough seas – which is why the games room is locked unless we're docked or in calm water. And there's a swimming pool that's seen better days – but it's okay. Now, I'm also supposed to tell you how to behave. For example, it's your responsibility to keep your cabins clean and reasonably tidy. It's no luxury cruise, this one. There are few cleaners and they only do general areas on board, not individual cabins. That means once a week you'll have to take used bed linen to the laundry and collect new sheets for yourselves. It's all good for the soul. There's a list a mile long of dos and don'ts – mainly don'ts. You know, no library books in the swimming pool, no skinny dipping, no mixed sexes in the cabins at night, and so on. Let's just say use common sense: if you're enjoying doing something, stop it. It's probably not allowed. Seriously,' he said after the laughter died away, 'I don't like having to tell you off all the time – it makes life miserable for everyone. So enjoy yourselves, and don't go too far.

'Now, what about questions? Not technical stuff about ships. You'll get that from a real sailor later. He's the one to teach you how to yell "Man overboard!" and the like.'

'You mean "Person overboard",' Toni shouted, resentfully.

'Sorry. I stand corrected,' Mr Beever replied. 'Now, what about questions? Surely I missed out more than I put in.'

Graham Squirrell put up his hand. 'I see,' he said, looking down at his timetable, 'that there are a few RE lessons but I can't see a time dedicated to worship. I assume there is one.'

'Ah, yes,' Mr Beever answered. 'There will, on Sunday mornings, be a sort of united church service. No particular denomination. And no compulsory attendance. Just a simple service which should fulfil spiritual needs but not cause inter-denominational fighting. Okay?' He paused then said, 'Well, if that's the only question from Cell Block G, let me ask one. What do you know of Norway? Say, its climate. Gabby? Any more bright ideas from you?'

'It's fucking cold.'

'Well … It's a direct, expressive answer. It could be more concise though – the adjective was inappropriate and unnecessary. But let's not quibble about it now. Think of Norway. And don't be fooled by its northerly location. The days at this time of year will be long and quite warm. What about ice? Do the ports get clogged up with ice? Anyone?'

'No.' It was Peter Fallick's quiet but confident voice again. 'The Gulf Stream keeps the coast warm. If you want to crunch through pack-ice you'd have to be going further north – Svalbard maybe. Where the polar bears roam. We won't see any icebergs except maybe in the north Norwegian Sea. We're off their normal tracks so if we see any they'll probably be tiddlers. A Russian cruiser once came to grief up there but that was a freak. Not really much chance of doing a Titanic.'

'That's all we need. A know-it-all. Someone who thinks he's God's gift to G Block,' a voice complained.

'Enough of that,' Mr Beever snapped. 'He's right. Away from the coast and at our northern-most point we might see floating ice and our course may be dictated by steering clear of trouble, but the ports remain ice-free.'

'Given the greenhouse effect and the Arctic ozone hole,' Alan said aloud, 'I'm surprised that icebergs aren't extinct.'

'Changing the subject to something important,' Gabby called out, 'what sort of night-life does this tub offer?'

'Oh, sitting out on deck gazing at stars, quiet reading, writing up your diaries. But,' Mr Beever added before he received another mouthful from her, 'there'll be the odd disco too. Given the people that run these things, it'll probably be very odd – all eighties and nineties stuff. Perhaps, though, you can get Charlton to donate a few of his tapes so you have some decent modern music too. I'll either keep away so you can enjoy yourselves, or I'll come for a while and you can watch me making a fool of myself. Anyway,' Mr Beever said, looking at his watch, 'time to split into smaller groups to sort out who's doing which topic, talk about yourselves if you wish, look at sea charts and so on. Oh,' he added as if it were really an afterthought, 'I'll also start seeing you individually too. Just for a few minutes so we can get to know each other.'

'Ah, Gabby. Sit down,' Mr Beever said.

'What for?'

'Humour me, Gabby, just for a minute. But don't get too comfortable. I haven't got much to say.'

'Good.'

Mr Beever smiled. 'I've a report on you as thick as a textbook. Now, I know you like being concise so let me summarize it. If I were the powers-that-be I'd do it in four words, "No respect for authority". And,' he added, '"Doesn't suffer fools gladly".'

'That's eight words. Mainly inappropriate and unnecessary, as you put it. So what?'

'So, that's fine. As far as I can see, the authorities you've met so far don't seem worthy of much respect. So ... there's no problem. At least there isn't a problem if, when you meet authority that *does* deserve respect, you're capable of giving it. You don't have to be antagonistic all the time.'

Gabby shrugged and rose. 'Are you done?'

'Yes. That's your lot. But don't forget it's a two-way thing, Gabby. You've got to convince me that *you're* worthy of respect as well.'

Gabby eyed him suspiciously. 'I don't need respect from a teacher,' she snarled and turned to leave.

'If,' Mr Beever asked Charlton, 'I were to ask you what I'd said in that briefing – don't worry, I'm not actually asking – you'd have some trouble. Right?'

Charlton did not look up. He just nodded.

Mr Beever laughed. 'It's all right. No criticism meant. You were miles away and I just wondered what you were thinking about.'

'This and that, I guess.'

'Music?'

'I suppose so.'

'Well, that's all right.'

'It is?' Charlton looked at Mr Beever for the first time during the interview.

'Sure. We all need to escape from our everyday lives sometimes. You know,' Mr Beever shuffled in his seat, 'I think it's important to tell you that I have been told what happened a year ago.'

Charlton's eyes dropped again. 'So you hate me for it as well.'

With candour Mr Beever replied, 'No, I don't. Charlton, if you remember only one thing from this trip, it should be that not everyone has the same view as the law. What you did was ... courageous and kind. There's no question of *blame*. Do you hear me?'

Charlton nodded, but without much conviction. His experience told him that a few kind utterances would be barely audible among the many shouts of condemnation. He brightened a little, though, because he felt that he might just get close enough to Mr Beever to hear his words of encouragement and support.

'Okay, I'm not going to go on about it. But let me just make a comment. You can escape from it by withdrawing only for so long. I want you to *construct* as well as escape. Get lost in music by all means but in a constructive way. You could begin to learn to play an instrument while you're on this trip, or you could try your hand at writing lyrics maybe. And you're something of an artist too, I understand. Let's work on that as well. Mix your escapism with construction. Okay?'

'Mike. Or can I give you your full name of Mike "The Hacker" Zlatkis?'

'You know about that, then.' Mike turned bright red.

'They tell me everything. Whether I want to know or not. Anyway,' Mr Beever said, 'I have a great admiration for people like you. Such persistence and lateral thinking required. I'd love to be able to do it myself. Not for greed and malice. I don't admire that sort of hacking, not hi-tech theft. I'd be like you – driven by curiosity and mischief. You've never gone in for financial swindles, have you?'

Mike shook his head. 'No.'

'Just the pleasure of cracking a system – like a code. Or doing cryptic crosswords. But you did wreak havoc with some sensitive Government data files, didn't you?'

'I guess so.'

'Well done.'

Mike looked surprised, amazed in fact. 'Is that all you're going to say about it? No lecture?'

'No lecture. I just wish we could exploit and develop your skills, but I haven't been able to lay my hands on a computer for you.' He leaned towards Mike. 'They know you and your aptitude too well.'

'They took my own PC off me before I came on board,' Mike moaned.

'Really? That was naughty of them – and uncalled for. I wish I could help, but the cupboard is bare. We'll have to discover different channels into which you can put your con- siderable energies.'

Trevor Beever buried his head in his hands. After his first day on board, he was still apprehensive about the OBTUSE ex- periment. He'd chatted with many of his charges and could describe very few of them as unsettled – whatever that meant. So what was OBTUSE all about? Probably nothing sinister, he thought, but he remained wary. The children were not so much unsettled as unruly – society's outcasts. That's all. There's nothing wrong with them, he said to himself, it's just the way they've been treated by adults or cheated by life.

There was Gail, who seemed to be regarded by her father as the runt of the litter. If the social services had got it right, she'd endured a lot at the hands of her father. When talk- ing to Gail, she had given little away to Mr Beever. He, and maybe men in general, didn't have her confidence. A separation from her father seemed best for Gail, but, given his position as a leading industrialist, it was even more convenient for him. Whilst Gail took it all and coped by withdrawing into herself, Gabby was strong enough to rebel. But that same strength of character that had allowed her to escape her father's attentions had brought her into conflict with all other forms of authority.

There there was Peter Fallick. Doctor's son and errant genius. A gifted child who had not been pushed enough, he'd become disillusioned. Unable to cope with him, schools – and most of his fellow pupils – shunned him. He'd reacted by shunning schools. He had the distinction of being expelled from three schools that couldn't offer him what he needed. And Cell Block G also housed the religious fanatic, Graham Squirrell. One whose faith was just a mite too fervent. He was not part of the conservative and powerful Christian Family Movement. His views were too off-beat to sit comfortably with the CFM. In fact, Graham's parents had called in the CFM in an attempt to deprogramme him, but it'd had the opposite effect. His quirky faith was strengthened by the experience. In desperation, they put him forward for OBTUSE.

These kids were hardly unsettled, just a class with more characters than normal. A handful, no doubt, and an interesting challenge. But what, Trevor asked himself, does OBTUSE have to offer them? He shook his head. There was no obvious answer. Perhaps he was looking for conspiracies where none existed.

The engine throbbed endlessly throughout the night. The *Queen* left behind her a perfectly straight trail of white water on black. Occasionally, every metal plate, every door and every nut and bolt seemed to rattle – apparently trying to shake free of the vessel – then the moment passed and the contented purring returned.

Several members of Cell Block G were still awake, chatting in the Common Room over mugs of coffee. 'It's not the constant vibrations,' Toni was saying, 'or the smell of paint, mixed with exhaust fumes. It's not even the size of the cabins. It's the whiteness of everything. Corridors, cabins and common rooms, even the plastic tables and chairs on deck – all the same whiter than white. I bet it was designed by a man. No imagination. Just slap a job lot of white emulsion over everything.'

'Perfect for graffiti,' Gabby noted.

'Yeah. That would help,' Toni agreed. 'It needs a bit of colour.'

'I reckon our Beever would call that going too far,' said Alan Splinter. 'Besides, the shop's not likely to stock aerosols. That would be tempting fate, as well as the resilience of the ozone layer.'

'It won't sell anything interesting – and the duty-free shop's not opening at all,' Gabby grumbled.

'We could do something about that,' Toni whispered.

Roger's ears pricked up. 'What do you mean?'

'Locks are made for picking.'

'Do you really do that sort of thing?' Gabby asked her.

'It has been known. Beever talked to me about it today in my counselling session. He knew all about my record.'

'Record?' Roger queried.

'Oh, nothing serious. No ram-raiding or anything like that,' Toni replied. 'Bit of shoplifting. Bit of bike thieving, breaking and entering. That sort of thing.'

'Bikes?'

'Well, I fix bikes for friends, you see. I have a knack with them. Some of the bikes I got brought weren't 100 per cent legit, though. You know. Take in four, do a pick and mix to produce three unrecognizable ones. It was profitable for a while. Till I got nicked.'

'No wonder you don't go in for ram-raiding. Not on your bike,' Gabby chipped in.

'What's Mr Beever say?' Roger asked. 'Did he give you a rollocking?'

'No. He was mega-sympathetic really,' she answered. 'Seemed to regard it as natural to expect a bit of charity from Tescos if you're broke and hungry.'

'Yeah. He was like that with me,' said Roger. 'I ain't short on cash but he didn't have a go at me for thieving, either.'

'If you've got the cash,' Toni asked, 'why do you do it?'

Roger shrugged. 'Mr Beever said I was after thrills and attention, like. I don't know. Just that I only feel alive when I'm thieving or joy-riding. Know what I mean?'

'Joy-riding? Really?'

'Yeah,' Roger answered. 'Once did over a hundred down the M1. Chased by cops, we was. Great! Crashed in Coventry in the end. It got reported on the radio. Me, on the radio! We was ... I don't know ... important for a bit. Know what I mean?'

'I know it means that Beever was right about wanting attention,' Gabby replied. 'But it sounds good to me. A radio star.'

Toni cautioned, 'Infamy isn't the same as being important.'

'It's not far off,' Gabby rejoined. Turning to Roger, she asked, 'Did you get hurt when you crashed?'

'Not really. You don't think of getting hurt – or caught. You just think of going faster and faster. It's great. Like when I was little. I used to jump out in front of cars, just to see them swerve. Wicked.'

'Bet your parents are ultra-respectable,' Toni surmised. 'You're just rebelling.'

'Dunno. They had pots of dosh. Used to tell me I'd never make nothing of myself.'

'Not nice,' Alan replied sincerely. 'Not nice at all.'

'Well,' Roger said, 'No problem now. They're both gone. I don't miss them. I'm more happier now.'

'Jolly Roger,' Alan commented.

Roger smiled infectiously. 'Yeah, why not? Jolly Roger. I like that.'

'What about your parents, Toni? Are you rebelling?'

'My father was ... er ... from a bank,' Toni said with a grin.

'Tell all,' Alan prompted.

'A sperm bank, actually. And my mother was a test-tube. Beever cracked a joke about breaking glass being a rebellion against my origins. Not bad for a teacher. You know,' she said, 'we got a good deal with him. Some of the other kids say that their teachers are dodgy, to say the least.'

'Come off it,' Gabby exclaimed disdainfully. 'I can see straight through him. Our Trev's trying too hard to be one of the lads. Eager to be cool. Eager Beever we should call him. Anyway,' Gabby asked Alan, 'what did he say to you, Al?'

'Oh, we just chatted politics. He's a good old socialist, you know. A union man. Feels there's a basic problem with the Government – it's become vicious and uncaring like a master when, in a real democracy, it would be subservient – a slave to the people. He's been in trouble through politics as well.'

'Politics!' Gabby exclaimed. 'Boring or what?'

Gail took advantage of her sister's killing the conversation. 'I'm going back to our cabin now,' she said quietly, mainly to Gabby.

'Okay.'

'Very secretive,' Alan said as Gail left the room.

'Is she a closet over-eater?' Toni asked Gabby.

'How do you mean?'

'Well, I saw her over dinner, stuffing bits of meat into her bag. Now she's taken it off to her cabin.'

'Ah. She's been found out, then,' Gabby admitted. 'She's brought her pet with her. Wouldn't leave him behind, so she smuggled him on board. Huggy the python. He's in our cell.'

'Really?' Toni asked incredulously.

'Really,' Gabby confirmed. 'She feels safe with a pet python around. A guard snake. But he's cuddly really.'

'Cor,' Roger said, clearly impressed. 'A python!'

Toni was still sceptical. 'Seeing is believing,' she muttered.

'Well, you'll have to ask Gail about that. But she doesn't say an awful lot.'

'Exciting, though,' Roger enthused.

'I thought that you only got excited on the job,' Toni commented.

Roger shrugged. 'Maybe not *only* then.'

'Well,' Toni said leaning towards him, 'I know how to get you some real excitement.'

'Now, now, children. Wait till you're on your own,' Gabby chuckled.

Toni's scowl showed that she did not appreciate silly jokes interrupting serious business. She resumed her conversation with Jolly Roger. 'Interested?'

'Yeah. Sure.'

Before Toni could continue, they were interrupted again. 'Hey, look!' Alan was pointing to something out of the window. It looked like a giant illuminated teapot, breathing fire from its spout.

They crowded around the window. 'An oil rig. Mega!' Toni saw the rig, and the ship that bobbed alongside, through eyes that had never before seen beyond Birmingham. 'It's enormous.'

'It would look even bigger close up,' Alan said. 'It must be at least half a mile away.'

They watched for a while – till Gabby got bored and went back to her seat. Toni nudged Roger. 'What do you think? Have you seen the duty-free shop?' she whispered.

'What about it? It's locked up and empty.'

'Right. But have you seen what's at the back of the shop?'

'What?'

'A door.'

'So?'

'Think about it,' Toni said. 'They wouldn't empty the whole shop just for this trip, then re-stock it for the next normal one. And how about the teachers? Can you see them

– and the crew – going without alcohol for the duration?'

'What are you getting at?'

'It's a stock cupboard. Bet it is. Full of mega-goodies. A few bottles just waiting to be liberated. Only a few, so they won't be missed, but enough to see us through a party or two.'

'Maybe.'

'So, are you with me? Do we get together to plan a raid?'

'A raid!' Roger's eyes sparkled. 'Sure. I'm with you.'

'Can you do Mike Zlatkis a favour if you're going to break in?' Gabby asked. 'The silly bugger's grumping in his cabin because of his damn computer. So, if there's one in the shop, swipe it for him, will you? He's suicidal without his own.'

Toni shrugged. 'Okay. You've obviously got a soft spot for our lonesome hacker. I don't care – as long as he takes the rap if he gets caught with a hot computer.'

Guardian Angels

Melvyn Ten Noever de Brauw sat in front of his monitor and sighed. It wasn't as if he lacked interest in his new learning programme but gaining the necessary momentum was difficult when all he was faced with was a cold green screen. He preferred the get-up-and-at-it sort of project. 'Oh well,' he said to himself, 'here goes.' Unwillingly, he reached for his electronic mouse and clicked on the 'Start info' window. He watched as a circle was drawn on the screen. Features, yellow and blue, appeared in the circle. Then the object began to revolve, showing that it was in fact a globe. To be precise, it was a planet with land masses in yellow and blue seas. A peculiar planet with more ocean than land. Immediately, Mel's thoughts turned to the shipful of human school children that he'd heard about. Their fate was one of the three disasters that his own race had chosen to review. As a result, it was one of the three subjects on offer as a project. Maybe he had been assigned to the project on the children from Earth. He hoped so because he felt a great empathy with those schoolchildren so far away. He didn't know why, but he felt it all the same. Anyway, if this plant revolving about its own axis on his monitor was Earth, it was no wonder that some of its inhabitants took to the seas in large ships. There was relatively little land.

As if to confirm his thoughts, the computer labelled the display 'Earth' and started listing facts in a box in the top right of the screen.

Almost spherical, *ca* 40,000 km circumference
Mass: 5.9×10^{21} tonnes
Moons: 1
Seas: 71% surface area
Countries: 229 different territories
Population: 5400 million
Average life expectancy: 69 earth years

And so it went on. Dry fact after dry fact. The globe occasionally changed to highlight different countries in different colours; some enormous, some tiny. At one point it showed climatic variations over the surface. Mel slowed the display at this point because he was interested. After all, temperature was a key factor in the disaster with the human children. He saw how a ship sailing north or south could soon meet floating ice which he knew was the cause of the shipwreck. His mind wandered as more facts sped by. From where did the ship set sail? Where was it going and why? He hoped that if he waited long enough, the programme would get around to specifics regarding the fated cruise and information about human children themselves. What did they look like? What did they do? How long was it before they were thought of as grown up?

Mel passed the time by opening the first of the boxes marked, 'Do not open until instructed by the programme to do so.' Inside, there was a variety of objects, all unfamiliar to him. He picked up a thin white sheet. On it, some writing had somehow been printed. 'Object A. Organic material called PAPER. It is on this substance that young humans in schools would laboriously record their observations. The material is made from living creatures called TREES, which were slaughtered to make paper. Strangely, young humans liked trees and even protested about their slaughter. Cross references: object B, writing implement called PEN; bottle C, writing dye called INK; object F, bound paper with human writing called BOOK; object H, graduated polymer strip called RULER; object K, hinged metal blades called SCISSORS.

Mel tore off a strip of the paper and dipped it into the black ink. Sure enough, the liquid dyed the paper. It also turned rather soggy. A wicked glint formed in Mel's eye. He rolled up the inky paper into a ball – finding, in the process, that the ink excelled also at dyeing hands. He scavenged in the box for something flexible. Object H, the ruler, seemed the most suitable. He placed the black blob on the end of the ruler, pulled it back, and flicked the inky ball at Malc. With a most satisfying splat, the paper thudded on Malc's back, stuck there for an instant and then dropped off, leaving a round black stain on his back.

As Malc span round, Mel tried to keep the smile from his face. 'If,' Malc said, 'you were a young human you would be in trouble right now because their teachers are organic.'

'You mean,' Mel asked his Mobile Aid Learning Computer, 'they're living creatures? Not neural chips and artificial intelligence?'

'Correct. They are older humans.'

'Isn't that inefficient?' Mel asked, hardly believing it. 'How can one creature know everything that a child is likely to ask?'

'They do not yet have the technology to accumulate all

wisdom and knowledge into a neural network interactive teaching unit,' Malc answered in his rather stilted voice. 'And they value human contact in their classrooms.'

'I see,' said Mel.

'They also appreciate the value of instructions,' Malc said pointedly.

'Okay, okay. I know. Back to the monitor,' Mel replied.

He learnt that the human children's misadventure was the unexpected outcome of an adventure, the type of project that he would have enjoyed himself. It wasn't clear to Mel why those particular children had been selected for the trip – perhaps they were particularly gifted, or perhaps they had won competitions for places on the cruise. In any event, they were travelling from their homeland called Britain to a neighbouring territory called Norway, though much of their time was spent on the ship itself – until a rogue iceberg, off northern Norway, brought their voyage to a sudden and disastrous end. None survived the sinking. Not a single one. Mel sighed. Such a waste of life. The more he thought about the human tragedy, the more it motivated, fascinated and saddened him. Mel really believed that he could make something of this assignment. This time, he'd been given a topic worthy of effort. He wouldn't just mess about as usual, he'd make a really good job of it.

There was a brief fanfare, then the stern face of the President appeared on the screen. Mel shifted in his chair, preparing himself for a full twenty minute lecture. He'd never been interested in the Presidential Broadcast before but this time was different. He had a vested interest.

'As you know,' the President's head said, 'each year, we are entrusted with the pleasant task of rectifying one natural tragedy somewhere in the universe. The first Supreme Leader in Moral Affairs placed this rewarding onus upon us on the occasion of his birthday many many years ago. The present Council would not wish to break our commitment to alleviating some suffering in the universe today. But remember, we do not and will not reshape deliberate acts of violence. The Council will not permit our intervention in loss of life through war or hostile action of any sort. Alleviating the symptoms of wickedness does nothing to remove its cause. Our help is pointless until the source is identified and cured.

'So,' she continued in a somewhat lighter vein, 'which tragedies has the Council considered? As usual, we were painfully aware of far more disasters than we can ever hope to avert. One of the Council's most arduous and uncomfortable tasks was to select three from the many. This year, the members of the Council were particularly moved by the death of two thousand of the Kinki tribe by the earthquake on Volkahagan. In considering this tragedy, we must try to put aside our natural revulsion of the physical appearance of the otherwise charming Kinki tribe. Second, the death of three hundred and fifty one children and fifty adult humans in the sinking of a ship on planet Earth. Here we must put to the back of our minds the human trait of settling disputes by war. This accident was caused by an iceberg when the ship's iceberg detection system was malfunctioning, and not by an act of hostility. Finally, and closest to our own planet, in our neighbouring galaxy, a meteorite impact on Sod has thrown into its atmosphere enough debris to blot out forty per cent of its sunlight. Much plant life will die and many emerging creatures feeding on those plants are likely to become extinct. While the exact outcome of the meteorite impact is not yet known, we must bear in mind that its repercussions on this primitive planet will be severe.

'There we have it. Three harrowing disasters. It is, of course, an invidious and impossible task to compare such events and judge one to be more tragic that the other two, more worthy of our intervention. The Council decided to assign each of our own young people to a project on one of these three tragedies. The best project submitted would decide which of the three equally worthy events would benefit by our intervention. In other words, the members of the Council felt that judging relevant projects would be more acceptable than assessing such widely diverse incidents, and perhaps more morally defensible. And now, the projects have been completed and examined by the Council. A winner has been selected.'

The President paused for dramatic effect. 'Come on,' Mel said to his monitor. 'Spit it out.'

'First, and much to the delight of many members of the Council, the project deemed most outstanding concerned the human children on Earth.' Mel let out a cheer but quickly quietened to hear the President's next words. 'Whilst the number of humans involved is actually rather small, the members agreed that the death of children – however few – invokes a particular abhorrence in us all. So much wasted potential. A great loss to the universe as a whole. So,' she continued, 'our eyes turn to Earth this year. And we can feel proud that we do so.

'The person submitting the best Earth project was ...' she inserted another histrionic pause, 'Melvyn Ten Noever de Brauw.' Mel realized that he had been on the edge of his seat only when he fell back into it as his name was announced. The effect was like a punch. But nicer. 'This project was notable not only for Melvyn's thorough comprehension and obvious compassion for the human children, but also for his unique and imaginative speculation on the likely effect on the humans of a visit by one of us and of our remodelling the course of their history – or, to them, their future. In fact, the project was so well received by Council that a break from tradition was contemplated.

'It is customary for us to transport one of our own Elders to supervise the intervention. Lately, this responsibility has fallen to Elders Posthumus, Popov and Kistemaker, who have ensured minimal interference with local life whilst still allowing the tragedy to be averted. The interest and compassion shown by Melvyn, that so caught the attention of the Council members, suggests a different strategy. Given that the Earth disaster involved largely children, it seems ... appropriate and poignant to send to that planet one of our own race in his formative years. If he is willing, Melvyn Ten Noever de Brauw shall be our envoy.'

Mel did not know whether to jump up and down with excitement or to sit motionless, agog. He did not know whether to shout, 'I'm willing! Of course I'm willing!' or merely to whisper incredulously, 'When do I go?'

'Clearly, Melvyn has immersed himself already in human culture, but he will need long and intensive training in life on Earth, language, customs, artefacts, and the like. And he will have to prove that he comprehends the prime need for minimal interference. It is a difficult and daunting task that awaits him. He must first prove to Council that he is equal to the task. If so, as his project suggests, he will make an ideal ambassador.

'With this splendid departure from tradition, I leave you. Melvyn's project can be accessed from your terminals using the code, MTNDB EARTH. I'm sure that it will fascinate you as much as it fascinated Council. I know that your hopes and wishes will go out this day to Melvyn, who will be entrusted with a great and wonderful gift from us to planet Earth. Goodbye.'

Mel still sat in a state of shock when Malc approached, saying, 'All my normal tasks have been subordinated. I have been logged on to an Elders' network – no less. Elders Posthumus, Popov and Kistemaker, to be precise. They intend to write you into their software, allowing you to become part of a three-dimensional picture – a simulator of human life for cyberspace training. This is not a passive game but a participation in a virtually real human world. Your agreement to begin training will signify willingness to oversee Earth intervention. You are requested to respond now.'

'I ... er ... I'd better not keep them waiting,' Mel replied. 'They might think I'm not bothered.'

Back to Earth;

Illegal Aliens

It was a clear, warm Sunday morning. The *Queen* chugged lazily from Stavanger towards Bergen – seven hours of weaving between the myriad islands. The coast of Norway was like an exploded jigsaw puzzle. Maybe once a jigsaw of Europe was whole and orderly but a giant clumsy hand must have dropped the puzzle. Most of it stayed together but the pieces at the edges were scattered, one hundred and fifty thousand bits of Norway being flung randomly into the sea. A chaotic coastline. No sign of sand or beaches – just rocks, moss, grass and trees.

Graham Squirrell had put aside his Stave Church project to attend the service. Mike and Gail were in their cabins. The others were in the Common Room. Peter Fallick and Alan were having a sharp exchange about the class system. Toni, tired of listening to the glorification of the working class by Alan, who had never experienced it, turned her attention to a crossword. Charlton was listening to a tape and drawing busily at the same time. Mr Beever was chatting with Jolly Roger about Norway, and Gabby was jotting down the required notes on the overland trips from Stavanger. Everyone else had completed their diaries. Gabby's was the shortest and most reluctantly written.

The front at Stavanger looked like toy-town. Twinned with

Harlow. Anagram of ants' grave. Enough said about Stavanger. Coach trips were all hair-pin bends, tunnels, snow-topped mountains, lakes, waterfalls, and educational rock carvings, stave churches, farms and glaciers in U-shaped valleys. Sights we weren't taken to see include naughty Norwegian films, football matches (even though Spurs were touring there), discos, bowling alleys, record shops and pubs.

Toni looked up and addressed the room as a whole. 'Where does winter last for forty-two years? Anyone know?'

'Probably that place up North,' Gabby replied. 'Hammerfest.'

Peter who had not apparently been paying any attention, looked up and said dispassionately, 'No. Uranus,' then returned to his discussion with Alan.

Roger smiled at Mr Beever and whispered, 'Clever, ain't he?'

Mr Beever nodded. 'Mm. Very bright is our Peter – academically. But one can be intelligent in other ways, Roger. Being streetwise, for example. It's all a matter of applying yourself to your own environment.'

'Yeah,' Jolly Roger said. 'I never thought of it like that. Even I can be clever like that.'

'Sure you can,' Mr Beever replied. 'But now I must go and have a word with Mike.' He stood up to go.

'Okay,' Roger said, then hesitated. 'Er … You mean you're going to his cabin?' There was more than a hint of panic in his voice.

'I think that's where he is.'

'Ah.'

'Yes?'

'But ... like ... he might not be there. Know what I mean?'

Mr Beever smiled wryly. 'It's all right, Roger. You don't need to protect him. I just want to have a quiet word with him.'

Mr Beever knocked at Mike's door, then went straight in. He didn't want to give Mike enough time for an embarrassing attempt to hide his contraband. Even so, Mike turned bright red when he saw who had entered. 'All right, Mike?' Mr Beever asked.

'Mm ... yes. Thanks.'

'You know why I'm here?' Seeing Mike nod slowly, Mr Beever continued, 'I thought you might. Mr Uunk has sent me to check Cell Block G for a computer that's gone missing from the shop. I thought I'd try your cabin first.'

With his hand still lingering on the keyboard, Mike said, 'Yes. I ... er ... I guess my innocence is going to be tricky to prove.'

Mr Beever laughed. 'Under the circumstances, yes. But I'm more interested in your honesty than your innocence.'

'What?'

'Are you going to do anything dishonest with it?'

'No. Of course not.'

'Can you do anything with it? It's only used for stock-taking, I dare say. Is it up to anything?'

'It might have come out of the ark – it's dead slow – but it's okay. I've got some compatible software. They didn't confiscate my discs, luckily. I've wiped clean its memory and put my stuff in it. I can link it into the ship's ethernet – look, there's a socket in each cabin – and log onto the ship's main computer. From there, via the satellite phone system, it's the world.' Mike stopped, realizing that it was bad form to enthuse about stolen property. He was digging his own grave, perhaps.

'And who pays for all this use of the phone lines?'

'I do – sort of. There'll be a big bill, but phone-phreaking will put it right.'

'What's that?'

'Well, it's sort of fixing the phone-bill by computer.'

'Computers are very versatile tools, obviously,' Mr Beever said sardonically. 'Are you saying that fraud isn't dishonest if it isn't the primary motive, that a little fraud's okay if it's needed to enable your quiet conspiracies?'

'I ... er ... suppose so.'

'Let me test your honesty in another way.'

'Yes?' Mike asked with trepidation.

'What do you think of the teachers on this boat? What are the other kids saying?'

'Honestly?'

'Yes,' Mr Beever confirmed. 'Honestly.'

'You mean, apart from you?'

'I mean honestly,' Mr Beever insisted.

'Well, we think you're ... great – really. Almost all of us, anyway. And there's a couple more like you, apparently. But most of the others are ... grim. The pits.'

'The pits?'

'Absolutely. That's what they're saying.'

'Yes,' Mr Beever said thoughtfully. 'That's what I think too.' He made a move as if to leave.

Mike stopped him, saying, 'Is that all? What about the ... er ...?' He nodded towards the computer.

'Did you steal it?'

'No.'

'It was a gift, then.'

'Sort of.'

'Mm,' said Mr Beever. 'Can't see the problem, then. Just ... be good. Or at least be ethical. And discreet. Okay?'

'Okay!'

Mr Beever opened the door, but before he shut it behind him, he said, 'I'm a great teacher but, as far as looking for computers is concerned, I'm very short-sighted.'

Back in the Common Room, Mr Beever checked Gabby's notes. 'Well?' she said aggressively, spoiling for a fight.

'Well,' he replied, 'short and to the point. Not exactly Tolstoy in degree of detail, but ... different.'

'Different? Is that what you call showing me respect?'

'No need to be so jumpy. I wasn't being sarcastic. I meant it. Your writing's fine – a different approach to the subject matter – but it's too brief. I'd like to see more of it. That's all.'

'No chance. Why should I? What's the point?'

'You're archiving your trip. Something to show your grandchildren. And, for a piece to turn out like that, you must enjoy writing, despite your reaction. So let's have more next time.'

'You can stuff that for a lark.'

'That doesn't help your cause, Gabby. Think about it. Anyway,' he added in order to escape before she said something that he could not ignore, 'I must go and have a word with Charlton.'

Mr Beever stood behind Charlton for a while, watching him sketching a stave church from memory. 'Charlton,' the teacher shouted so his voice would penetrate the personal stereo. 'That's good. In fact, it's excellent. Fantastic detail. Well done.' He mimed the removal of the headphones so that he could talk without the whole ship hearing. 'You settling in all right?'

'Suppose so.'

Quietly, so no one else could hear, Mr Beever asked him, 'Better than ... the last place you were in?'

'Has to be. No strip searches, no endless lock-ups. No banging of doors and clanking of keys. No bullying.'

'And you get some privacy here.'

'Yeah. The bedrooms have locks on the *inside*.'

'That's right.' Mr Beever beamed. 'Here, you can build up your self-esteem again.'

He left to make his report about the missing computer. He felt able to reassure Mr Uunk of Zlatkis's honesty without compromising his own. He could state categorically that Mike Zlatkis had not stolen it. Mr Beever felt reasonably in control of his situation even though he was little nearer to explaining the OBTUSE experiment. He was unaware that, back in Cell Block G, his future and that of his charges was being transformed.

Mel materialized in a bland corridor on Deck 3, just around the corner from G Block. His first sensations were the vibrations, the slight pitching of the ship, and an atmosphere that was rather more acrid than he had anticipated. Not even the exhaustive simulations could prepare him for the fine detail. He had grown used to Earth's gravity and the limited capabilities of his earthly body. He felt almost human and, like a human, he could see and hear only narrow ranges of frequency. His eyes could not even cover infra-red and ultraviolet wavelengths. And his new sense of touch was woefully inadequate. Yet, despite the meagre human sensory input, the contact with earthly materials like the metal floor still surprised him. The real thing was more solid than the simulated – almost abrasive. Back home, the imitation atmosphere of Earth was pure. Here, on Earth itself, the traces of impurity in the air stung his human eyes and burnt his human lungs. He hoped that he would lose his sensitivity as he acclimatized to the strange environment. Apart from the physical discomfort, he felt alone and vulnerable. A fish out of water. His own people and, although they didn't know it, the humans on board were relying on him. The responsibility weighed heavily on his mind.

From the adjoining corridor where he stood, Mel heard a door open, a scrambling noise as if a scuffle were taking place, and a muttered curse.

Cautiously, he peered round the corner into Block G. He saw a girl in some distress.

'Damn!' she muttered. Then she called, 'Alien! Alien!'

Mel quickly withdrew. He was stunned. How had she found out so quickly? He looked over his body, but it looked perfectly humanoid. It was as near to human as modern technology could make it. A sixteen-year-old boy to blend in with his surroundings. How then ...?

Suddenly, the girl dashed along the corridor, turned, and appeared in front of him. She was startled to bump into Mel and let out a cry. 'Oh! I didn't know anyone else was here,' she said anxiously. 'Look, I'll have to trust you. Have you seen my Alien?'

For a moment Mel was staggered. Then, after carefully analysing her question, he realized that she could not possibly be referring to himself. But any relief that he felt was short-lived. There must be another alien on board! Why? Who? How? 'What species of alien should I have observed?' he asked her.

'Oh, sorry,' she replied. 'Alien's my dog. He's a stowaway – shouldn't really be here. He just escaped from my cabin.' Still seeing puzzlement in Mel's face, she added desperately, 'Dog. You know, hairy and walks around on all fours. Did he run past you?'

'Er ... No. No, he did not.' Mel remembered about dogs. Strange looking life-forms, some breeds were quite like the Kinki tribe.

Gail's eyebrows rose. The boy's accent was strange and he spoke oddly – too correctly to be natural. 'Okay,' she said. 'Don't tell anyone, though. Oh, look,' she said. 'There he is. Alien,' she called. 'Come here, boy.' The dog walked placidly towards her, wagging his tail. Gail said to Mel, 'Don't worry about him. He growls a bit at boys but he won't bite.'

The dog looked at Mel suspiciously, then approached him and smelled his legs with great interest. 'What is he doing?' Mel asked.

'Getting to know you. He seems to like you. Tell him your name.'

'Will he understand?'

'No, silly! But he likes the sound of a voice.'

'My name is Mel,' he said, patting Alien's head. The dog immediately sat to attention.

'Funny,' said Gail. 'He's never done that before. Anyway, I must put him away before he's seen.'

'Can I come and talk to you a little more?'

Gail looked unsure. 'No. I ...'

'It will not be for long. It is important. I need your help.'

'You're sure it's important? You're not having me on?' The boy looked genuine and innocent enough. Also, her dog's reaction to him vouched for his good character. Alien protected her by growling at all males, yet he seemed not to sense any threat at all in Mel. 'Okay,' she said. 'This way.'

In cabin G1, Mel first asked her name, then went on, 'Gail, you said that your dog was ...'

'Alien?'

'No. You said that he was not supposed to be here.'

'A stowaway.'

'Yes. That is the word. A stowaway. I am one too,' Mel admitted.

'You mean, you're not from one of the other Blocks?'

'No,' Mel replied. 'I am strange here.'

'Oh, I get it. You're Norwegian. Bet you came aboard at Stavanger. Hitching a ride.'

'Yes. A foreigner. I need one of these,' he indicated the room, 'in which to hide.'

'A cabin?'

'Yes.'

'Well ... er ... I don't know,' Gail said. 'It's not easy ...' She didn't know if she should trust this stranger. She suspected that his outward timidity hid an inner audacity but, unusually, she was not intimidated by it. There was something about him that distinguished him from other boys. She sensed within him absolute integrity. 'I guess we could find you something,' she continued. 'But it's not up to me. Charlton Ng has a cell ... cabin to himself. Maybe you could share that. No one'll notice the extra mouth to feed. I suppose you'll blend in if you don't speak too much. The only problem is Mr Beever. He'll notice you.'

'Who is Mr Beever?'

'Eager Beever. He's our teacher.'

'Yes. I know of teachers,' said Mel. 'I will conceal myself from him. If I am seen by him, I will explain myself. Perhaps he will understand.'

'I don't know about that. But first we'll need to check it out with Charlton. He's a quiet lad. Very private, so he may not be happy to ... Anyway, we'll see. I'll take you to him, okay?'

'Yes. That is, as you say, okay.' He smiled at her, the endearing smile of a lost child beginning to warm to unfamiliar territory.

Jolly Roger was in his element. He'd taken up the post of look-out at the door of the Common Room. With the exception of Mike, who was deep into his computer in his own cabin, the whole of the Splinter Group had turned up for the secret tryst. Roger loved the atmosphere. It reeked of conspiracies. Lowered voices, plans being hatched, the risk of being discovered, the adrenalin. Anything really exciting was on the limit of, or beyond, what was allowed. Like joy-riding, all-night raves and alcohol. Like harbouring a stowaway.

'His English isn't too good,' Gail was explaining, forced by Mel's intrusion to come unwillingly out of her shell for a moment. 'Or rather, it's too good. But, apart from that, he'll blend in.'

'When there's a crowd – like for meals,' Toni added. 'It's easy to go unnoticed among three hundred kids.'

'Three hundred and fifty one,' Mel muttered sadly.

'What?' Gabby cried.

'Before coming on board, I carried out much research. There are three hundred and fifty one children and fifty adults.'

'He knows more than we do!' Gabby exclaimed.

'Well, there are three hundred and fifty two now, and we're getting ahead of ourselves,' Alan remarked. 'Before we discuss tactics we all have to agree, or not, to help hide Mel. It'll have to be a joint effort. It only takes one snake in the grass to drive a coach and horses through this particular monkey business.'

'Excuse me,' Mel interrupted. 'I am unaware of these animals on board. I do not understand.'

'No, no,' Alan said. 'It's not to be taken literally.' Amid the sniggers, Alan tried to explain the idiosyncrasies of the English language, but failed. 'Anyway,' he addressed them all, 'we're trying to decide what to do. Are we all agreed? I'm more than willing to do my bit.'

'Me too!' Roger uttered keenly, then put his hand over his mouth, realizing that he'd spoken too loudly.

Everyone but Graham and Charlton nodded in agreement and murmured their approval.

'You are all very kind,' said Mel.

'But Graham didn't agree,' Peter pointed out.

'I haven't disagreed either. I'm thinking about it.'

'It doesn't need much thinking about,' Peter retorted. 'Surely the Bible has something to say about friends in need and good Samaritans.'

'True,' Graham replied, unruffled by Peter's comment. 'But whether he's a friend or not is irrelevant. Or why he travels. "The wolf will live with the sheep, and the leopard will lie down with the kid, and the calf and the young lion all together; and a mere boy will be leader over them".'

'We've had enough animals!' Toni groaned.

'What's he talking about?' barked Gabby.

Calmly, Graham replied, 'Isaiah eleven.'

'Okay,' Peter said. 'At least he's agreed, even if it's cloaked in the sort of religious claptrap that makes my hackles rise.'

'Does it?' Gabby retorted. 'I like seeing the odd hackle rise but I'm not sure it's worth it in your case.'

'Oh, shut up, Gabby,' Toni snapped disapprovingly. 'Let's get back to the point. Graham's agreed – we think – so it's down to you, Charlton,' she said. 'We're stuck without you.'

'Yeah,' Alan added, 'But Charlton *has* got cause to think on it because he's got most to lose – half a cabin. He'd be bearing the brunt of it.'

'We'd all help out, though,' Roger said willingly.

'Yeah,' Gabby agreed. 'What do you think, Chaz?'

'I express my gratitude,' Mel said to Charlton, once installed in his cabin. 'I am sure that you accepted me because of a sense of duty to your friends. In wanting to help and protect me, they coerced you.'

'No,' Charlton replied. 'It wasn't that.'

'Then why was it?' Mel asked, as he bounced experimentally on the top bunk.

'Because you are an outsider. You don't belong.'

Mel ceased for a moment his exploration of the bed. 'Do you mean that you do not belong either?'

'I feel alienated from the others, yes.'

'Why?'

'I'd rather ... er ... It's a long story.' Charlton said no more.

Strangely, the *Queen*'s fittings were not continually creaking. The ship was deathly quiet and still. She must have docked. But the silence was deeper than that. There was none of the sounds that humans make. Not even the sound of breathing.

Mel dangled his head over the side of his bunk. Where Charlton should have been sleeping, there was only an empty bed. The sheets were badly ruffled. It was a bed of someone who had tossed and turned all night. Mel climbed awkwardly down the insecure ladder and got dressed. He knocked on the door of the shower room but there was no reply. Clearly, Charlton had left the cabin.

Eventually, Mel found him on the Sun Deck. Despite the dawn, it was still quite dark. The *Queen* was moored in the shadow of Bergen's house-studded mountains. 'Sunrise,' Mel commented gingerly. 'Beautiful.'

Charlton did not seem perturbed by Mel's intrusion. 'Maybe,' he replied reservedly.

'Each dawn is a genesis. A new beginning.'

'Brick wall dawn is more like it.'

'Sorry. I do not understand.'

'Another day, another obstacle. It's the title of a song.'

'I estimate,' Mel said, 'that it is not a happy song.'

'Sad songs speak louder.'

'I would have thought that they would be quieter than happy songs.'

'No,' Charlton said. 'I mean ... Never mind.'

'You like music.'

'Love it.' He tapped his Walkman, as always attached to his belt. 'Better than telly any day. How about you? What sort of music do you like?'

'We do not ...' Mel shrugged. 'It is not easy to explain in your language.'

'From what I've heard of Norwegian music, it's hard to explain in any language.'

Mel looked at Charlton. 'It is good to see you smile,' he said.

Immediately, Charlton stopped smiling. Humour, he thought, did not become him. It was inappropriate to his situation.

They leaned on the rails of the walkway and watched the town wake up. 'Where are you going to, anyway?' Charlton asked Mel. 'You didn't say yesterday. Not here – Bergen.'

'No. Not Bergen. North.'

'North Norway?'

'Yes.'

'Hammerfest?' Charlton suggested.

'Yes. Near Hammerfest.'

'Is it important for you to get there?'

Mel hesitated. 'Yes. It is a pilgrimage, a vital mission.'

'Why? What have you got to do there?'

It was Mel's turn to smile. 'How did you say? It is a long story.'

'Okay. No inquisition.'

Below them in the harbour, vans scurried about, delivering tray after tray of sea-trout and salmon. The fish market was rapidly coming to life. Behind them, the Kleppestö car ferry had docked and was disgorging Norwegian commuters onto the main road into Bergen.

'I had trouble,' Mel confessed, 'to understand the talking of Graham.'

'Don't we all.'

'What did he mean by the talk of lions and of sheep?'

'No idea,' Charlton replied. 'I couldn't make anything of the bit about a boy being leader, either.'

'That,' Mel said, 'did not surprise me.'

'No? How do you mean?'

'Perhaps I should not have …' Mel paused to think. 'In any group, some person always emerges in the role of leader.'

'Well, Graham's just a religious nut.'

'I do not understand. A nut is a fruit, or a metal collar into which a screw is driven.'

'No,' Charlton interrupted, 'I mean he's crazy about religion. That's all.'

'Religion?' Mel queried. 'That is a belief in some power outside of your own nature?'

Charlton looked surprised. 'Of course. God and all that.'

'God. Yes. I have read of Him.'

Charlton shrugged and put it down to the language barrier. He didn't respond. He had no wish to prolong a conversation about religious groups. He'd had his fill of their prejudices. He let go of the rail and rubbed his hands together to wipe away the salt. Everywhere on deck was coated with a layer of salt. The rails, the seats, the tables. Borne by the wind, brine impregnated everything. Perhaps, Charlton thought, that's why everything's white – so it won't show the salt.

'Sodium chloride,' Mel declared, looking quaintly proud of his knowledge.

'Right. It's a pain.'

As they talked, people collected around the canopies of the market stalls, and the morning became increasingly misty.

'I like to ask about you, Charlton,' Mel said. 'Why did you opt to undertake this cruise? Why did any of your friends choose to come?'

'Choose? There wasn't a choice. We were just told we were selected for it.'

'You must be "unsettled". What does it mean?'

Charlton shrugged. 'I guess in my case it means I'm not making progress. I don't belong in a normal school, I didn't get on in care, and I couldn't cope with a Young Offenders' Institution. Anyway,' he said before Mel could ask another question, 'it's all part of the long story. And now,' he said, looking at his watch, 'it's time for breakfast. Then it's dry land for us. One of our trips into Bergen.'

'Yes. It will be a difficult few days alone in your cabin. I will be perfectly adequate, however.'

'Yeah, you'll be okay. The others'll rustle a stockpile of food for you at breakfast. The cabin'll be like a larder before we go.'

A fine drizzle had set in by the time that they turned to go indoors. On the way to the dining room, Charlton asked, 'What's Bergen like – any good?'

Mel paused, then said, 'I have not a great amount of knowledge on Bergen. It is far from my home.'

Yellow and Black

It was a filthy day. A day for staying inside, for staying dry.

Mike put his head around the door of the Games Room just as Toni called, 'Twelve!'

'Twelve?' he said admiringly. 'That's not bad.'

'Yellow and black with three reds.' On the receiving end of a thrashing, Alan's comment was more complaint than explanation.

'Hush!' Jolly Roger asked for quiet as his eyes flitted between white, black and the corner pocket.

'Nineteen,' Toni enthused as the black ball dropped into the pocket with a satisfying thump.

'Just the colours, then,' Roger taunted Alan.

Watching the game from the corner, Peter added a whispered commentary, 'Cyclone Klotts has it all sewn up. With twenty-seven left on the table, Alan Sea-breeze Splinter would need nine snookers just to come close in this match.'

'I can manage without that, Peter,' Alan said tersely. Then he turned to Mike and asked, 'Do you want to take on the Cyclone next?'

'No. I'd be hopeless.'

'Well, none of us has got anywhere near him either,' Alan replied.

'Twenty-one,' Toni yelled.

'Mike Zephyr Zlatkis,' joked Peter.

'Zephyr? What's that?'

'No more than a slight breeze,' Peter answered.

'That's about right for me,' Mike agreed. 'No, I came for help. You might know this, Alan. Are you any good at chemistry?'

'Never heard of it. Consult the oracle. Ask Peter. He knows everything around here.'

Mike showed Peter the structure of a chemical that he had copied from his VDU. 'Do you know what it is?' he asked.

'No. But it's an organophosphorus compound of some sort. Probably a pesticide. Why?'

'Any chance it's a nerve gas?'

The green wobbled in the mouth of the pocket but did not drop. 'Now you've made me cock it up,' Roger moaned.

Absorbed in his conversation with Mike, Peter was too intrigued by Mike's question to commentate on the failed pot. 'Sure,' he confirmed. 'Phosphorus compounds are a bit that way. Pesticides, nerve gases. They're all much the same. Designed for killing.'

'Oh, good,' Mike said with glee. 'I'm on the right track, then.' He turned and began to walk away.

'Come on!' Peter exclaimed. 'You can't leave now without telling us what you're up to.'

'Well,' Mike said, waving his piece of paper in triumph, 'I got this from MoD files. Data on chemical weapons, I reckon. I'm nearly into the hard stuff. When I've cracked the West's files, I'll have a go at the Middle East and the rest.'

'What for?' Alan queried.

Peter put up both hands quickly to stop Mike replying.

'Don't tell me,' he said. 'You're going to save the world by arranging an exchange of information on chemical weapons via computers.'

'You got it! Let them all develop antidotes to each other's weapons. That'll speed up the disarmament process.'

'While you're at it, why don't you exchange all their nuclear secrets as well?' Peter asked dryly.

Mike took the question seriously and replied, 'The info's better protected. Besides, I'm a realist. We've only got a few weeks.' Having stunned the others into silence, he turned and left.

After the door closed, Toni sniggered, 'Silly sod.'

'Not necessarily,' Peter responded. 'He's obsessive but very sharp.'

'And well-intentioned,' added Alan.

'Mm. I call it naive,' Toni replied, 'like most recluses.'

'I like him,' Roger piped up.

'On the topic of recluses,' Alan said, 'How's Charlton getting on, do you think?'

Really, he was asking Toni but it was Peter who answered. 'Our punky, angry but silent young man? Dangerous, I'd say. Anger and silence is a dangerous combination in one person. A little push and he'll be into self-destruct mode. The trouble is, you can't trust these tortured artist types to destroy just themselves.'

'Well, I think he's improved since our weird Norwegian friend joined the crew. At least Charlton talks to Mel even if he doesn't talk to anyone else,' Alan countered.

'True. Maybe Mel will sort him out, get him to talk about whatever's bugging him.'

'Yeah,' Alan agreed. 'Sort of … repaying the debt on half of Charlton's cabin.'

'A good clout would bring him to his senses soon enough,' commented Toni. 'Best thing for self-pity.'

'Has your school always been strong in psychology, Toni?' Peter replied.

'I just hope Mel's in a fit state to do the shrink's job,' Alan said. 'He's doing more throwing up than talking.'

'Well, it can't be sea-sickness. Not in Bergen harbour,' Toni joked. 'It'll be some of that breakfast stuff that was left around too long before he ate it.'

'I hope that's all it is,' Alan said. 'Charlton's quite concerned.'

'Believe the son of a doctor,' Peter put in. 'He's got an infection and probably a bit of food poisoning. Bet he's fine in twenty-four hours.'

'Prepared to nail your colours to the mast on that, eh?' Alan scoffed.

'Colours?' Roger queried. 'What about the green, then?' He handed the cue to Alan. 'Your shot, and it's right over the pocket. Can't miss.'

'Let's call it your game. Besides, it's not ecologically sound to put down the green.'

'Ah,' Peter quipped in an old man's voice. 'A long time ago, green was just a colour, you know, not a philosophy or a hopelessly outnumbered party.'

'Talking of parties,' Toni rejoined, 'we must sort something out now we have a bit of booze stashed away from the raid.'

'Yeah,' Roger said as he collected together the snooker

balls, 'we done our bit getting it. Let's not waste it.'

'Okay,' Alan conceded. 'I'll organize something. The moonshine thrash.'

'I could help,' Peter volunteered.

'No,' Alan put in quickly. 'It doesn't matter. I wouldn't want to waste your talents on a mere party.'

Peter did not take offence. He had long since become reconciled to constant sniping. A freak of nature had endowed him with more than his fair share of grey matter. He never set out to flaunt, but almost everything that he said glittered with cleverness and that irritated his classmates. In the past, he'd even tried to win friends by concealing his intelligence but the other kids then accused him of patronizing them. He could not win. He might as well have been gifted with the plague. Socially, his intellect had the same effect. He expected unpopularity even if he felt that he did not deserve it. 'Well,' he replied, 'at least I offered.'

Mel languished on the lower bunk. Charlton had swapped bunks with him for fear of his falling during a particularly restless sleep. Actually, it was more like stupor than sleep. Sometimes, Mel's body writhed alarmingly. And his cough came from deep down, like a smoker's. Sometimes, he was so still, he might have been in a coma. But all the time, sweat rolled from him, saturating the sheets. 'Cold,' he would mumble. 'Cold!' Yet his body was hot. Too hot. He only left his bed – frequently and with Charlton's help – to go to the toilet.

Much of the time, Charlton could make nothing of his words – if they were words and not just noises. Occasionally, though, a word, phrase or sentence made a kind of sense. Even in his fever, Mel must have known what was happening to him because he struggled to say, 'Virus. I am useless to the humans in this state. I must fight it. Cannot return home with a human virus. They cannot help or take me back. If only I could produce antibodies.' Nothing coherent followed.

Charlton shook his head. 'Food poisoning like hell!' He went to find help.

'This,' Mr Beever said, weighing the papers on his palm, 'feels a bit more substantial than the last effort, Gabby. Let me have a quick read.'

'If you must,' she replied in a wicked tone of voice.

> *Bergen is in Norway. It is on the south-west coast. It is a city. It is the second biggest city in Norway. It is the chief port of Norway. It was founded in 1070. It was founded by King Olav Kyrre.*

Mr Beever stopped reading and squared up to Gabby. 'What's this?' He shook her notes in exasperation.

'My account of Bergen. Like you wanted,' she replied impudently. 'Lots of detail. Facts, glorious facts.'

'Does it carry on like this all the way through?'

'Sure does. Good, eh?'

Shaking his head sadly, Mr Beever lamented, 'You know it isn't. Where's the invention of your first piece? I can get a list of facts from anywhere. From you, I expect more – a bit of imagination. I wanted to see Bergen through your eyes.

And,' he added before Gabby had an opportunity to butt in, 'don't just tell me to sod off again.'

'I wasn't going to,' she replied. 'I would've been more blunt than that.'

For the first time, Mr Beever became annoyed with her. 'Perhaps I was wrong about you, then. Perhaps this,' he said, throwing her notes angrily onto the table, 'is the best I can hope for.'

'It's all you're bloody well going to get.'

'Okay, Gabby,' he retorted. 'It's up to you. I just thought... Oh, forget it. I can't force you. If you're not prepared to make an effort... Why should I care about you wasting your time?'

Before Gabby could reply, Charlton came into the Common Room asking, 'Is Peter around?'

'Library,' Mr Beever answered brusquely. As soon as he had spoken, he knew that he'd adopted the wrong tone. He had no quarrel with Charlton. More calmly, he said, 'Before you go, Charlton, have you seen your sketch? It looks great. Pride of place on the wall.' He pointed to the poster board where Charlton's intricate drawing of a stave church had been pinned.

'Oh, yeah,' Charlton replied disinterestedly.

'Are you okay?' Mr Beever asked him.

'Yeah,' he said. Realizing that a more convincing response was called for, he added, 'Sure.'

After he'd gone out again, Gabby scoffed, 'Teacher's favourite gets flattery, then.'

'Flattery suggests insincerity. But I mean it,' Mr Beever stated. 'I always give praise when it's due. And when I give it, I always mean it.'

'Teachers!' she hissed. 'All venom or too bloody smarmy by half.'

'Teaching!' he rejoined. 'All brickbats and blunt instruments.'

'That's what you teachers deserve.'

Peter stroked his chin thoughtfully. 'You've got a point, Charlton. He *is* worse. What do you reckon, Alan?'

Charlton had found Peter in the library and bumped into Alan in the corridor on the way back. He had persuaded both of them to examine Mel's worsening condition.

Alan shrugged. 'You're the expert. Mind you,' he reminded Peter, 'you were the one who said he'd sleep it off in twenty-four hours. Now look at him. A hospital case if ever I saw one. But we can't even take him to the nurse. Not a stowaway.'

'He could go under a false name like Alan Splinter or Peter Fallick,' Peter suggested.

'Maybe ...' Alan began.

'No!' It was the first clear utterance from Mel. 'Biological details will not match.'

For a moment the three boys looked quizzically at each other. Then Alan said, 'I think he means medical records. And he's got a point.'

Mel pushed himself up a little on his elbows. With a faraway look in his eyes, he said, 'I must survive.' Coughing violently, he dropped back onto his bed. 'Not for my benefit,' he mumbled. 'For them.'

Peter looked closely into Mel's face. 'He's delirious. And

there's some sort of goo oozing from his eyes. It doesn't look good.'

'Well, what are we going to do?' Charlton asked solemnly.

'If only we knew what was wrong with him,' Peter pondered. 'Perhaps he should be quarantined.'

The boys looked at each other as if they had realized for the first time that they could be at risk as well. In fact, it had already occurred to all of them, but the possibility somehow became more real when verbalized.

'Hang on!' Peter cried. 'What have I been playing at? We have a computer whiz-kid on board and my dad has a self-diagnosis package on-line in his surgery. Don't dig out the yellow and black flag yet.'

'What?'

'In the good old days,' he explained, 'ships carrying a contagious disease would fly a couple of flags, warning others to keep clear. One was yellow and black, the other was plain yellow, I think. Anyway,' he said triumphantly, 'time to pay Mike a visit. You stay and look after him, Charlton, and keep your eye on symptoms. We'll need to know exactly what they are.' Peter leaned towards the unhearing Mel and said, 'Leave it to us. Soon have you jogging round Deck 2. And we've got three days to get your stuff into strutting condition for the Kristiansund disco.'

It didn't take much persuasion to enlist the help of Mike The Hacker. For a new challenge, he gladly abandoned for a while his quest for world disarmament. With Alan sitting quietly on the bed and Peter peering over his shoulder, Mike entered the directory. The list of services that appeared on screen seemed endless. Abattoirs, accountants, advertising, agriculture. 'What's it going to be under, Peter?'

'No idea. But it's not abattoirs, I hope.'

'Okay. Just yell if I scroll past any possibility. Here,' he stopped the stream of terms, 'How about "clinical chemists"?'

'No. Keep going.'

Hobbies, holding companies, holidays, home improvement, horse breeding and training, hosiery, hospital services.

'How about that? Hospitals.'

'Maybe,' Peter said. 'But let's carry on for a bit. It's not quite right.'

Marriage bureaux, marital arts, massage, meat products, mechanical engineers, medical practitioners.

'Stop,' Peter cried.

'Yes, I see it,' Mike said. He put the cursor on 'medical practitioners' and pressed 'return'. 'My God!' he exclaimed. 'There's a lot of it about.'

The VDU screen showed yet another list. Accident, accouchers, acupuncture, alienists, alternative medicine, anaesthetists, aurists, bacteriologists, bone specialists, brain specialists, chiropodists, chiropractor.

'I haven't heard of half of these,' Mike said.

Clinical psychologists, clinics.

'How's that? Clinics?' he asked.

'No,' Peter answered. 'It's all family planning and VD.'

Dental surgeons, dermatologists, diagnostic services.

'That's the one!'

The computer responded to the request for further information with a list of locations. 'Where is your dad's practice?' queried Mike.

'Milton Keynes,' Peter replied, his tone slightly apologetic.

Mike hit a few more keys, then he beamed. 'There you go. Three services. Which do you want?'

Peter cheered. 'Yeah! Home and dry. Netherstone's the one.'

'Okay.' Mike hit 'return' with gusto.

The screen responded with a logo and, underneath it, the words 'Netherstone Health Centre. Self-diagnosis programme.' At the bottom of the screen in small letters, it read, 'Do you wish to log on? Y/N.'

'We certainly do,' Peter chimed.

Mike clicked on the Y box. But as soon as he saw the response, he sighed. Just one word at the top of the screen. 'Password.' He turned to Peter and asked, 'Well, do you know it? We're nobbled if not.'

'I've no idea,' said Peter, suddenly crestfallen.

'There's many a slip 'twixt cup and stiff upper lip,' Alan commented from the bunk.

'Aren't you one of his patients? You should have the password,' said Mike.

'No,' Peter groaned. 'Doctors don't treat their own families. All I know is, he gives each patient a code. It's probably their name followed by a number.'

'He's bound to have a Smith on his list,' Alan suggested. 'Put in Smith and try a few numbers.'

'There are a lot of numbers in this world,' Mike replied.

'And if it's like other systems, it'll only give me five or ten random tries then it'll shut me out. To discourage illegitimate use. Then it won't give me further attempts to log on for ... I don't know ... five or ten minutes, maybe. It depends how keen it is to deter hackers.'

Neither Alan nor Peter replied immediately. The silence spoke for them all. Eventually, in an attempt to cheer them up, Alan said, 'The molehill that broke the camel's back.'

'It's hardly a molehill,' Mike replied. 'It's more like a mountain.'

Peter moaned, 'We're kaput, then.'

Mike looked aggrieved. 'Do you give up if you don't get the first clue of a crossword? There is something I can do. Let me think.' He sat back for a moment. 'I don't like trial-and-error methods. So inelegant. Look, Peter, how often is this programme used by his patients?'

Peter shrugged. 'Before I came away, Dad said it was catching on. But he's the optimistic sort. I don't know.'

'Clearly your dad specializes in diseases of the rich and computer-literate,' Alan baited him. 'The sort of service the poor have to do without since our beloved Government dismantled the NHS and welfare state all those years ago.'

Mike was not to be diverted once an idea had struck him, so he ignored Alan's comment. 'I can get in there,' he said. 'But it could take time. I can write a nifty little routine that will store someone else's password whenever they connect to the system. That's the way to do it! I'll write a capture programme into the log on procedure. Next time a legit user logs on, his password will be captured and stored in my file. The computer will reject the user because I've hi-jacked his password but he'll just think he's mistyped his password because, for security, nothing appears on the screen while he's typing it. No way of checking if he's got the password right. He'll try again and the second time, my file will pass him through to the normal log on programme and he'll be connected. After he's finished, I recall my file and there will be a lovely password.'

'Great,' Peter said. 'How long will it take?'

'Oh, I've done similar corruptions before. It won't take long to establish my file in this operating system – it's unlikely to be that well protected. But how long before a legit user shows? That's what we rely on.'

Peter and Alan went to give Charlton the news with mixed feelings. It could be an hour or two, it could be a day or a week before Mike made any progress. Mel's condition could worsen a lot in that time. 'Or,' Peter reminded Charlton, 'he might get better.'

'I wouldn't hold your breath,' Alan said.

Charlton was woken by a quiet knock at his door. With a weary sigh, he climbed down from his bunk, glancing at Mel's listless body, and crept to the door. 'Who is it?' he asked in a hushed voice without opening the door.

A whisper answered his own. 'Me. Gail.'

'Okay.' He fumbled to open the door. She slipped into the cabin but neither of them spoke till he had closed the door again. 'What is it?' he asked.

Gail hardly glanced at Charlton in his pyjamas. By the night-light she was looking at Mel. 'I wondered how he was.'

Charlton looked at his wrist but he wasn't wearing his watch. 'It's the middle of the night.'

'I was exercising Alien in the corridor. I couldn't sleep. Hope you don't mind.'

'No. I don't sleep much either.'

Gail peered closely at Mel. 'Asleep,' she noted.

'Yeah. Unconscious maybe.'

'At least he looks peaceful.'

'For a change,' Charlton answered. 'He's been twitching and all sorts.'

'Twitching?'

'Sort of contortions, I guess. Sometimes his whole body, sometimes just his face. It's very off-putting.'

'Is there still a discharge from his eyes?' Gail asked.

'It comes and goes.'

Gail sighed.

'Why did you come?' Charlton asked quietly.

'I don't know,' she whispered hesitantly. 'I feel ... to blame. In a way. I brought him into Cell Block G.' She did not admit that, ever since Alien had befriended Mel so curiously and quickly, she had been intrigued by him. In a sense, she thought, both her dog and Mel were aliens. Both were forced to remain hidden in a place they didn't belong. Perhaps she had a weakness for stowaways.

'I should go,' she said. 'Keep me in touch, Charlton. Especially when Mike has some success.'

'Okay,' Charlton said as he opened the door for her. 'And thanks,' he whispered.

Before he climbed back up to his bunk, Charlton gazed through his port-hole across Bergen harbour. It was quiet and still, hardly a ripple on the water. No ferries and, for once, it wasn't raining. On the island across the bay, yellow lights glinted like decorations on a black background. Yet he felt anything but peaceful inside. He was scared for Mel, disconcerted by his occasional ravings, and he was haunted by the spectre of living again in the stifling presence of serious illness. Memories loomed ever closer.

He knew that he wouldn't be able to get back to sleep so he sat at the table and continued his latest sketch. It was a bed and, amongst the crumpled sheets, a distraught figure. It wasn't clear from the unfinished face whether the subject was Mel or some other victim.

Charlton tapped Mike on the shoulder and enquired, softly but urgently, 'Are you sure you've checked that password?'

'Yes,' Mike replied, somewhat impatiently.

'But it's been twenty-four hours and he's getting worse.'

'Charlton!' Mr Beever called. 'You're the last person I thought I'd have to ask to be quiet.'

Charlton's head sank. If he could not concentrate on the sheet of figures on his table, at least he could hide behind Mike Zlatkis.

At the front of the class, Eager Beever was fighting a losing battle over fractions, proportions and percentages. 'Right,' he said resolutely. 'Let's do it this way. Think of something we all do every day. Like eating or sleeping but neither of those.'

A voice from the back of the class shouted, 'Going to the loo.'

After the sniggers had died down, Mr Beever accepted the

suggestion. 'Okay. Let's work out how much of our lives we spend in the loo. Via percentages. First,' he instructed, 'we need to know how long we spend in there each day.'

Inevitably, Gabby remarked, 'That depends what you do in it.'

'I suppose I asked for that. But since you haven't come up with a helpful response, let's call it, say, ten minutes. Now, what percentage of a day is that?' On the board, he went through all the maths, converting hours into minutes, and finally arriving at a figure of 0.69 per cent. 'Let's call it 0.7 per cent,' he said. 'Now, if you live to be a hundred, how much of it's been in the toilet? Think about it. But not too much. Don't find complications where there aren't any. Point seven per cent of one hundred.'

Mr Beever was smarting because Peter had not graced the class with his presence but at least it gave the others a chance to think. For a change, they were not overawed and frustrated by Peter's academic flair.

Eventually the answer came. '0.7 per cent of one hundred years must be 0.7 of a year.'

'Exactly!' Mr Beever beamed. 'And how long's that in days? After tapping the keys of his calculator, he announced, 'Two hundred and fifty five days, roughly. And that's ... over eight months.' He paused for effect then said enthusiastically, 'There you are. Applied maths tells you that you're likely to spend eight months of your life in the loo.'

Gabby piped up, 'That's a lot of ...'

'Yes. Thank you, Gabby,' Mr Beever interrupted. 'I think we can guess for ourselves what it's a lot of. Let's leave something to the imagination.'

Trevor Beever breathed in deeply, coughed and pretended to choke.

'All right, all right. Unsubtle point taken,' replied one of the three smokers amongst the staff.

'I don't know why you light up in here. Just breathe in like the rest of us second-hand smokers.'

The staff room was littered with off-duty teachers. The tables were littered with coffee mugs, newspapers and lesson plans. The walls were littered with timetables and duty rotas. Each of the dozen forms had its own schedule and each one was colour-coded. The wall looked like a giant shade chart and Form G, Beever's bunch, was a bright yellow blob on the chart. The scheme had been organized elaborately, immaculately and, Trevor believed, unnecessarily by the Deputy Head, Mr Brown. Mr Brown was obsessed by colour. He also seemed, like Mr Uunk, to lack a first name. They were Mr Brown and Mr Uunk to pupils and staff alike. Perhaps that's why the pupils had taken it upon themselves to christen Mr Uunk. Cueball was a good name for someone so perfectly bald.

From the rows of mugs, Trevor carefully selected a yellow mug, filled it with coffee, as thick and black as the sea water at night, held it up towards Mr Brown and said, 'Cheers. Good colour scheme.' It wasn't the first time that he had ribbed his colleague over the matter of the colourful display.

'Don't start that again, Mr Beever,' warned Mr Brown, as if he were threatening one of his pupils.

'I've already finished, Mr Brown.' Trevor took a gulp of coffee and sat down. The two teachers had long since ceased to disguise their mutual lack of respect.

Mr Brown turned to one of the other teachers and asked, 'Any news on who's responsible for vandalizing books in the library?'

'No.'

'I hear,' Trevor said, 'that one of the Brown group put a snooker ball through the TV room window. Left the brown ball as a calling card.' He couldn't resist provoking the Deputy Head.

'If you gave them Black and Deckers,' Brown said, 'they'd be drilling through the sides of the ship. Some of these hooligans are ram-raiders and drug dealers. Some are even on arson and firearms charges, you know. And there's the animal liberation yobs. The little horrors are unstoppable and unfathomable.'

'Nonsense,' Trevor retorted. 'If you label them as irresponsible, they'll act irresponsibly. That's not un-fathomable. It's what you'd expect.'

'So you just trust your lot and they never misbehave?'

Trevor laughed. 'Children will be children, not angels! And I don't promise what I can't deliver. I wouldn't really want to, anyway. In fact, something's brewing right now in Cell Block G. Secret machinations and all that. I haven't been able to put my finger on it yet.'

'Only now it's brewing?' Mr Brown snorted. 'Don't fool yourself. Your lot are as destructive as the rest. They just haven't been caught yet.'

'You may well be right. But I doubt if they'll be in-volved in any really nasty business. More mischief than malevolence.'

'You must tell the rest of us,' Mr Brown said, his own

tone midway between mischief and malevolence, 'this magnificent method of control that you exert.'

'It's hardly that. But I do try not to antagonize them.'

'Yes, I've noticed,' Mr Brown replied. 'We know why they call you Eager Beever. I can't say I like all this liberal camaraderie. It's more to do with trying to be popular than with teaching. You have to court unpopularity to educate effectively.'

'Oh. I didn't know that. I simply try to develop them in whatever captures their imagination. At least they're attentive then. Let's face it, we're being used to give society a break from these kids for a while. That's what OBTUSE is all about. It's not really about their education, so we might as well let them enjoy it. They're not so much unsettled as cheated – in lots of different ways. Some abused, some misunderstood, some are just too astute. They're not write-offs, though. There's hope for them. But it's no use forcing them where they don't want to go. Or their grudges will really come to the surface. You'll get more than balls through windows.'

'Then we'll spend all our lessons on the inane thump thump thump of pop music. That's all those Philistines care about.'

'There are worse things to be interested in.'

Mr Brown was astonished. 'Really? I've banned my kids from playing those pop video things. They're ... diabolical.'

'You can't judge modern music by what appears in pop videos any more than you can judge journalism by reading the *Sun*,' Trevor argued. 'And, yes, I've got a lad who might just come out of his shell through rock music and art.'

'Art! He's probably responsible for the graffiti.'

Trevor shrugged. 'I don't know. I doubt it, though. Not his style. But at least it gives the corridors a bit of colour. That felt-tip drawing of Uunk's head is beautifully drawn.'

'What!' Mr Brown exploded. 'It's crude and grotesque. It's offensive.'

'That depends on your point of reference. I think it's got a ... lovable rogue quality to it. Do you remember,' he said, 'that programme, *Spitting Image*, before it got censored into oblivion? Our kids' images of Cueball ... sorry, Uunk ... are similar to those puppets. Naughty but nice. It's a good vent for their feelings, and ultimately harmless.'

'Well, I'm sure that Mr Uunk has been hurt by this malicious graffiti. And I have every sympathy.'

'Oh,' Trevor jibed, 'you're just grumpy because of that "Cueball kissed the Brown" slogan on Deck 2.'

Mr Brown flared up immediately. 'That's the worst slur of them all! That will be painted out tomorrow. I will not tolerate that sort of innuendo. It makes my flesh creep.' Sweat appeared on the Deputy Head's brow.

'All right, all right.' Suddenly, the pleasure of taunting Mr Brown evaporated. The Deputy Head's over-reaction suggested a bigotry that would be unpleasant to reveal. Besides, Trevor thought, it was a pity to drive anyone to the end of his tether with a mere joke. Even the righteous Mr Brown. 'If you let them know that you're outraged by their exuberance or minor misdemeanours, how do you react to their major misdeeds? How will they ever learn the difference between mischief and malice? So far, it's just been high spirits,' Trevor said. He also wanted to warn Mr Brown that persecution would only escalate their misbehaviour, but decided against. He felt that any more preaching to Mr Brown would probably escalate the Deputy Head's efforts to play the Grand Inquisitor. Mr Brown was physiologically incapable of leniency. Kid gloves simply did not fit him.

Also, his blood had an unusually low boiling point. 'High spirits!' he ranted. 'There's hardly a working fire extinguisher left. They've all been let off. And do you know how many tables and chairs they've thrown overboard?'

'They do seem to like seeing the white plastic ones bobbing on the waves, I'm afraid,' Trevor said in a conciliatory tone.

'And another thing,' Mr Brown complained. 'The Government is kind enough to give each of them a grant and what do they do? They pocket the money and steal from the shop. The crooks!'

It occurred to Trevor that Mr Brown lacked the one essential characteristic of a teacher: he did not like children. 'I gather,' he said, 'that you belong to the children-should-be-seen-and-not-heard school.' At the same time, Trevor thought, 'He certainly doesn't belong on the *Queen of the Fjords*. I wonder why he was selected.'

'Even in a modern world,' Mr Brown said, 'there's room for good old-fashioned values.'

Trevor groaned. He was always saddened by those who try to make time stand still. He himself had always been fond of change and welcomed the unknown lurking round the next corner. Traditions, he believed, should be challenged constantly. Besides, only the King Canutes of this world tried to resist the times a'changing. And they soon found themselves all at sea. Trevor took a drink of coffee and relaxed in his chair. He was too dismayed and frustrated to embark on another futile argument with the Deputy Head.

Instead, Trevor took out of his bag some scraps of paper that he had retrieved from the bin in his classroom. He did not make a habit of scavenging in dustbins but the sight of Gabby tearing up some of her work and throwing it away had aroused his curiosity. It was not his normal behaviour to lose his temper with his pupils either, so he was desperate to salvage something from his clash with her. On the table, he shuffled the pieces of paper until he had in front of him a completed jigsaw of a page from Gabby's diary.

In Bergen it rained. In Bergen it always rains. In Bergen the rich own Kagool shops. Bergen has a grey roof at tree-top level and it's made of thick cloud. Bergen's houses are straight out of Amityville but built on slopes. Bergen's schoolkids speak better English than what we does. At least the ones that they wheeled out to meet us did. An overland coach trip from Bergen means a bit of narrow bumpy road between ferries. A trip means staring at stave churches, views from tops of mountains (the funicular was fun), the house that was featured in the film Psycho *– otherwise known as Grieg's home (where we were subjected to a horrifying recital; write heavy metal tunes he certainly did not), and a million museums (by far the biggest bundle of laughs was the Leprosy Museum).*

What is the big deal about fish? Fish to eat, Bergen Aquarium to visit, the fish market to stroll around (more or less a biology lesson). Thank God the Fishery Museum was closed for building repairs.

Summary: Bergen = water + fish.

A broad grin of relief spread across Trevor's face. 'I knew it!' he said to himself. 'Weak on detail and accuracy but strong on atmosphere and inspiration. She *has* got something!' He sipped his coffee and considered how he might make her proud to use her talent. He knew that it would be unprofessional for a teacher to show favouritism to one particular pupil but he was beginning to be obsessed with Gabby. He relished the task of ensuring that she made a success of her life.

Sternhell dismissed his Parliamentary Private Secretary before picking up the telephone. He dialled, then waited for a response. 'John,' he said, oozing charm. 'How are things?' he asked as if the Defence Secretary could sum up the state of the nation in a single sentence. 'Yes, well,' Sternhell remarked after he'd heard the reply, 'I'm phoning to keep up to date on the military exercise near Norway. You know the PM asked me to keep in touch. And,' he slipped in, 'I think we both know what she has in mind, given the imminent cabinet reshuffle.' Sternhell listened patiently and politely to the Defence Secretary, then said, 'Yes. All very good, but there is also something specific I need to pursue with you. Were my suggestions regarding submarine activity heeded?' After listening avidly to the answer he replied, 'Good. And, as I recommended, it's Captain Mallet in charge?' A moment later Sternhell smiled and repeated himself, 'Good.' Then, to emphasize his contentment, he added, 'Excellent.'

The sky blue paint around the swimming pool was beginning to peel away. The water was heated even if, to the blubberless children of Block G, it felt decidedly arctic. Trevor Beever came up to the surface, wiped the water from his face and rubbed at his bloodshot eyes. Peter, fully clothed, stood above him. 'You wanted me?' Peter asked him.

As soon as Mr Beever had noted that Peter was avoiding yet another lesson – this time, in the swimming pool – he had sent out a search party for him. 'Ah, Peter,' he said, grabbing hold of the edge of the pool. 'Just a second.' He heaved himself out of the water and into a sitting position on the lip of the swimming pool. Only his legs remained in the water. He groaned as he rubbed at his eyes again. 'Heavy on the chlorine in there,' he complained.

'Chlorine isn't used,' Peter returned. 'It was a chemical weapon in the first world war, so they're hardly likely to put it in swimming baths. It's a solution of hypochlorous acid and hypochlorite.'

'Well, whatever it is, it stings the eyes.'

'That's something else, I think,' Peter replied. 'Reaction between organic waste and the hypochlorous acid gives this stuff that causes eye irritation.'

'I'll take your word for it, Peter. But right now,' said the teacher, shivering, 'there's something else that's irritating me. You know, I don't appreciate you bunking off my lessons. What are you up to?'

On the other side of the pool, Mr Beever's helper yelled, 'Head down, Graham! Breathe to the side, not the front.'

'Looks like a struggling whale,' Peter chuckled.

Perhaps one of the Cell Block G inmates did have enough blubber to protect him from the cold.

'That's enough of that,' Mr Beever admonished Peter. 'Besides, I want an answer to my question.'

'What do you mean?'

'I mean, I don't like to see you wasting the opportunities I try to give you.'

'I ... er ... wasn't wasting time, though,' Peter defended himself.

'Why? What were you doing?'

'I was in the library.'

'Yeah?' Mr Beever looked into Peter's face in an attempt to decide if Peter was telling the truth. 'What were you reading about?'

'Chemistry. Pesticides, pollution. Chemical weapons. That sort of thing.'

'Like the use of chlorine in World War One?'

'Mm.'

'You'd better write me a report on it, then, hadn't you? The benefits and risks of chemicals.'

Peter did not seem put out. He might even relish the task. 'Okay. No problem.'

'But before you go, Peter. Don't neglect other aspects, like this lesson.' He indicated the swimming pool. 'Don't neglect the body. It needs as much exercise as the brain.'

'I don't,' Peter replied resentfully. 'But I don't like swimming. I do my own exercises. In privacy. My body is a finely tuned instrument.'

Startled, Mr Beever watched Peter retreating from the pool. He was not sure whether he'd witnessed bravado as a cover for fear of water, a simple joke, or a lad with self-assurance and hidden strength.

No one went on deck to wave goodbye to Bergen, the wettest place in the known universe. It was raining and a blustery wind did its best to shred the Union flag. Inside, in cabin G9, a disease did its best to shred Mel's human body and mind.

Every muscle in his body ached. He felt as if he'd been pummelled for three days. Reverting to his natural form would offer relief but, in that guise, the Earth's atmosphere would destroy him in a minute or so. Anyway, Charlton stood sentry, as faithful and protective as Alien at Gail's side. Yet Mel longed for the release that his own form could provide, if only it were available to him. If only it were not the ultimate release. He knew that he had to persevere, to defeat the earthly infection. Over and over again, he told himself that he must recover, but the bouts of pain and confusion became longer and more frequent. Control over his strange body and belief in deliverance became increasingly difficult.

Suddenly he yanked himself upward in panic. 'Where are we going?'

'Out to sea.' It was Charlton's voice.

'To sea? North?'

'Yes.'

How long had he been in bed? They could be near the end. Trying unsuccessfully to control the movements of his face, arms and legs, he shouted, 'It could be soon! I must save them. Without me they will not survive.' His arms flailed about, trying to grab Charlton. 'How near are we to my destination?'

'I don't know. You've never said exactly where you're going.'

'In the sea, near Hammerfest.'

'In the sea?' Charlton was mystified. 'I don't know,' he said again, shrugging. 'But we've only just left Bergen.'

'Bergen?' Mel looked puzzled for a moment, then relaxed. 'Bergen, yes. South-west of Norway. The meadow by the mountain. Second city. The next port is Kristiansund. There is still time.' He flopped back onto the bed, coughed violently, then shut his gritty eyes.

If Mel was going to save them, someone would first have to save him. The fight had exhausted his spirit.

The pouring rain washed the salt off the *Queen*'s deck and fittings. The heavens were as threatening and virulent as Mel's disease. Through the downpour, the yellow flares of Mongstad refinery could just be made out against the black clouds.

A Dog's Life

The *Queen of the Fjords* shook, rattled and rolled through the obstacle course between Bergen and Kristiansund. The sodden Union flag hung limply against the mast as if fatigued by the storm. For most of the journey, the ship was protected from the swell of the open sea by the islands on her port side. When she was exposed for a while to the Norwegian Sea, the gentle pitching did not even upset the most delicate of stomachs. There was sickness aboard, of course, but it travelled incognito in cabin G9. Unseen, unchecked and untreated.

Charlton opened the door just wide enough for Gail to edge her way into his cabin. 'How is he?' she whispered anxiously.

'Calm now but he's been real bad. And saying some real weird stuff. You know,' Charlton said as Gail peered closely at the sleeping patient, 'I think it's important that he gets somewhere in North Norway. I think he's got to save someone there.'

'Save someone? From what?' asked Gail.

'From dying. "Without me they will not survive." He's said it, or something like it, lots of times. And he's been reciting facts about … everything – us and Norway in particular – as if he'd learnt it parrot-fashion.'

'Do you think he's going to be all right, Charlton? Really?'

Charlton shrugged. 'Dunno. He doesn't look good. All

the writhing and contortions are the worst. It's like nothing on earth ... unnatural. Then sometimes he seems to try to move but can't – as if he was paralysed.'

Gail sighed. 'Well, we'll just have to hope that Mike Zlatkis comes up trumps. Gabby and some others have gone to his cabin to try again.'

'Aren't you going?' Charlton asked her.

'They don't need me. I'd rather be here.' She sat down but then realized that she had presumed Charlton's consent. 'Do you mind?'

'No. You're welcome. Being alone with disease is ... no fun.'

'No, I guess not. It can't be very nice for you. Do you want to go to Mike's while I stop with him?'

Charlton thought about it but declined. 'No. They can get on okay. They'll soon be along if they get anywhere.'

'I don't blame you. These cells are small enough without cramming lots into one of them. I hate being closed in.' Her voice trailed away.

'You don't like to talk much, either,' Charlton observed.

'This could be my longest conversation.' Gail smiled a little. 'You're hardly a chat show host yourself.'

'I guess not.' He did not elaborate. They shared their mutual concern for Mel in silence.

A posse of the Splinter group was packed into Mike's cabin. Anticipation was running high. Mike was hitting keys, muttering encouragement to his PC, and occasionally addressing the others. 'A bit back, when hacking presented very little challenge, passwords were straightforward. Car regist-rations, wives' names and the like.' He sighed and tapped a few more keys. 'The main ones were "sex" and "Marilyn Monroe".'

'A male-dominated business, or what?' Toni commented over Peter's shoulder.

'Easy to crack. The computers allowed unlimited at-tempts so you just had floppies with all known names and words. Or an algorithm to generate all car number plates. You set it going and waited. Now computers shut you out after a few tries, and passwords are usually a combination of numbers, words and symbols like the dollar sign. But once you've cracked them, they usually make sense.'

Gabby put her hand on Mike's shoulder. 'I'm having second thoughts about that date of ours – if I'm just going to be lectured about computers all the time,' she said with a grin on her face. 'So stop pissing about and give us the password.'

Mike exonerated himself. 'It's not an easy business, you know. Anyway, nearly there. I'm just retrieving my capture file now. Let's see if there's anything in it.' He hit the return key and sat back in triumph. 'Yes!' he exclaimed. 'Someone's accessed the programme. And there,' he said pointing to the VDU, 'is his password. I told you – a number, words and, in this case, underscores.'

They all cheered. For fear of attracting attention of any passing member of staff, it was a quiet cheer.

'And given it's Milton Keynes,' Peter noted, 'it *does* make sense.'

The screen showed, 'Password: 5_concrete_cows.'

'Let's not hang about,' Gabby said. 'Let's get in there!'

Peter added, 'Who's nearest the door? You'd better get down the corridor and bring Charlton. He'll have to tell us all the symptoms.'

The VDU went blank for a couple of seconds after Mike entered the password. Then a screenful of script appeared. 'Welcome to the Netherstone Self Diagnosis Package. There are bound to be times when you are anxious about your health. But you may be unsure whether it is something serious that needs attention, or something that will pass without treatment. By going through the series of checks in this programme, you can find out whether you are really ill, or just mildly unwell. This service does not replace a consult-ation with your doctor but it can calm fears over minor ailments without the expense of a visit to your doctor. Unusual or potentially serious symptoms will be identified and referred to the doctor. An appointment or immediate referral is completely automatic when necessary.'

Mike pressed 'return' to scroll the screen. 'The system is designed to be used anonymously and in total confidence. It is most important that you respond to questions as carefully, accurately and honestly as you can. The programme will require you to respond first to questions about age, weight and similar general characteristics. These questions are im-portant to your diagnosis. The programme then asks you to enter specific signs of illness. Clear instructions are given on how to respond at all points. Press *return* to begin the pro-gramme.' At the bottom of the screen there was a logo and the words, 'Sponsored by Fitness Drugs Limited.'

'Are you ready, Charlton?' Mike asked.

'I guess so,' he replied.

'Get on with it!' Gabby cried.

'All right. Here we go.' Mike read the first question aloud. 'Sex. Male or female? I don't think we need Charlton's advice on this one. Next, age in years. What do you reckon? Fifteen, sixteen?'

'Put in sixteen,' someone suggested.

'Right. Now weight, in kilogrammes. Any guesses?'

'A lot less than when he came on board,' Alan said.

'Try fifty kilos,' said Charlton.

'Okay. Now, height in centimetres.'

'He's my height,' Alan interjected. 'And I'm a hundred and sixty or thereabouts.'

'History of illness? How do we know?'

'Just say no,' Gabby said impatiently, 'so we can get on to the juicy stuff.'

'Smoker or non-smoker? Non, I think,' Mike answered himself and keyed in the response. Immediately, the next question appeared on screen. 'Do you suffer any allergies?'

'Who knows? Put in no or it'll ask us which allergies.'

'We could make one up,' Gabby said. 'Like an allergy to seawater.'

'Are you taking any drugs at this time?' Mike read from the screen.

'Does this thing have a "don't know" box?'

'Give it another N for no,' said Alan.

The programme moved into the second phase, gathering data on symptoms. 'Temperature' the screen read. 'Enter temperature in Celsius, if known. If not, enter N for normal, C for cold, H for hot, or F for feverish.'

'Might as well go the whole hog, eh, Charlton? Feverish, I'd say,' Peter said.

Charlton nodded. 'Yes. F.'

'Sickness?' Mike read from the screen.

'Yes,' replied Charlton.

'Lots of heavy breathing into the big white telephone,' Alan quipped.

'Diarrhoea?'

'Yes.'

'Wouldn't it be easier to list what he hasn't got?' Gabby uttered.

Ignoring her, Mike continued, 'Look, this is more interesting. We choose a part of the body from this list and report what's wrong with it.'

'Where do we start?' Charlton asked.

'The order doesn't matter.'

'Let's go for eyes, then.'

The programme allowed a choice from a list: sore, bloodshot, impaired vision (e.g. blurred vision, double vision), discharges from the eyes, foreign object in the eye, blindness.'

'How does your dad expect the blind to cope with this programme, Peter?' Alan asked.

'With the help of a friend, I guess.'

'Let's get on to the interesting parts of the body,' Gabby urged.

They reported the problems with Mel's eyes, his spasms, the abnormal facial contortions, occasional paralysis, and violent coughing. Once they had come to the end of the programme, the screen showed the Fitness Drugs logo and the message, 'Please wait a moment.'

But it was more than a moment.

'Come on,' Charlton exhorted under his breath.

'It's thinking about it,' Mike explained. 'Quite a large data base to check against, no doubt.'

'I must tell Dad to get it to play a tune to soothe the troubled spirit whilst waiting,' said Peter.

'Or it could just show a meter ticking away showing how much money the thing's guzzling,' Alan suggested.

Suddenly, the VDU showed a different display. 'The computer has failed to recognize your illness. It may not be serious but you have been referred directly to Dr Fallick who wishes to check a few of the facts before suggesting whether treatment is advisable. Simply type in your response to each of the doctor's questions, and when you have finished, strike the return key to transmit your answer.'

The first question Peter's dad asked was, 'Hello, caller. Do you wish to identify yourself?'

'Here,' Peter said to Mike, 'Let me take over.' Mike moved aside to let Peter tap in the answers. 'Hi, Dad,' he typed. 'It's Peter. I'm well but there's someone on board with those symptoms.'

The reply came back, 'How did you break into this system?'

'We have a hacker on board.'

'You also have a misplaced sense of humour. Those symptoms fooled my computer because they are a joke. Right? You are wasting my computer time, Peter.'

'No,' Peter replied. 'He is really ill.'

'Yes, I know. He has a warm and dry nose, I imagine.'

'What do you mean?'

'Classic symptoms of distemper. Canine distemper. A virus causing an incurable disorder of the nervous system.'

'That's Gail's pet python for you,' Alan cried. 'She said that Mel patted her poxy pooch.'

'Shush!' Peter cried above the clamour in the room. He typed, 'Can humans get it?'

The reply was short. 'No.'

'Sure?'

'Absolutely. The virus belongs to the measles group but cannot spread to man. It cannot penetrate a human cell, I suspect. Admit it is a dog, Peter.'

'Well,' Peter addressed the others in the cabin. 'What do I say?'

'Tell him it *is* a real person,' Charlton urged. 'Try again.'

'But he's convinced,' Peter replied. 'I can feel Dad's confidence hundreds of miles away.'

'That's right,' Alan added. 'We're not going to get any further here. Just tell him it's a dog and have done with it. Anyway, we've learnt all we need. Even if medical science isn't ready to accept a human with distemper, we can treat it like measles.' He hesitated, then asked Peter, 'Can't we?'

Peter shrugged. 'I don't know. Not many get measles these days. Vaccination rules. How do you cure measles anyway?'

'We could vaccinate,' Alan exhorted. 'The nurse is bound to have a measles vaccine.'

'But biochemistry doesn't work like that,' Peter objected.

'Perhaps Norwegian biochemistry is different,' Alan said.

'Don't be ...'

Alan interrupted the rebuke. 'It was a joke, Peter.'

'Oh. Well, it won't work anyway. It's no good preventing a disease when he's already got it.'

'I suppose not,' Alan admitted. 'Bolting the stable door after the horse has been led to water.'

'Look,' cried Charlton in frustration. 'We need an answer. We've got to help Mel. He's on a special mission of some sort – to save someone near Hammerfest. So let's sort it out.'

Dr Fallick was also getting impatient. The screen showed, 'Well?'

'All right,' Peter said. 'Let's try this.' He typed, 'You have us beat, Dad. We have a smuggled dog on board. But how should we treat it? Antibiotics?'

'No. Antibiotics will arrest secondary bacterial infection only. They will not halt the virus.'

'So what do we do?'

'Such cases are usually hopeless. Have it put down.'

Charlton would have cried out but he was stunned into silence.

Gabby was less inhibited. 'Great move, Peter! You made a right balls-up of that.'

Peter knew that any esteem that he had enjoyed arose only because he'd been indispensable. Once he'd made a mistake, he was no longer useful. And when he was no longer useful, his popularity would hit rock bottom again. He drooped, but not enough to let them trample all over him. 'At least I tried,' he muttered. Shaking his head, he typed into the computer, 'Thanks for those kind words.'

'Sorry. It should not be allowed to suffer, though. And please don't hack into my system again. Particularly not over a dog.'

'Sorry, Dad.'

'Have a nice cruise. Behave yourself for a change.'

Mike took over and logged off the system while the others skulked away.

Peter's attempt to take the sting out of Mel's predicament had failed. Yet any satisfaction that the kids in the Splinter Group derived from Peter's comeuppance was tempered by concern for Mel.

'We want to put Mel out of his misery,' Gabby remarked, 'but that's a bit extreme. Have him put down!'

Charlton alone thanked Peter for his efforts.

'I'm sorry,' Peter replied.

Towering behind them, Roger said, 'Ain't your fault. Good try.'

'Thanks.'

'But ... er,' Charlton put in, 'what do we do now?'

'I'm thinking,' Peter answered. 'I haven't given up yet. You see, he's got a virus. Distemper or not, it's a virus. And if it's getting the better of him,' he concluded, 'it means he hasn't got antibodies for it.'

Charlton brightened a little, recalled something that Mel had once muttered. 'That's right. He said he had to produce antibodies. I remember now.'

'Where do you get them from?' Roger asked as if they could be plucked off a supermarket shelf.

'Well ...' Peter hesitated. 'Charlton, you'd better go back and look after Mel. I need a visit to the library.'

Roger's admiration for Peter, and his faith in him, was undiminished. 'I'll come with you,' he volunteered.

'Okay,' Peter replied more cheerfully. In a world that often spurned him, Peter was glad of the company.

As they strode along the white corridors, Roger asked him, 'You know all about sickness and stuff, don't you?'

'Not enough, apparently. But this one's really weird. I don't know, but my memory tells me to check on something called gamma globulin.'

'Sounds horrible.'

'You'd be in big trouble without it,' said Peter. 'I'm wondering if that's why Mel's in trouble.'

'You're probably right,' Jolly Roger replied encouragingly.

Mel was not the only one in trouble. When they got to the library their way was blocked by a couple of boys from one of the other classes. 'You can't go in there,' they ordered.

'Why not?' Peter responded.

'Because you can't.'

'It's important,' Peter said. 'I've got to get in.'

'Yeah,' Roger confirmed.

'Well,' the bigger of the two boys said, 'what we're doing is more important.'

'You're not tearing up books, are you?'

'Now, would we do that?' one boy asked the other with a sneer on his face.

''Course not,' his companion replied, also sniggering.

'A little burning, maybe, but no tearing.'

'Burning!' Peter was outraged. 'But I like books.'

'Hear that? He likes books!' Addressing Peter, the boy said, 'What are you going to do about it? Run and tell Cueball?'

'No,' Peter replied, 'I'm going in.' He took a step forward resolutely but was pushed back. Still not intimidated, he tried to force an entrance again.

The bigger boy's fist clenched threateningly.

'All right, Peter,' Roger said, pulling him back. 'I'll take care of it.'

'No ...'

Two fists landed in Roger's stomach and, with a groan, he dropped to the floor, winded.

Peter shook his head. 'You shouldn't have done that,' he said to them as he helped Roger to his feet.

The boys laughed. 'Oh, we shouldn't have done that,' they echoed.

'I'm going in now,' said Peter firmly. 'Don't try to stop me.'

As he stepped forward, a fist was aimed at his stomach too. Peter's left arm flew down and parried the blow. His attacker's face showed amazement when his jab failed to connect. The second boy threw a punch at Peter's head. Peter did not duck or sidestep. Instead, his right hand shot up and caught the fist in midair, just before it hit his face. The boy cried out as if he had landed a blow on a brick wall. Peter's hand enveloped the fist and squeezed it.

'Ouch!' The boy's knuckles became white and his nails bit

into his own palm as Peter maintained the pressure. 'You ...' In a despairing effort to free himself, the boy aimed a kick between Peter's legs.

Peter's right hand remained clamped around the boy's fist. The left chopped downwards and struck just above the rising knee. The would-be assailant shrieked in agony and, with his free hand, clutched at his wounded leg.

'Now,' Peter said. 'I advise you to call your friends out of the library and let us in.'

The smaller boy reached into his pocket and pulled out a knife. The blade was pointed at Peter.

'Don't be silly,' Peter warned him. 'If that thing comes any closer to me, I'll break the arm that does it. Understand?'

'You're bluffing,' the boy returned nervously.

'Try me.'

The first boy yelped as Peter applied yet more pressure. 'He's not bluffing, Kev. Ow! He's crushing my hand! Get them out of there. He's crazy. He's doing my hand in.'

'Sure?'

'You'd know if he had your hand,' he whined. 'Quick, before he breaks something.'

Peter did not release his grip on the fist until all of the boys had traipsed sulkily out of the library. Finally, when he did let go, the boy groaned with pain as he slowly unclenched his throbbing fist. Cradling his injury with his good hand, he repeated, 'You're crazy.' He limped a few steps away then turned to reinforce his point of view. 'A nutter!'

'I just like books,' Peter replied. 'That's all.'

As the gang shuffled down the corridor, Roger breathed, 'Wow!'

Peter smiled at him. 'Are you okay? I tried to stop you getting hurt.'

Roger was not thinking of himself. 'I ain't never seen anyone fight like that.'

'What you saw,' Peter chided him, 'was the avoidance of a fight. I don't like fights.'

'Could you really have broken his arm?' he asked in wonderment.

'No,' Peter said. 'Not really.'

Jolly Roger did not believe him. 'I bet you could've.'

'Come on,' said Peter. 'Let's go in.'

'Yeah, but how did you learn to fight like that?'

'Learn to avoid fighting like that,' Peter corrected him as they entered the library. 'People like me,' he answered, 'often have a rough time at school, you know. Especially with a name like Fallick. See that?' he said, pointing to his scarred cheek. 'I got it from a boy who thought I was too clever by half. My existence offended him, so ...' Peter made a slashing gesture near the side of his face. 'I wasn't offended by boys physically stronger than me, but they were offended by me being brainier. Odd, this stigma about intelligence. Anyway, after this,' he indicated the scar again, 'Dad made sure I learnt how to protect myself. Defence against budding Mr Bigs.'

'Cor! It was great to watch.'

Peter smiled. 'Antibodies, Roger. We're here to cure someone, not to create casualties.'

Inside, Peter drew Roger's attention to an untidy pile of books that had been assembled on a table. 'That's their intended bonfire,' he said. 'Would you believe it? Look.' He pointed to the ceiling above the pile.

'What?' Roger asked.

'It's a smoke alarm. They wouldn't have got very far. Wallies.'

It didn't take long to find a book on prevention and treatment of disease. From the section on immunological products, Peter read excitedly, 'Immediate protection against certain infections can be obtained by injecting immunoglobulins.'

'Was that what you said before?' Roger asked him.

'More or less. Listen. "Gamma globulin may be used to mitigate or prevent measles." That's it!' Peter exclaimed. 'Basically, gamma globulin contains antibodies. I knew it! It'll give him the protection he doesn't seem to have. And because it's used for measles and the like, the nurse should have some. Let me read up the details, then we can go.'

'Why not just nick the book?' Roger asked.

Peter shrugged and grinned. 'Why not?' He hesitated then added, 'Just a minute.' He browsed around for a book on caring for pets. 'Here we are,' he said glancing at the index. 'Canine distemper. Page 131.' He flicked through the volume. 'Got it! "Prevention is the best policy but the course of the disease may be modified by administration of gamma globulin".'

'Nick that one as well?'

'No. It just confirms that I'm not a million miles away. Mel's no dog. It's that health book we need.'

As they made their way back to Block G, Peter suggested, 'Why don't you go ahead and round up the Splinter Group?

They'll respond better to you. Organize a meeting while I read up the details. Then we can sort it out between us. That's if they haven't lost faith in me already.'

'No,' Roger responded loyally. 'No chance.'

Everyone had assembled except for Charlton and Toni. Charlton was looking after Mel in his cabin. Toni was nowhere to be seen. Roger stood in the crow's nest position at the door, and Peter had taken charge.

News of Peter's feat outside the library had spread rapidly among the inmates of Cell Block G. Embellishments by Roger ensured that the new light in which Peter was viewed was particularly bright. With the realization that Peter combined brains with unsuspected brawn, he acquired a certain respect. At the least, his cell-mates were prepared to give him another chance.

'So,' he was saying to Gail, 'your dog *has* come into contact with distemper?'

'Yes,' she replied dejectedly. 'In some kennels a few weeks back. Another dog died from it. But Alien had had his jab. He hated the kennels. That's why I had to bring him.'

'So he's a carrier, not a victim. And somehow, despite obviously being a human, not a dog, Mel's caught it.'

In cabin G9, a very different explanation was forming in Charlton's mind. If humans can't catch distemper then Mel can't be ... No, he told himself. That's a ridiculous idea.

Back in the Common Room, Gabby was surprised by the extent of her sister's misery. After their father's treatment of her, Gail did not waste much pity on any male. Yet now she seemed almost fond of Mel. Perhaps, Gabby thought, any compassion Gail felt for Mel was compounded by guilt. Perhaps she felt responsible for his condition.

'As far as I can see,' Peter continued, 'he's got no immunity to this disease – measles, distemper or whatever. His own body isn't fighting it. No antibodies. Gamma globulin contains antibodies. We inject it, the antibodies do the business.'

'If humans can't get distemper,' Alan protested, 'how come this gamma globulin will work?'

'I'm not sure it will,' Peter replied. 'Dad said the virus can't get inside human cells, but if it did – like with Mel – we might well have antibodies that would deal with it. We can't tell. But human immunoglobulins might do the trick. It works with dogs, apparently.'

'Look what happened last time we listened to clever clogs,' Gabby muttered.

'The point is,' Peter stressed, 'that it *might* work. I haven't got any other ideas. Have you?'

'He's right,' Alan admitted. 'It's our best shot, you might say.'

The Splinter Group murmured agreement.

'All we have to do is get hold of some and then inject it,' said Peter.

'Well, injecting it isn't much of a problem,' Alan said. 'You can do it, Peter.'

'Me? I've no idea how to do it. I only know that if you get it wrong, you can paralyse an entire arm – permanently.'

'But you know everything. Your dad's a doctor,' Gabby commented.

'If your dad was a nuclear physicist, would you be able to build a neutron bomb?'

'All right,' Alan intervened. 'Peter can't do it. Can anyone else? We need a heroin addict. Surely there's one somewhere on board.'

All around the Common Room, heads shook. 'God will decide,' Graham said, 'not medicine.'

'Oh yeah?' Peter thundered. 'God's track record on saving people from death, disease and despondency is not exactly terrific.'

'Watch out!' Roger whispered urgently. 'Someone's coming.'

Never had so many projects been taken out quite so eagerly. Never had so many G-Block children been absorbed completely, immediately and simultaneously in their project work. But the panic was unnecessary. The door opened and Toni walked into the room. Amazed at the sight of all her colleagues scribbling furiously and in unnatural silence, Toni guffawed. 'Well, aren't we a mega-studious lot! This can't be for real.'

They groaned, 'Oh, it's only Toni.'

As soon as she had been briefed on the situation she said, 'Well, it serves you right for holding meetings without me.'

'What do you mean?'

'If you'd waited for me, you wouldn't have had a problem.'

'You don't mean you're the elusive heroin addict?' Alan asked.

'Don't be daft. My mother is diabetic. In case of emergency, I learnt how to do the insulin jabs for her.'

'Hang on. Hang on.' Peter tried to quell the celebrations. 'It's easy to inject insulin in the thigh, stomach or whatever. Gamma globulin's put into the arm – as far as I know – where you can hit the shoulder joint, a nerve or even an artery.'

'Oh, don't be such a wet blanket,' Gabby groaned. 'She's the best we've got. At least she's for action and not all talk.'

'Okay,' Peter conceded. 'You're right. All we have to do is get the globulin. According to this book,' he said, 'it'll be in a vial. A solution. We've just got to hope it's part of the nurse's standard tool kit – for treatment of measles and the like.'

'Ah,' Toni said, milking the moment. 'You're after another of my skills, then.'

'I guess so.'

'Fair enough,' she replied. 'Are you in on this job, Roger?'

'Yeah,' Jolly Roger answered. Then he added, 'What job?'

'The medical room. That's where medicines are kept, I understand,' said Toni. 'The nurse is in there all day but not at night. If someone dies in the night, you ring the bell outside the sickroom to get her out of bed, next door to the surgery. We'll have to be quiet, in other words, but it shouldn't be difficult. I doubt if the surgery's built like Fort Knox.'

'The stuff shouldn't be hard to find either – if it's in there,' Peter added. 'It'll be stored in a fridge. Just find the fridge.'

'I never done a medical room before,' said Roger. 'A doddle. When do we do it?'

'As soon as poss,' Peter replied. 'Mel isn't getting any better.'

'Besides,' Alan added, 'tomorrow we'll be dragged, kicking and screaming, into Kristiansund. We ought to give him his jab before we have to leave him for the day.'

Toni looked at Roger. 'Tonight, then?'

Roger nodded. 'Great.'

'And when we've cured him, we'll celebrate with our other contraband. Won't we, Alan?'

'Sure. The moonshine thrash to celebrate his recovery,' Alan responded.

'We're a long way off yet,' Peter warned. 'Maybe the globulin won't be there, maybe we'll cock up the injection. And there's the little matter of whether it'll work.'

'Totally bloody saturated blanket!'

The open promenades on each side of Deck 2, immediately below the Sun Deck, housed the safety equipment. Lifejackets and flares were stored in long white boxes that doubled as benches, and lifeboats hung ominously from gantries. In case of emergency the galleries were always well lit. At night the *Queen* looked like two parallel strings of light on a pitch black sea. She had not yet sailed so far north that the night was stripped of its darkness but already sunset and daybreak had squeezed the night-time into just four hours. When the *Queen* edged her way through the narrow strait by Måløy fishing centre, the wind rushing through the bridge that linked the centre to the mainland hit a perfect high C.

Inside on Deck 2, the white corridors were dimly lit and quiet. Two a.m. No rowdy kids, just gentle vibrations and the faintly audible scream of the wind. Only Toni and Roger creeping silently to the sickroom encroached on the emptiness.

'Here it is,' Toni whispered. 'Come on.'

The door to the waiting room was never locked so when Toni tried the handle tentatively, the door swung open. 'Told you,' Roger said in hushed tones. 'A doddle.' Quickly, they slipped into the waiting room where they felt less vulnerable. Neither of them had been to the sick bay before so they took a moment to look around. By the dim glow of the night light, they saw a small waiting room, chairs around three of the walls, posters on dental care, safe sex, alcohol and smoking, and the door to the medical room itself. 'Over here,' Toni breathed. But when she saw the combination lock she uttered a quiet curse. 'Not quite a doddle after all. And look, they've built the door frame so we can't slip the catch with a library card.'

'I thought you was good at this sort of job,' Roger murmured.

'Give me a lock to pick, and I'd be in like a shot. But there's nothing here to go at,' she said in frustration. 'We could be here all night guessing the combination.'

'So what do we do?' asked Roger.

'Don't know,' she replied. 'Just a minute.' She was reading the notice next to the door. 'If you need medical attention at a time when the nurse is not here, ring the bell.' Underneath, a nameplate read, 'Nurse on duty: Emma Richardson.'

'Emma Richardson,' Toni said quietly to herself.

'What?'

'Nothing,' Toni answered. 'It's just that I know that

name. I think. Anyway, look, all we have to do to get the combination is to be here watching as she opens the door.'

'What, in the morning?'

'We ... Mel can't wait that long. I mean now.'

'But, like ...'

Roger's objection was too late. Toni had pressed the button and on the other side of the wall, an alarm could just be heard.

'But ... what are we going to say to her?'

'We've got a couple of minutes to come up with something,' said Toni. 'Don't panic. Just follow my lead. And keep your eye on her as she unlocks the door. Memorize the number.'

'I was never no good with numbers.'

'It's time to change your ways. I can hear her coming.'

It wasn't long before a bedraggled Nurse Richardson entered the waiting room. She screwed up her eyes and said in a deep Birmingham accent, 'Hello. What have we here? *Two* problems in the middle of the night?'

'No,' Toni said. 'Two people with one problem.'

'What is it?' she asked, approaching them. 'Not another knife wound or broken nose?'

Toni looked around the room as if struggling for the right words. 'It's a bit embarrassing,' she said. Roger looked thunderstruck, really lost for words.

'Okay,' the nurse said, resigned to an interrupted night. 'Come in.' With Toni and Roger on either side of her, she tapped out a five-digit code to open the door. She turned on the light and told them to sit down. She sat herself at the opposite side of a large table and picked up a Biro. 'At this point,' she said, 'I'm supposed to note your names. My guess, though, is that you wouldn't be here in the middle of the night if you were the type to volunteer names. Right?'

'Right,' Toni looked down at the floor in a pretence of shame. Roger simply stared.

'Tell me the problem, then,' the nurse said in a nothing-you-can-say-will-shock-me voice.

'Well, we ... er ... went a bit too far this evening. Didn't we?' Toni looked at Roger for support.

'Er, yes,' he confirmed.

'You had sexual intercourse? Is that what you're saying?'

Toni nodded sheepishly. Roger looked aghast, distinctly less jolly than usual.

'Were you protected?' the nurse asked.

'We thought so,' Toni responded. 'But it split. You know. Now I'm worried.'

'I see. Have you had ... relations before,' she asked Toni, 'with this young man or others?'

'My first time,' Toni answered, convincingly timorously.

The nurse turned towards Roger. 'And how about you?'

Roger shuffled in his seat and said, 'I never ...' Toni kicked his leg and he hesitated. 'Er ... No. This is the first ...' Roger became dumbstruck again.

'All right,' the nurse said in a kindly, maternal way. 'I don't think you have much to worry about. I'll give you a morning-after-pill, young lady. I guess that's what you're after.' Whilst the nurse got the prescription, she explained its use, then finished with some advice. 'I do suggest that you both retire to your separate beds. And I also suggest that you think carefully about your future behaviour. I can't dictate to either of you but I do ask you to think it over. Okay?'

'Okay,' Toni agreed.

Roger merely nodded.

'Right. Off with you!'

'Come on,' Toni whispered to him. 'We'll give her half an hour to settle down again, then we'll go back. Did you get the number?'

'Nearly,' Roger said.

'Nearly?'

'It began five, one, something.'

'You're hopeless,' said Toni. 'Five, one, two, one, nine. It's a good job I'm with you.'

Roger was still thinking of the pill. 'You ain't going to take that pill, are you?'

'You've got to be joking! What for? I don't need that sort of thing.'

'Chuck it overboard,' Roger suggested.

'No chance!' Toni uttered. 'I know girls on board that would pay mega-bucks for this!'

It was while they sat in silence in the deserted Common Room that she remembered how she had come across the name of Emma Richardson. Local newspapers in Brum. Nurse Emma Richardson had been found to be too generous with clean needles for addicts, and too helpful to young girls in trouble. In an increasingly moralistic society, it was deemed that she had cared when she should have condemned. She was adjudged to have encouraged undesirable behaviour. As Toni recalled, she had been reprimanded and moved to a new area. Toni grinned. Even those in authority for the OBTUSE experiment were 'unsettled', she thought. A shipful of outcasts! Even the officers were buccaneers.

The second visit to the surgery was less eventful than the first. Toni entered the code number and the door opened immediately, welcoming them to Nurse Richardson's inner sanctum. 'Leave the light off. The fridge's over here,' Toni whispered. 'I noted it earlier.'

They sat down together in front of the open fridge and, by its own light, went through it carefully, shelf by shelf. 'Cor,' Roger intoned, 'there's some funny stuff in here.'

'Yeah,' Toni agreed. 'We could set up a chemist's shop. Make a bundle on some of this stuff.'

'Yeah, but ...'

'I know,' she muttered. 'Mind on the job. Mel's treatment, then out as soon as possible.'

'Look,' Roger said. 'There's some syringes in packets.'

Toni went through the packages one by one. 'Bingo!' she said in a hushed voice. 'This one's got a vial of gamma globulin, syringe and needle. All pre-packaged in the right amounts. Mega! Let's tidy up and get out.'

Peter, Roger, Toni and Charlton peered at Mel. 'He's been like this all night,' Charlton was saying. 'At least he's not writhing around.'

'Mm.' Peter looked closely at him. 'He's deathly white, and far too still. More paralysis, I guess. Well,' he said to Toni, 'the sooner we get it over with ...'

'The sooner I can get a couple of hours kip before break-fast.' She opened the polythene package, pushed the needle onto the syringe, then thrust it through the rubber septum into the solution. Slowly, she withdrew the plunger to suck the liquid into the barrel of the syringe.

Peter pulled one of Mel's arms out from under the crumpled blanket. 'We'll use his left arm – just in case.'

'In case of what?' Charlton asked.

'Complications. If Toni hits a nerve, she'll paralyse his arm. Better his left than his right.'

'How do you know he isn't left-handed?' Charlton queried.

'Shut up,' Toni snapped. 'Both of you.' She was tapping the inverted syringe to ensure it was free of air bubbles. She squirted a little of the liquid out of the needle till the plunger was exactly on the mark. 'Okay,' she said. 'Here we go.' Without hesitation, she jabbed the needle into Mel's upper arm. A slight groan came from Mel, reassuring them that some part of him could still feel external events. Slowly, Toni depressed the plunger, easing the vaccine into him, then withdrew the needle. Only a tiny red mark on Mel's arm remained as evidence that he had been injected. 'That's me done,' Toni said emphatically. 'You volunteer to chuck this stuff overboard, Peter.' She handed him the syringe. 'I've done my bit.' As she left, Charlton said softly to her, 'Thanks.'

She smiled. 'Don't count your chickens.'

'She's right,' Peter agreed, as he gathered up the bag and vial with the remains of the globulin. 'It could be a long haul – even if it works.'

Outside it was already dawn, just light enough to see the snow-capped Romsdal mountains.

There were several pairs of bleary eyes over breakfast, including Roger's. Even so, in hopelessly unrealistic anticipation of Mel's recovery, but with great skill and dexterity, Roger had stolen a complete breakfast to take to cell G9. Charlton peered into Roger's bag then nudged him, saying, 'He'll never eat that lot. He's hardly stirred since ... you know.'

Good naturedly, Roger replied, 'Just in case. Anyway, got to keep my hand in.'

'Thanks. I'll try him on the fruit juice at any rate.'

'Cheer up, Charlton,' said Alan. 'You know what they say – worse things happen at sea.'

Some time between the nocturnal theft, therapy and Thursday morning, the *Queen* had been navigated carefully through the narrow channel into Kristiansund. She was, as Gabby put it, parked between a picturesque wooden fishing boat and an iron vessel that was certainly no oil painting but that served the oil industry.

Mr Beever breezed past his charges. 'Ready to cast off your sealegs?' he asked one and all. On receiving a communal groan and murmur as a reply, he said, 'I see Roger's ready. Look, he's got his bag with him right now.'

'Er ... yes.' Roger put his hand on the bag protectively. He did not relish explaining the hot breakfast secreted inside.

It was Alan who distracted Mr Beever. 'What's on the cards for Kristiansund, then?' he enquired.

'Oh, a set of caves today, a modern church for a change,

and a shipyard-cum-museum. And quite a bit of free time on land too. Disco tomorrow, of course.' Mr Beever wiggled his hips without spilling a drop of the coffee that he was holding. 'We're having a fjord trip and a visit to a local school to mix with the natives, as well. All good stuff.'

After Mr Beever had gone, Roger let out a breath that he'd been holding. 'Close!'

Peter put his tray on the table and said brightly, 'Morning!'

'Do you have to be so cheerful?' Toni retorted.

He looked concerned at her response. 'Is there a problem with ... you know who?'

'No. Just that some of us didn't sleep much.'

'Oh, I don't need much sleep, especially with these short nights. Anyway,' he asked Charlton, 'how's the patient?'

Charlton shrugged. 'Same. No change.'

'Does he move at all? What about that arm?'

'He stirs a bit, that's all.'

'Including his left arm?'

'Yes. It's very swollen near the jab,' Charlton said quietly, 'but he has moved it.'

'That's a relief. And I guess the swelling's a normal reaction. So far, so good.'

'Not exactly jogging round Deck 2 yet. Eh, Peter? That's what you promised, wasn't it?' Alan reminded him.

'Yeah, well. That was before. When I thought Dad would come up trumps. I'm beginning to think he won't be strutting his stuff tomorrow night after all.'

'Let's hope you cracked it this time,' said Alan. 'After a storm comes a silver lining, and all that.'

Gabby joined her fellow inmates, saying, 'I see old Cueball's been active.'

'Oh?'

'Have you seen the queue outside his room this morning?'

'The Plimsoll line,' Alan called it. 'All those boys he'd just love to take a plimsoll to. Persistent smokers and those he caught nicking things from the shop.'

'Well, I heard that last night there was a competition to see who could pee over the Sun Deck rails into the sea. Not exactly what Cueball considers dignified behaviour,' Gabby replied. 'The whole row got caught.'

'Why do you boys always do that?' Toni carped. 'Something to do with manhood, is it?'

Before any of the boys could reply, Gabby said, 'Well, I wish I'd been there. Good laugh.'

'Forgive me, Gabby,' Peter responded, 'But wouldn't you have found it rather difficult? You're not exactly equipped …'

'To watch,' she interrupted. 'Anyway, the moral is that Cueball's stamping his dainty little feet. The wally. Lucky Rog and Tone didn't cop it last night, though.'

'Luck,' Toni objected, 'has nothing to do with it. Mega skill.'

Mel winced involuntarily as he turned over. His body was sluggish and unwilling, his head felt light. He felt confused. But at least he was no longer cold. His chest was taut and hot. It felt as if a rope had been coiled around him and was being pulled tighter and tighter. Another clamp seemed to have been applied to his upper left arm. It squeezed so much that the rest of the arm and his hand seemed deprived of blood. They blazed with pain. He understood why humans called it pins and needles, but it had gone several stages beyond a pleasant tingle. Every nerve ending was being jabbed systematically by invisible, microscopic needles. He was a nervous wreck.

His eyes opened but took a while to focus on the empty cabin. The room receded, deformed and rearranged itself several times before it became all shipshape again. Mel moaned, then called, 'Charlton? Charlton!' He was so hot and dry. He needed a drink but his minder had gone missing. The look-out was no longer at his post. Mel dragged himself into a sitting position. 'I will have to get it myself – when this cabin has stopped revolving.' In the wake of his own movement, the room bobbed about. It took a minute to come to a stand-still. Mel pulled aside the sheets with his good arm and, despite his legs' reluctance, forced them out of the bed. He found himself sitting on the edge of the mattress, his head crammed against the bottom of the upper bunk. He groaned again and rested for a while. Then, gripping the top bunk with his right arm, he yanked himself to his feet. But not for long. His legs were too weak and uncooperative. They could not support his weight. His fingers slipped from their lifeline to the bunk and he collapsed. His left side hit the deck first. He cried out with the pain that racked his arm. A second later he sank into unconsciousness.

When the kids are ashore, the crew will take the floor. During the children's day in Kristiansund, the *Queen*'s decks were hosed down and she took on fresh water. The cleaners swept through the dining area and corridors. The man with the job lot of white emulsion provided a clean slate for the graffiti artists. When the seven coaches rolled up to the quayside, the *Queen* groaned and the crew shuddered. When the kids come back on board, peace and quiet are overawed.

Before they embarked each youngster had to submit to a bag search, instigated by Uunk and Brown. The aim seemed to be to confiscate any aerosol paints bought in Kristian-sund. None was found, but a video tape that was no Disney film, an air gun, several packets of cigarettes, a few dubious magazines (including Gabby's newly acquired copy of *Play-girl*), and a Swiss army knife were rooted out.

'I suppose the search is the teachers' idea of a good lark,' Gabby complained bitterly to Mr Beever.

'That's right,' he replied. 'We're a bunch of sadistic kill-joys.'

She chose to ignore the sarcasm in his tone. 'I knew it!'

The characterless corridor to Cell Block G that, most of the day, had been an eerie deserted haven, was transformed into a seething mass of unsettled humanity. Among the returning children, Trevor Beever's cries of 'Quiet, rabble, quiet!' were lost in the hubbub – mostly disgruntled voices raised against Cueball and his sidekick. As the pairs of children entered their cabins, the noise gradually diminished, but doors were left ajar so that friends could shout to each other across the corridor. Charlton, though, slipped surreptitiously into his room and immediately shut the door behind him. When he turned, he let out a cry. He saw Mel sprawled on the floor of the cabin. Fearing the worst, Charlton dashed to his side and put his hand on Mel's chest. He was warm and still breathing. Charlton sighed with relief. But he was unable to elicit a response from Mel or lift him on his own so he went out into the corridor for help.

He rushed out and bumped straight into Mr Beever. 'Hello?' the teacher said. 'What's wrong? Looks like you've seen a creature from outer space.'

Charlton hesitated. 'Outer space?'

'A joke, Charlton. It's a joke.'

'Oh,' Charlton muttered. 'I'm sorry, sir. I didn't see you. That's all. Nothing's wrong. Nothing at all.'

'Okay,' Mr Beever replied, clearly aware that something *was* wrong. 'But remember that you *can* come to see me when there's trouble, when you really need help. Yes?'

'Yes,' Charlton said. 'Thanks.' He waited till Mr Beever had disappeared from the corridor before running into Peter's room. 'Come on,' he said urgently. 'Mel's out of bed. On the floor. He needs help.'

The two boys bundled Mel back into his bunk. He moaned somewhat, turned over and exhaled noisily, like a tired old man. 'Look on the bright side,' Peter said. 'He couldn't have got into that position just by falling out of bed. He must have got up on his own. Could be good news.'

'Maybe,' Charlton mumbled fretfully.

It was a restless night. For Charlton it meant a lack of sleep. For Mel it was a hopeful sign of life. For Mr Brown's form it meant retaliation.

The first sign of trouble was the news at breakfast-time

that the trip to the fjords and the evening's disco had both been cancelled. 'A day-long detention on board,' Mr Beever complained irritably.

'And whose fault is that?' Gabby asked accusingly.

'Some of Brown's lot have gone too far, but it's all come from the atmosphere he and Uunk have created.'

Gabby had expected him to blame just the kids so she had to shelve the abuse that she'd prepared. 'What happened exactly?' she asked.

'Some time last night,' Mr Beever explained, 'everything that was not screwed down in Mr Brown's form-room disappeared into the harbour.'

Gabby could not keep a grin from her face. 'Everything?'

'Everything. His room is bare. Haven't you seen what's happening down on the front?'

Sure enough, the locals had salvaged from the water the plastic chairs and anything else that had floated. The flotsam and jetsam were lined up on the wharf and Mr Brown strode back and forth along the rows, stopping occasionally to examine something in greater detail, as if he were inspecting the troops. He did not look pleased.

'It must have been a well planned operation,' she laughed. 'Cover of darkness doesn't last long.'

Mr Beever did not share her amusement. 'All their work, books, bookshelves, posters, cupboards, display boards. The lot.' He shook his head. 'It infuriates me. All that work and effort gone to waste.'

Gabby took a good look at her teacher, then said, 'You're annoyed for the kids, aren't you? Not at them.'

A wry smile appeared on his face. 'Have you only just realized whose side I'm on?' he answered. 'I hate it when someone's best endeavours are squandered. Like real ability going unrecognized or not given a chance. We should all hate that, Gabby.'

'That's why you lost your cool with me before, is it?'

He looked at her askance. 'Of course. I don't like to see you chucking your talent down the drain, either. Oh, I'm not looking for miracles. I just don't like to see crap writing from you. Too many people can't see what you kids are worth. It's stupid for you to join them, Gabby. Don't let them turn you into a waster as well. Believe in yourself. The chap down on the quay – and ones like him – won't. It's up to you. And I'm turning this chat into a lecture,' he chided himself, 'so I'm going to shut up now.'

Gabby did not reply. Instead, she turned her attention back to the farce on the dockside. After a few moments of relishing Mr Brown's discomfort, she nudged Trevor Beever and said, 'It's funny to see him panicking down there, though, isn't it? You've got to admit it. If there's trouble, he's the right one for it.'

Mr Beever admitted it. 'Couldn't have happened to a nicer fellow.'

Reading, Writing and Repression

Confined to class all day, Gabby asked impertinently, 'Aren't you going to check if any of us were involved?'

Mr Beever looked surprised. 'Is there any reason to? I imagine Mr Brown will find the culprits amongst his own.'

'What'll happen when he finds out who did it?' Toni asked with a grin. 'He can hardly expel them!'

'Make them walk the plank,' Alan suggested. 'That seems appropriate.'

'Or he'll take them to more Grieg recitals,' Gabby put in.

'All right,' Mr Beever said, trying to dampen the high spirits a little. 'I really don't know. I can't read his mind. They'll probably lose a lot of privileges – miss out on some of the best bits of the tour. That sort of thing. But for now,' he added, 'we're all punished. We have to think how we can use today's extra time constructively. More constructive, I hope, than writing out one hundred times, "I am learning that it's a bad thing to throw bits of my classroom overboard".'

'Is that what Brown's lot are doing?' someone asked from the back.

'You never know. It seems a long way to come to sit in a classroom writing, but *c'est la vie*, as they say in Norway. But what about us? Let's put your experiences so far to good use. I want you to expand on some aspect of your project. Or, even better, simply write a passage on something that means a lot to you. Happy or sad, it doesn't matter. Just something that you feel strongly about – especially if it's also to do with Norway. Alan might choose politics, Charlton might go for music or art. And it's got to be computing for Mike. Anyway, you get the idea. I'll move amongst you to discuss topics. Have a think about it till I get to you. Or simply get cracking on your own. Remember, I want commitment – a subject that interests you, annoys you, excites you, or whatever. Okay?'

By the time Mr Beever got to Charlton he had not only started but also finished. 'You look ... er ... knackered,' the teacher said. 'Are you all right? You weren't up all night, were you?'

'How do you mean?' Charlton replied defensively.

'Shifting furniture.'

'No. 'Course not.'

'Another joke, Charlton. I didn't think for a moment that you ... Oh, never mind! Can I read your ... what is it? A poem?'

'Well ...' Charlton clutched his composition protectively. 'I got carried away. I'm not sure ...'

'I'd like to read it, really.'

Charlton handed over his notebook reluctantly. 'I'm not sure I should have written it.'

Mr Beever scanned the page. 'It is a poem, then.'

'I don't know. It's supposed to be lyrics, I guess.'

'Let me read it quickly,' said Mr Beever.

I am sick of stagnation. I want to control my being.
I am sick of constant pressure. I want time to mean nothing.

I am sick of solemnity. I want to hear laughs, see smiles.
I am sick of imperfection. I want to go out in style.
I am sick of sympathy. I want to slip from memory.
I am sick of ill-health. I want to flee this broken body.
I am sick of dependence. I want some detachment.
I am sick of medicine. I want nature's judgement.
I am sick of shackles. I want to fly.
I am sick of torment. I want to die.

Mr Beever was silent for a while, apart from a sigh. He knew what Charlton must have put himself through to write those lyrics. Eventually, Mr Beever returned the notepad to Charlton and said quietly, 'No wonder you look knackered. I don't know what to say. I can't say it's good. Good isn't the right word. It's raw and powerful. Painful, even. I asked for emotion and I got it. What can I say?' Mr Beever shrugged. 'Just, well done, I guess.' Even more quietly, so no one could hear, he asked, 'It's a description of motor neurone disease, isn't it?'

Charlton nodded. 'I'd rather not ...'

'Sure. Actually, you still look pale. Do you want to go to your cabin to take a break?'

Charlton bucked up at the suggestion. 'Yes.'

'Want anyone to go with you?'

'No,' he replied hastily, then changed his mind. 'Well, maybe ... if Peter ...'

'Peter?' Not anticipating that Peter would prove to be popular with a classmate, Mr Beever was pleasantly surprised. 'Okay. I can spare him for a bit.' Mr Beever called for Peter but, before he dismissed the two boys, he read through the beginning of Peter's offering. Following his accomplished account of chemistry and the environment, Peter's new essay was packed full of facts. It read almost like a scientific journal.

If a cottage had been built at the edge of the Norwegian Sea straight after the last Ice Age, and assuming no change in sea level, the same holiday home would now be 100 metres above the coastline. In fact, the whole of Scandinavia is rising as much as 1 cm per year. During the Ice Age, the mass of ice on the land pushed it down. When the ice melted away 10,000 years ago, the weight was lifted and the land started to rise again, like a float pushed underwater then released. The only difference with a land mass is that it is a slower process. Norway is still rising today. It has not yet bobbed up to its equilibrium position.

Mr Beever smiled. 'The float pushed down in the water is ... an interesting metaphor.'

'You mean lousy,' Peter replied. 'But people have been writing for hundreds of years, you know. All the good ones have been used. Besides, it's a simile, not a metaphor.' He grinned cheekily.

'Just testing. Go on, escort Charlton back to his cabin.'

The topic of Graham Squirrell's essay offered no surprises either. It was an elaboration of his stave church project.

Real church is in the soul. Concrete or wooden buildings are just convenient places of assembly for people with church in their minds. It is as easy to be righteous in your bedroom as in a stave church. It is just a series of vertical planks of wood. It is a construction of dead timber, protected with pitch. Real church, which is God's purpose, is protected in the minds of the righteous.

In the sea off Kristiansund there is an island. It is called Grip. It has a lighthouse and a stave church. The church is almost five hundred years old. Life on Grip was not easy. About one hundred souls used to live there. They built their houses near the stave church for protection. There was wickedness around Grip. The islands and reefs had names like "The Killer" and "The Devil". The waves swept over Grip many times. Only the stave church was left standing after the poundings of 1640 and 1820. The people thought that a wooden church would protect them. The last islanders deserted Grip in 1974. It is now a desolate place. The people had only a wooden symbol, which is not a substitute for a personal relationship with Jesus. They could not really have had God's purpose in their souls.

'Good,' Mr Beever said to Graham. 'A good offshoot of the project. Can you develop this idea of God's purpose? I'd like to learn a bit more. Like, what it means to you, what it means to others, and how it affects your future.'

'Well, all right.' Even when he was enthusiastic, Graham seemed lugubrious. He turned his attention back to his exercise book.

Apprehensively, Mr Beever turned his attention to Gabby. 'Well, young lady, have you decided to write something?'

She sniffed. 'Don't know why but, yeah, I've done something.'

'Will I want to read it, or will it make me lose my cool again?'

Gabby merely shrugged in reply.

Mr Beever looked into her face and pronounced, 'Well, I feel confident. How much have you got so far?'

'Not a lot. And what I've got so far is all you're going to get.'

'I appreciate that it takes a lot of effort to get prose to seem effortless.' He grinned. 'Come on. Let's hear it, then.'

'What? Aloud?'

'Why not?' Mr Beever replied. 'I want you to see the reaction of your colleagues. To see that you can entertain them too with your writing.'

'You don't want to see it – or vet it – first?'

Mr Beever shook his head. 'I said I feel confident. I trust you.'

'Okay, then. It won't take long.' Gabby read aloud for the whole class to hear. 'It's not hard to see why we're not staying long in Kristiansund. It's a young town – somewhere with life. A place where history is history. In recognition of the fact that Adrian Mole is now nearing retirement age, there was no sign of his books, not even Norwegian translations, in Kristiansund bookshops. The town had no dead musicians to resurrect, no disused leprosy colonies. Not even many monuments to dead fish. More hunky oil workers than withered fishermen. One stroke of luck: we missed the annual opera festival.

'P.S. Some unnecessary detail to keep Eager Beever happy. Kristiansund is a sprawling mess. Houses built on terraces rising up from the harbour. If the one at the top topples, the rest have had it. In 1940, when bombs were not laser-guided and collateral damage was the aim rather than the by-product, Kristiansund was smaller but an even bigger mess. Since, it has been rebuilt, outgrown one island, invaded two others. Three islands' worth of mess, separated by straits, bound by bridges. That's all the detail you're going to get.'

The reading was interspersed with laughter. 'There you are,' Mr Beever said. 'They enjoyed it. So did I. There's something there, Gabby. You should work on it. Write up your version of the OBTUSE cruise. It would go down in the annals of history.'

'You're very keen to get me to do this writing lark,' Gabby observed. 'Why?'

'Because you have a certain knack. It should be developed.'

'What if I put you into the story?' Gabby inquired wickedly.

'If you like.'

'I wasn't thinking of being complimentary.'

'I wouldn't expect you to,' Mr Beever replied. 'As long as it's the truth as you see it, I don't mind what you put.'

'That's what you say,' Gabby rejoined. 'But you really try and cultivate that pally image of yours. You'd squeal soon enough if I dented it – or demolished it.'

'We'll see ... when you write it.'

'No chance. I was only teasing.' Defiantly, she murmured, 'I'd rather chuck the whole bloody lot ...' She picked up her account of Kristiansund and screwed it up, but she stopped short of throwing it in the bin.

Mr Beever frowned. 'What is it about you, Gabby?'

'I'm special. That's what it is. There's no one else like me.'

Mr Beever could not argue with *that*.

'You didn't mind me getting you out of the class, did you?' Charlton asked Peter on the way to cabin G9.

'Hardly!'

'It's just that I thought you could help if Mel's bad again.'

In fact, Mel had not taken a turn for the worse. When they entered the cabin his eyes were open and he was breathing steadily. His face and body seemed to be free of contortions, but he lacked colour and vigour.

'Hello!' said Peter brightly. 'Back with us?'

There was no answer. Charlton tried to attract Mel's attention, saying, 'Mel? Mel?'

He stirred. 'Mm?'

'Are you okay?' Charlton asked.

'I am winning.'

'That's the stuff!' Peter cried, but Mel said no more. 'Ah well, it's a start,' Peter said to Charlton. 'Look, I'll go back and tell the others – quietly. You're staying here?'

Charlton nodded.

'By the way,' Peter said, as he left, 'It was a good stunt that you pulled to get out of class. You looked quite shaken for a while.'

'It wasn't a stunt.'

Peter echoed Mr Beever's words. 'Just testing. I didn't think it was.' For a short while in the classroom Peter believed that he had witnessed Charlton approaching self-destruct mode, apparently brought on by the writing exercise. If so, the distress was self-imposed because Charlton had chosen the painful topic himself. He'd decided to spill out some of his anxiety, remorse, grievance or whatever else he needed to unburden. Charlton still made Peter feel uneasy but, since leaving the class, he seemed to have composed himself.

After his guest had returned to the form-room, Charlton sat near the bunk and worked on his latest sketch. All he could hear was the music pounding from his personal stereo. He lost track of time as his pencil scratched busily, incessantly.

Suddenly he became aware that Mel had turned towards him and was saying something. He stripped off his headphones and said, 'What? What did you say?'

'Drink.' Mel's voice was weak but clear. 'Thirsty.'

Some of the contents of the glass of water ran down Mel's chin, but he swallowed almost the whole glassful before falling back onto his pillow and groaning.

There was a knock at the door. 'Damn.' Charlton put his mouth near the crack in the cabin door and said, 'Who is it?'

'Me.' It was Gail's voice.

When he'd let her in, she explained, 'Peter said he was on the mend. I had to come and see. Beever thinks I'm in the loo so I can't stay long.'

Mel opened his eyes again on hearing their voices. 'Home,' he said. 'Will I ever go home?'

Gail went to the bed. 'Of course. You'll be okay.'

'You do not understand. We have not illnesses. We have not doctors.'

'You won't need one soon. Anyway,' Gail replied, 'everywhere's got doctors.'

'Not my home.'

Gail and Charlton glanced at each other with puzzled faces. 'Where *is* your home Mel?' asked Charlton.

'Far ...' His eyes shut and immediately he was asleep.

'What was all that about?' Gail queried.

Charlton sat down, looking first at Mel, then out of the window, before answering. 'Can you keep a secret, Gail?'

'I'm a great keeper of secrets,' Gail replied wistfully.

'Well, you're going to think I've cracked,' said Charlton, 'but ... I don't think he's from here.'

'Where? Norway?'

Charlton shook his head. 'He doesn't really know about Norway. He's just memorized facts. He's memorized facts about us and about Earth as well.'

'What are you saying?'

'He's not from here.' He hesitated, then added, 'Not human.'

Gail did not respond immediately. She just stared at Charlton. 'That's ...'

'Crazy?'

'Yeah. Crazy.'

'So how come he's got distemper? Humans can't catch it, remember. And he's talked about having an earthly virus – as if he wasn't from Earth. Actually,' Charlton explained, 'he called it a human virus, but the point's the same. I don't think he's human.'

'I still can't ...'

'I know. It's a bit much. But ... you must admit, it could explain a few things. Like not having doctors, and your dog's reaction to him.'

'I don't know,' Gail said. 'I suppose so.'

'Don't tell the others, will you?' Charlton asked anxiously.

She shook her head again. 'I wouldn't dare.' As if suddenly aware of the time, she added, 'Look, I've got to get back. And maybe you should too. Eager Beever's getting worried about you. You don't want *him* knocking on the door.'

'Okay,' Charlton replied. 'I'll follow you soon. But promise you won't tell the others?'

'Promise. When he's better, we'll have to find out, you and me.'

'How?'

'I don't know. We could always ask him.'

'Mm. I guess so.'

Charlton waited for five minutes after his second guest had left before heading begrudgingly back to the classroom.

Mr Brown seemed to believe that turning the ship into a floating graveyard was an effective punishment. Having failed to persuade him to reinstate the disco, Trevor Beever sat in the staff room instead of bopping the night away, embarrassing himself on the dance floor. In front of him he had spread his pupils' compositions. Only Charlton's piece surprised him. Was Charlton beginning to come to terms with his past? Trevor hoped that the harrowing lyrics were good therapy and not simply the ravings of a disturbed lad. Either way, Trevor wondered what had precipitated the outpouring of such emotion. Why here and now?

The other offerings saddened or delighted him. Gail had had so much stuffing knocked out of her by life at home that she was virtually empty. Her exercise book was the same. On the other hand, Mike's devious brain had compiled a devious crossword. All of the across answers were places in Norway, and all of the down clues referred to computer terms. One day, Trevor thought, Mike will be working for a bank, showing the company how to improve its security, or for a designer of computer games. His lateral thinking and his penchant for computers would eventually make him respectable, then, shortly after, wealthy. How about Alan Splinter? Any future he might have had in politics had been tainted by his unfashionable views. He did not have the right politics for his day, for these entrepreneurial times. The new Dark Ages. It was years since the nation admired or tolerated its rebels, or regarded them with curious and cautious affection. Alan had blown it. He was born into the new world order but he was certainly not born for it. Trevor read the beginning of Alan's lengthy essay with a rueful smile.

British society has an ultra-respectable exterior. Everyone must conform to the God-fearing, profit-seeking, western ideal. The new world order means the big western Christian democracies, the policemen of the world, come first. Outspoken non-conformists disappear. Not like the police death squads of Guatemala or Brazil. The kids on our city streets disappear into 'youth centres' or 'special schools' but it would not be out of character for the Government to improve its disappearing tricks. Junkies, jobless, gays, lame ducks and those of the wrong religion are all swept under the carpet.

Take lame ducks. The end of the NHS began with a rationing of treatment. Varicose veins and removal of non-malignant lumps were not cost-effective, and they cluttered the waiting lists. They were struck off. The money stretched only to urgent clinical needs and lucrative diseases. Then slow attrition set in. Now, private hospitals discharge patients when their insurance money runs out. And if you don't have it in the first place, don't get ill.

If we had an irresponsible press, adverse publicity might open a few eyes – and several cans of worms. But the media have been nobbled. The Privacy Law, designed to protect the private lives of the powerful, became a vehicle for State censorship. Only the really unstoppable, undeniable critical reports now reach the public.

Take gays. AIDS made it easy to subjugate gays and drug users. Such outcasts, and those who display their bigotry too openly, are too embarrassing to be tolerated. Humanity is no longer an essential part of being human. Britain has a ruthless, uncaring, rotten interior.

And so it went on. Some would call Alan's views extreme. Trevor Beever simply called them right. In the essay it was easy to detect the headstrong character that, whilst orchestrating an inner city riot, had put a match to a Government building. As Alan had intended, the office was closed so no one was hurt but much census information went up in smoke and the building had to be demolished.

Toni was rebellious in her own way. Her composition was a diatribe against education. She claimed that it did not exist. School, she maintained, just groomed girls for the wearing of aprons. Toni's rebellion was the realization that women, as much as men, could enjoy themselves and plan their own lives. Then there was Roger's meagre piece of paper. Roger had real strengths but writing was not one of them. Education was failing him because it never put him into a situation in which he could shine.

Trevor collected together the papers and books, then raided the staff's secret store of gin and tonic. Toni's protestations, Roger's bumbling, and two large drinks could not put out of his mind Alan's crude analysis. Even the third gin and tonic sharpened his senses for a while. Were the kids and his colleagues too embarrassing to be tolerated? Was the OBTUSE initiative a giant exercise in sweeping under the carpet? A brief but expeditious disappearing trick? Certainly, many on board might be categorized as outcasts or bigots. And Trevor Beever himself? He knew that he'd broken one fundamental rule of life. It was expected that the idealism of the young gave way to the dignity of age. But as Trevor got older he found himself more in tune with his disaffected charges, and more outspoken. Dignity had not moderated his idealism.

The fourth drink did the trick. Anaesthetized against Alan Splinter's words, he headed back to his cabin and untroubled sleep.

Deliverance;

God's Whispers

Once, when the years could still be counted in three digits, there was a Viking raider and pillager who, on a visit to Greenland, took a wrong turn and discovered part of America. When this accident-prone traveller returned home, he founded Trondheim. The people of Trondheim did not live happily ever after. In the fourteenth century, the population was reduced almost to zero by the Black Death. The buildings of Trondheim were reduced repeatedly to ashes by great fires. The status of Trondheim was reduced when Oslo took its title of capital of Norway. And now, for a whole week, the unfortunate city was to play host to three hundred and fifty-one British ruffians. Some places just don't get the luck.

Many of the invasion force were on deck as the *Queen*, hardly out of breath after the short passage from Kristiansund, entered Trondheimsfjord and later the sheltered harbour of the city itself. Trondheim was so sheltered by the convoluted coast that it did not have the feel of the seaside. More Windermere than Weymouth. Toni nudged Roger and said, 'Just think of all those lovely souvenirs waiting to be liberated.'

'Yeah. Lots of shops.'

'Time to get my own back for all that raping and pillaging.'

Roger looked concerned. 'I'm sorry. I didn't know ...'

'Not me. The Viking ... Oh, never mind. Just remember there might be another search when we come back on board. Be careful.'

Soon, the unsettled marauders were told to prepare themselves for a reconnoitre of Trondheim.

As Gail left her cabin, Alien made a dash for freedom, eager to reconnoitre Trondheim himself. As he ran out between Gail's legs, she cried, 'No!' He scampered a little way down the corridor, then hesitated because Peter was walking towards him. While he crouched low, preparing to defend Gail against Peter, she grabbed him from behind.

'Wants a walk in Trondheim as well, eh?' Peter guessed.

'I'm afraid so. He knows he's going to be left again.'

'Quick,' Peter whispered. 'In here. Beever's coming.'

They barged unannounced into cabin G7 where there was another accident-prone traveller whose mission had taken a wrong turn. Charlton looked startled as they tumbled into his room. 'Sorry,' Peter said quietly. 'Eager Beever's out there. Had to hide Alien.'

The dog wriggled out of Gail's arms, then walked up to the bunk. He cocked his head on one side and viewed the prostrate Mel curiously, even sympathetically.

Gail frowned. 'Alien really shouldn't be in here,' she said. 'In case he does any more damage to Mel.'

'There's no problem,' Peter reassured her. 'Not now he's had the immunoglobulin.'

'Are you sure?' she checked.

'Of course I'm sure,' Peter replied.

Charlton, protective of his cell-mate, reminded Peter of

his fallibility. 'You also said Mel couldn't catch distemper from a dog.'

He deflected the criticism, saying, 'That was my dad.' He looked at Mel, conscious yet apparently unhearing, then added, 'He's on the mend all right. Don't you think?'

'He certainly seems a lot better,' answered Charlton. 'Not so many convulsions.'

Suddenly, Peter had an idea. 'Look,' he said to Gail, 'if you're worried about leaving Alien on his own, why don't you let him stay in here? They'll be company for each other while we're on shore. Mel and Alien — the two stowaways together.'

'I don't know,' she replied. 'Alien's sparked off enough trouble already. He really has taken to Mel, though.' She liked the notion of a friend for Alien in her absence, but she did not want to cause further mayhem.

'I'm not sure either,' Charlton agreed.

'Let's ask Mel, then,' Peter suggested. Kneeling by the bunk, he whispered, 'Mel? What do you think?'

'What?' Mel replied absently.

'Do you want Alien to stay with you?'

'Alien?'

'The dog,' Gail explained.

'Are you leaving?' Mel asked.

'A few hours, that's all. In Trondheim.'

Mel nodded. 'Trondheim, yes.'

'Is there any harm leaving Alien with you?' Charlton asked. 'Would you like that?'

'He may stay. I have antibodies now. He cannot do harm to me.'

'There!' Peter stood up, his opinion vindicated. 'Problem solved.'

Gail shrugged. She still felt some trepidation but was willing to be persuaded by Mel himself. His sanctioning of the arrangement absolved her from further responsibility. 'Well, I suppose that clinches it.' Gail knelt by Alien and stroked him. 'You stay here and look after our Mel,' she said. 'And this time don't ...' She could not finish her sentence because Alien jumped up and licked her nose in reply.

After the fledgling horde had departed the ship and calm was restored, Mel tried his strength again. This time, when he'd got to his feet, he clung to the bunk, tottered forward, and stayed vertical. The few steps into the bathroom seemed like a marathon. He broke into a sweat and his body shook. Even so, he persevered. Always steadying himself with one hand, he slowly removed his underclothes. The rail around the shower was meant to offer support in rough seas but Mel gripped it tenaciously as the hot water powered over his soiled body, the water washing away the seediness. He had no energy to use soap or sponge, he just let the water do the work. Afterwards he could do no more than dab himself ineffectually with the towel. Refreshed, but exhausted, he sat on the toilet seat to recover.

The bathroom door was nudged open and Alien peered in. 'Ah,' Mel said to him. 'Are you a brave dog?' Wagging his tail, Alien sauntered up to Mel. 'There is a decision that I have made. I hope that you are an understanding dog.' Mel stood in front of the full-length mirror and examined his temporary body. 'It will only take one minute,' he said to the dog. 'You will see ... a metamorphosis: caterpillar to butterfly. I must become a caterpillar again within one minute. Like your butterflies, I would not live long here.' He breathed in deeply, closed his eyes, then slowly exhaled, letting out an inhuman groan.

Alien took three steps back but did not shift his gaze from Mel. The dog's face betrayed both wariness and wonder. He retreated further, trembling in the corner of the shower unit, but did not bolt for the door.

Mel felt the disease slipping from him, the warmth and luxury of his own form. It was like returning home safely after a long, difficult and frightening journey. If only ... But it was no use wishing. Out of the confines of the body designed for living on Earth, he could not even breathe the air. For those few seconds, though, he could relish his full faculties. The air, toxic to his lungs, held many secrets that humans could not detect. Well above 20 MHz, the air pulsated with messages. Normally, his brain could disentangle all signals transmitted simultaneously, but at different frequencies. This time, he could unravel the songs and chat from radio stations but the less distinct messages from satellites, private radios and radar scans were garbled. His mind was still clouded after the transformation. Even so, it was wonderful to hear properly again.

At the lower frequencies, he could feel the vibrations of the wind and waves on the ship's side, the beatings of seagulls' wings above the ship, the rhythms of canine and human life — there was a cluster of humans somewhere to the fore of the ship, perhaps some of the ship's crew relaxing together — and the drone of passing ships. Only one of the noises puzzled him. It seemed to be the throb of a ship's engine but its timbre was quite unlike the rest. He placed a hand against the wall of the bathroom in an attempt to detect the vibration through touch. Even though the ship was almost deserted, its walls were full of activity. Mel could not easily deconvolute one vibration from another, but the mysterious sound persisted weakly. A distant, unusual craft was in some way scanning the *Queen of the Fjords*.

He moved out of the shower and back into the cabin. The metamorphosis had removed his human blindfold. Out of the porthole, he could see the Earth in its true colours. He could see that the sea was cold and the harbour buildings were warm by their infra-red signatures. He could see the stray cosmic and ultraviolet waves high in the sky, and the beautiful spectrum of white light. Yet, he needed to be on the other side of the glass to see clearly the dim signals of distant heat sources. Any such frequencies from the strange sea-craft must have been absorbed by the material of the window.

Alien's whimper from the corner of the bathroom reminded Mel that his fascination with the human world threatened his existence and his mission. 'You're right. Time to revert,' he said, re-entering the shower room. The dog whimpered even more and Mel smiled, realizing that he had spoken in his native tongue, frightening the animal even more. He translated, 'You are correct. The time to change has come.' He resisted the temptation to experience the Earth through his own senses for a few moments more, and to inhale strongly as a means of steeling his body for the trauma. Instead he leant against the wall and let the humanoid form envelop him, shrouding his senses and infusing the remnants of disease.

He groaned with fatigue. Eager to lie down again, Mel pulled on his underclothes, gripped the rail and then groped his way to the door. He stumbled out of the bathroom and almost fell onto the bed. Alien followed him faithfully then sat at the edge of the bunk, happy that Mel had resumed his familiar shape and posture — flat out on the bed. Mel felt deflated and deprived. Deprived of his home, even his own identity and the comforts that it offered. But he also felt enriched by his experience of Earth and its people. And, of course, he'd conjured up sixty seconds of respite from the ailment that had stolen much of his time on Earth and much of his human capabilities.

It was late evening before the rabble returned to the ship, though sunset was several hours away. Mr Brown and Mr Uunk stood by the gangways, looking out for anything suspicious but not implementing another search. Toni flushed as she walked past Cueball. She wasn't nervous, she was just hot. Under her English jumper, she was wearing a traditional Norwegian sweater — one more garment than she had on when she disembarked. Mr Beever clutched a carved wooden troll (which, unlike Toni's sweater, was accompanied by a receipt) and talked to Charlton as they boarded the *Queen*. 'Well, does it remind you of anyone? What do you think?'

'Er. Not really.'

'Come on, use your imagination.'

From behind them, Gabby commented, 'Pull its hair out and I can think of one good candidate.' Her head jerked in Cueball's direction.

'Mm,' Mr Beever pondered. 'I see what you mean.'

'But,' she added, 'one of them's awfully appealing, the other's appallingly awful.'

'I think we'd better leave it there, Gabby. I want to have a word with this young man. No need to panic, Charlton. I just want to talk about your artistic endeavours.' Really, Mr Beever was puzzled by Charlton's behaviour. He felt sure that something was going on in Cabin G7 and was trying the back-door approach. 'Let's chat on the way to your cabin.'

Now there was something to panic about. 'To my cabin?'

'Don't worry, I won't intrude for long. Just a quick chat.'

'I don't really feel like it.'

'That's something you'll have to work on. The professional can turn his mind to his work even when he doesn't feel like it. He anticipates inspiration, he doesn't just wait for it.'

'Okay,' Charlton agreed, unable to find a solid excuse to refuse. 'But ... er ...' He was thinking of Gail, who had just gone on ahead with his key to transfer Alien to her own cabin. And he was thinking of Mel. 'It'll be meal-time soon. Do you want to go to the canteen straight away?'

'No, I want to freshen up first. Now, about your skills ...' Mr Beever was not to be shaken off by Charlton's twists and turns. 'Have you ever thought about a direction for the future? Making a career from art.'

'A career? I've never thought of it like that.'

'Why not? You're good at it. You enjoy it. You could make it if you really want to. Just a matter of deciding what'll pay the food bill.'

'I've no idea. I've only ever done what I want to do.'

'There's another mark of the professional. If what he fancies doing is not what the world wants, or will pay for, he takes steps to become commercial.'

'That's professionalism?' Charlton queried. ' I have to be interested ...'

'Just a little prostitution of your art,' Mr Beever said as they descended the stairs to Deck 3 and Cell Block G. 'It buys time for the world to get used to you. Once they're hooked, *then* you do what *you* want.'

'What sort of thing had you got in mind?'

'I don't know,' Mr Beever replied. 'It's a matter for you, really. Sketching? Something to do with music? Art!' Suddenly, the teacher stopped walking. 'Hello. What's this?'

Gail was backing out of Charlton's cabin. In an urgent whisper, she was coaxing someone within, 'Come on. Quickly. Come on out.' Furtively, she glanced along the corridor and saw Mr Beever. For a moment she hesitated, then quickly slammed shut the cabin door. Her cheeks turned as red as the Norwegian flag. Mr Beever looked first at Gail then at Charlton. He seemed more disappointed than angry. 'Okay, you two. Out with it.'

When neither Gail nor Charlton said anything, Mr Beever continued, 'I knew something was going on. I'm surprised it's you two, I must say, but let's hear it.'

Charlton looked at Gail and shrugged. They could no longer protect both stowaways. 'Might as well bring him out,' he said.

'Who?'

'Alien, of course,' Charlton replied. The dog seemed

more expendable than Mel, and harbouring a dog seemed the lesser of the two crimes.

Gail opened the door and called, 'Alien, come on out now! No! Not ...' She shook her head and sighed. 'Come on, dog.'

'Dog!' Mr Beever exclaimed.

'I'm sorry, Mr Beever,' Gail said as the small dog padded out into the corridor, wary of the door that had been shut in his face. 'I couldn't bear to leave him at home.'

When Mr Beever approached Gail, Alien snarled at him. 'It's all right,' she said, kneeling by the dog. Realizing that with a few more steps, Mr Beever would be able to see into Charlton's cabin, she stood up again and closed the door.

'So he's from home. You didn't get him in Norway?'

Gail shook her head. 'He's my pet.'

'You haven't taken him ashore, have you?'

'No.'

'Good. But ...' Mr Beever sighed. 'Didn't you think of the dog? It can't be much of a life for him here.'

'My parents wouldn't ... Anyway, it's better than kennels. I exercise him each night.'

'And what about going to the toilet?'

'He's well trained. Dog litter.'

'I see. But,' Mr Beever asked, 'why was he in Charlton's cabin?'

'Er ...'

Charlton interrupted, having anticipated this question. 'It got a bit cramped in Gail's cabin with Gabby there too. I have a little more room.'

'I see,' Mr Beever repeated. 'At least I understand now

why you reacted so badly in Kristiansund when I said you looked as if you'd seen a creature from outer space. Alien indeed! What are we going to do about it?'

'You won't send him away?' Gail looked with alarm at Mr Beever.

'Nowhere to send him to. Or you. So I guess we'll just carry on. I'll have to report it, though. I'll have a word with Mr Uunk when he's in a good mood. But you must be responsible for him, Ms Grobb. The dog, that is, not Uunk. And no trips ashore for him. Okay?'

'Of course. Thanks.' Gail still looked ashamed but she felt relieved — like the deliverance that accompanies a confession or pronouncement of a sentence. And she could have imagined far worse outcomes. It was a light sentence.

Mr Beever grumbled, 'First a computer, now a dog. Is there anything else you want to confess to?'

Gail and Charlton looked blankly at each other, then at Mr Beever but said nothing. They both sighed with relief when he turned and left. 'Phew! That was close,' said Charlton.

'Close? It was more than that.' Gail knelt down and patted Alien.

'I meant it could have been worse. He might have found Mel. How is he, anyway?'

'Better. You go in and see. He's hungry — that's a good sign. Can you get Roger to pinch some food? I have enough to worry about feeding Alien.'

'Yeah, okay. There is a good side to all this, I think. If Mr Beever catches any of us pinching food for Mel, we can say it's for Alien.'

'Great. Blame it on Alien. By the way,' Gail stood up close to Charlton and lowered her voice. 'Earlier, when I said, "Come out, Alien," Mel began to get out of bed.'

'Yeah? So you believe me, now?'

'I don't know,' she whispered. 'He could still be confused, or maybe he didn't understand.'

'But he could be ... Couldn't he?'

'I guess so.'

Mel put down the empty plate and took a drink of water. 'Better?' Peter asked him.

The patient nodded. 'I unknow the reaction of the body to this food, but I need it. I may still display sickness but I am considerably more well. I feel ...' Mel hesitated. 'Where is Charlton?'

'Oh, he's wandered off alone again. Thinking great thoughts.'

'He thinks troubled thoughts, I estimate.'

'You've noticed.'

'Yes, but I think he too is a little better. My problem, and recovery, have also eased his burden by some unknown mechanism.'

'Maybe,' Peter said. 'Anyway, is there anything else you want?'

'Yes. I hoped Charlton would help me to the fresh air.'

'Out on deck?'

'Yes.'

'Okay. I'll help instead. Let's get your clothes on.'

'I need only a few of your minutes,' said Mel as he struggled out of bed and into his clothes.

'Yes. You shouldn't overdo it just because you feel a bit better.'

'I am aware of my limited capabilities.' Mel smiled wryly.

'Even at this hour, there are a few kids milling about on deck — as well as teachers and crew. We'll have to hope you blend in. If we get stopped, let me do the talking. Okay?'

Mel smiled again. 'Okay. It is the talking at which you are good.'

When no one was looking, Peter supported Mel in his efforts to walk at a normal pace. Whenever others were nearby, Mel did his best to walk alone. A slow stagger was less suspicious than an aided amble. They did not attempt the two flights of stairs to the Sun Deck but stayed on Deck 2. Mel flopped gratefully against the gallery rail and breathed in deeply. 'That is good. Fresh air, as you say, at last.'

Peter smiled. 'It's good to see you back on your feet.'

'Yes. I must thank you. I believe that my chances of survival were small without you.'

'I don't know. Did the globulin help? Or were you on the mend anyway? Perhaps I didn't help at all. One thing's for sure, though — it wasn't just me. There was Charlton, Roger, Toni, and Mike.'

'Your language is imprecise. It does not distinguish the singular you from the plural you. I thank you all,' Mel said. After a few moments of reflection, he continued, 'What happened to me, Peter?'

'It's quite a story. As you know, although it should be impossible, you caught this disease, distemper, from Gail's hound, Alien. Your insides must be mighty peculiar. Distemper! Very odd. Anyway, you'll have to be nice to our Gail,' he said. 'She's a sensitive soul and she's feeling guilty about it. Thinks the whole thing's her fault.'

Briefly, Peter filled in the story and Mel interrupted only when he did not understand something, or wanted to make an observation. The first thing that he did not understand was hacking. 'I have seen Mike not often and do not know of the process of hacking.'

'No. Mike'll spend most of the voyage in his cabin with his computer, no doubt. He's an obsessive hacker — that's breaking into computer systems.'

'Accessing restricted programmes? What is the objective?'

'Fun. Challenge,' Peter answered. 'And in Mike's case, to save the world from war by exchanging enemies' military secrets.'

'He interrupted this worthy mission to help me. I am grateful to him.'

Peter waved his arm in front of his face to scatter for a while the gnats. 'Then there's the ship's best buccaneers: Toni and Roger. They nicked the antibodies for you. And Roger's also good at meals, as you've seen.'

'They nicked the antibodies?' Mel queried. 'I do not comprehend. They made a notch in them?'

Peter laughed. 'No. Nick means pinch, steal, rob. Take without the owner's permission.'

'Yes. I understand. I hope that I do not get them into crime.'

'Oh, I don't think so,' Peter replied. 'They're only too willing to nick things!'

It was then that a track-suited Mr Beever came past and greeted Peter. 'Hi, there. Hello, who's this?' he said, nodding towards Mel.

'Don't worry,' Peter smiled. 'You're not suffering from amnesia. He's not one of yours.'

'Didn't think I recognized him.'

'I'm fraternizing with the enemy camp tonight. He's from J Block. Aren't you?' Peter nudged Mel.

'That is right.'

'Ah well. Not everyone's lucky enough to get into G Block.' Mr Beever trotted backwards away from them. 'Going to jog off all that fatty food.'

'Don't fall off the end of the promenade,' Peter called after him.

Mr Beever laughed, turned and jogged out of sight.

'Who was that?' Mel asked.

Feigning nervous exhaustion, Peter collapsed onto the rail alongside Mel. 'Phew! That was what we call a close shave.'

'Pardon?'

'Mr Beever. Our teacher. He's okay. He turns a blind eye … I mean, he forgives a stolen computer and a smuggled dog, but it would be a bit much to expect him to stay cool over a gatecrasher … stowaway like you.'

'So the chances of more close shaves are high. Will Roger remain committed to the nicking procedure?'

Peter could not help but grin. 'It's a fair bet, yes. He won't need much encouragement. Risk is something he relishes.'

'Roger is good.'

'Yeah. Despite the sun not shining the day he was born.'

'But your sun always ...'

'No,' Peter explained, ' I mean he's had a rough life. And he's not the world's greatest brain. You know, the sort that thinks phlegmatic describes someone who spits a lot. But you can't fault him on loyalty. He won't see bad in anyone. Not even me. And he's got a mean cueing action.' Peter paused on seeing Mel's puzzlement. 'Never mind, that last bit's got nothing to do with it.'

'He may have had an unhappy life but I hear people calling him jolly.'

'Ah, yes. That's because the Jolly Roger is the name given to the black flag of piracy,' Peter explained.

'Piracy means robbery at sea.' Mel smiled mischievously. 'It is a good name for him.'

'True.'

'There is Toni also who, I think, travels under the same flag.'

'Yeah. The brains behind the pirates. Life's landed a low blow or two on her. She's been forced into crime by circumstances. She's an independent girl — though she does like someone, Roger mainly, to agree with her before she gets stuck in. Independent, but likes someone on her side. Anyway, you'd be sunk without Toni.'

'Sunk?' There was a degree of alarm on Mel's face.

'Sorry, another colloquialism. I mean, in deep trouble. She gave you the injection. Not exactly a trained nurse — a bit hit and miss — but you're still with us.'

Mel rubbed his upper left arm, still sore after Toni had punctured it. The whole of the arm was stiff and too painful to raise above chest height. But his discomfort was a small price to pay for his life — and for a chance to save everyone else's on board. Thoughtfully, Mel remarked, 'I have many debts. Perhaps I can repay one day.' He stretched and sighed. 'It is very good here, but I think that we take the risk of close shaving. Also, I have tired my strength. Shall we return?'

As Peter helped Mel back to cabin G9, Mel began to shiver. He leaned more and more heavily on Peter. Peter took the strain without complaint and apparently effortlessly. His size belied his strength and sense of balance. By the time they reached the cabin, Mel's shiver had become an uncontrollable shake. When he dropped onto his bed, Mel said weakly, 'Thank you, Peter. I asked you to devote a few minutes of your time and in fact used 16.922.'

Peter was taken aback. Mel did not even have a watch. '16.922 minutes, eh? Not 16.923?' He grinned.

'No. It was ... I ... er ... have a good sense time.' Mel looked confused. 'Sorry. I believe that I am still unwell and confounded.'

'You're not kidding,' Peter replied. 'You need to rest.'

Mel did not bother to undress. He did not have the energy. He fell asleep moments after lying down.

There was a convergence of ways outside cabin G9. Having got Mel back to his bed, Peter was departing. Charlton was returning from his walkabout. And Mr Brown was arriving in a quest for Peter Fallick.

Asked if he knew where the said Peter Fallick could be found, Peter was tempted to give the Deputy Head some wayward directions. Even with the dreaded Mr Brown, though, Peter was honest. 'You've found him,' he admitted.

'Show me the key to your cabin,' Mr Brown ordered.

'Why?' asked Peter.

'Just show me.'

Peter shrugged and searched through his pockets. After a fruitless exploration of the depths of each pocket, he looked at the teacher and said, 'Strange. I must have lost it.'

'Right!' exclaimed Mr Brown, like a man who had just had all his suspicions confirmed. 'Come with me.'

'Why? What's it all about?' Peter queried.

'You know perfectly well what it's all about,' Mr Brown returned irritably. He grabbed hold of Peter's sleeve to drag him away but when he yanked, Peter did not budge. He was a slight boy but he seemed to be rooted to the spot like a statue.

Peter and Charlton looked quizzically at each other. 'Want me to do anything?' Charlton asked his mate.

'I don't think so,' Peter replied. 'It's obviously a misunderstanding. And,' he said pointedly, 'as long as I'm not manhandled, I'll go and sort it out.'

'Don't be funny with me, boy,' Mr Brown retorted. 'Come on!' He let go of Peter's sleeve.

Peter shrugged and followed him towards his office.

Charlton stood and watched with a frown on his face. Something told him that Peter was in deep water. He resolved to go and find Mr Beever. As form-teacher, Mr Beever should at least know that one of his pupils had been collared by the Deputy Head. After all, Mr Beever once said to Charlton that he'd always be available for a chat when trouble loomed.

In his office, Mr Brown made Peter sit at a table, then he picked up a key from his own desk. He waved it under Peter's nose. 'Know what this is?'

'It's a key,' Peter could not resist replying.

'Careful, lad! Just answer me this. Is it your key?' His questions sounded like accusations.

Peter peered at the code on the key. 'Yes,' he said. 'Looks like it. G4. So what?'

Mr Brown put down the key and instead occupied his itching hands with a plastic ruler. 'So, what have you got to say to me?'

Peter considered for a moment. 'Not a lot. Nothing, in fact. I don't know what this is all about.'

'Huh. Well, let me tell you where your key was found. The library!'

'Yeah? I'm not surprised,' Peter responded.

Mr Brown, though, did look surprised. 'You're not going to deny it?'

'Deny what?'

Mr Brown circled Peter like a shark, slapping the ruler into the palm of his left hand. 'It was found among a pile of vandalized books,' he barked.

'Oh.'

'Oh. Is that all you have to say? Admit it. The game's up.'

'I don't intend to admit anything. If my key turns up in the library, it proves that I've been in the library, that's all. I'll admit to going to the library. Frequently.'

'The key — your key — wasn't just in the library.' Mr Brown built up to the denouement. 'It was right in amongst the books that had been ripped and burnt. So,' he cried, 'How do you explain that?'

Peter shrugged. 'I don't know.' He sighed. 'I guess someone nicked my key and planted it there.'

'Ha!' Mr Brown exclaimed derisively. He came to a halt threateningly at Peter's shoulder. 'Think you're inventive, don't you? Far-fetched is more like it. Tell me, who would want to go to the trouble of stealing your key and placing it among books that had mysteriously been vandalized?'

Of course, Peter knew perfectly well who would want to plant his key as evidence at the scene of the crime. The boys he and Roger had confronted outside the library were unlikely to be the types to forgive and forget. Even so, there was an unwritten code of honour that would not permit him to point the finger. Especially not to a teacher like Mr Brown. Peter also knew that, if he did shop the guilty parties, they would only make matters worse for him later.

'Cat got your tongue?' Mr Brown jeered.

The Deputy Head was so close that Peter could hear his rapid heartbeat. Peter remained calm. 'I just think you've jumped to a conclusion that someone wanted you to come to. You probably won't listen to what I have to say anyway.'

'You ...' Suddenly, Mr Brown struck out viciously with the ruler, aiming at Peter's left hand on the table. But the plastic did not swat Peter's flesh. It thwacked the table. In a flash, Peter's hand had darted out of the way. In the next instant, it was on top of the ruler, fixing it to the table-top.

'Why, you ...' Mr Brown was incensed. He slid the ruler out from under Peter's hand and crashed it down again. He was never quite sure what happened in the next two seconds.

The ruler hit the table then somehow Peter hit it. The Deputy Head's unbreakable ruler fell to the floor in two pieces. He stood and stared at the fragments like a man made impotent.

'Now,' Peter said, taking charge of the situation. 'Why don't we take a look at the facts. Much more productive than turning nasty. You see, I spend half my waking life in the library. I'm hardly going to smash it up. So what's your evidence against me? Just the prize exhibit of my key?'

Mr Brown was recovering slowly from the shock of the destruction of his ruler. Tamely, he stammered, 'Not more than thirty minutes ago, one of my pupils came to me from the library to say that he'd witnessed what was going on. He'd seen the culprit in the act. The description fits you perfectly.'

'Two things,' Peter replied. 'One. Is it usual for your kids to run to you, dying to inform on someone? How many times has that happened? Hardly ever, I suspect. Don't you think there's more to it than meets the eye — a bit of vindictiveness creeping in? Two. Half an hour ago, I was up on Deck 2, talking to … a friend.' Peter stopped, realizing that his alibi was straying perilously close to Mel.

'And who was this friend?' Mr Brown asked. 'So I can check your story.'

Peter's spirited defence was momentarily in tatters. 'Well…' Peter hesitated. 'I could give you the names of ten kids who'd swear blind they were with me. His name's not important. You'd only accuse him of lying to protect me, anyway. But I'll tell you one thing. Mr Beever saw me. He was jogging round Deck 2 at the time.'

'Mr Beever?'

'Yes.'

Mr Brown was taken aback. He did not expect the defendant to call a fellow teacher to the witness box. 'Okay,' the Deputy Head conceded. 'I suppose you'd better go while I check this out with Mr Beever. But if you've lied about this, believe me, you'll be in even bigger trouble.'

'I know, I know,' Peter replied. 'Please can I have my key back now?'

Mr Brown slapped the key into Peter's palm in a final gesture of defiance.

Out in the corridor, Peter nearly bumped into Mr Beever, still in his tracksuit, as he strode towards Mr Brown's office. 'What's going on here?' he asked Peter.

'Nothing,' Peter replied. 'I've sorted it out. I've been allowed out on bail. You're too late. You missed all the action. But he,' Peter pointed at Mr Brown's door, 'may have a question or two for you.'

Eager Beever shook his head. 'Well, clearly I'm not going to make sense of it from you. I'd better go in and see him.'

'Good luck to you if you think you can make sense of *him.*'

While the children toured Trondheim, Mel and Alien were confined to quarters. As Mel's disease ebbed, his curiosity and infatuation with the Earth flowed. Despite occasional dizziness and shivering, the lingering inflammation of his left arm and a touch of indigestion, he walked unsteadily but unaided to the port-hole. Instinctively, he placed his fingers on the glass but they told him nothing. After all, they were only human. He left his hand on the window to steady himself. Something out there still perturbed him. Yesterday, he had heard its rumbling, propagated through water. But why should it disturb him? He had seen and felt many new sensations yesterday. He was like a baby, experiencing everything for the first time. Perhaps he felt threatened because the vibrations came from an unknown source. Yet he had not seen the birds, and the beating of their wings did not fill him with apprehension. He had not seen a radio or TV station but their signals did not invoke uneasiness. Mel had never been intimidated by the new. So why now? He had no reason for suspicion, other than unreliable intuition. Just the distant rumble of some unseen earthly device. In the Earth films that he had watched as part of his training, he could tell when something ominous was in the offing by the threatening nature of the background music. Now he regretted that real life on Earth did not come with a musical score.

He resisted the temptation to shed his human cloak and probe the object for a short while with his own senses. He needed all of his energy to complete his recovery. From the canine perspective, no doubt, Alien was grateful for Mel's restraint, for immutability. Mel patted the dog and tried to persuade himself to forget his irrational worries. He had a more important task to consider: the fate of the *Queen* and her passengers. His limited strength did not allow much activity for the moment but at least he could prepare himself for the action to come. Yesterday's sensory exploration had not located the ship's iceberg detecting radar. Presumably, it was operational only at sea. Mel resolved to probe the system soon after the ship set out for Trondheim. All he needed was health, a dark night and a bit of luck. During his virtual reality training, he had learned as much as possible about the primitive radar technology. His plan was to rectify the detection system whenever it suffered catastrophic failure. Mel squatted down and spoke to Alien, 'As they say here, no problem.' But Mel was soon reminded of his own frailty. When he stood up, the room span before his eyes. He staggered, and had to clutch the chair to steady himself. Even so, he could not help but smile. 'Perhaps there is just a little problem. It will be solved soon, though.'

In the evening, Mel fell asleep directly after eating a hearty, pirated meal. By midnight he was awake again and in need of a stretch and some fresh air. The nourishment must have helped because he felt clear-headed, and his various pains had become merely aches. Quietly and carefully, he dressed and slipped out of the cabin without waking Charlton. To his earthly guise, the ship felt quiescent. The silence and inactivity was strangely calming and attractive. He trudged up two flights of stairs, tiring not only his legs but also his arms, which he used to haul himself up each step by pulling on the banisters. When he reached the Sun Deck, he paused to get his breath back.

Outside, it was a warm, peaceful night. Hardly a breeze. It was dark but a bright moon, the lights of Trondheim and the northerly location delayed the true blackness of night. Towards the aft, Mel recognized a plump figure standing with his back to the town, gazing out to sea. There was nothing out there but the vastness of sea and sky. As Mel made his way laboriously along the walkway, Graham turned and saw him. 'Mel,' he whispered, 'Are you okay?'

Joining him on deck, Mel said, 'I am fine. A little tired, perhaps.'

'What are you doing out here?' Graham asked, looking around to see if anyone was watching them.

'I am doing what you are doing.' Mel indicated the view. 'I am appreciating this wonderful planet.'

Graham relaxed somewhat. 'Yes. It is ... tranquil. Awesome.'

'Awesome?' Mel queried.

'Yes. The world. God's work.' Graham breathed in deeply, then stood in silence for a while. 'You know,' he said, 'sometimes it's so quiet and lonely here, you can almost hear His whispers.'

Earlier in the evening Mel had refused to entertain his own illogical and uncertain instincts. He preferred something more substantial than a hunch. He did not now relish a discussion with someone whose life was built on an impulsive, but probably unshakeable, belief. 'Graham,' he said, 'before my illness, you suggested that a mere boy will become leader. What was your meaning?'

'It's not my meaning. I simply applied it.'

'To which person?'

'To you, of course.'

'Me?'

Graham nodded, then looked out to sea again. 'It just came to me,' he said without looking at Mel, 'when I saw you.'

'A whisper from your God?'

'Perhaps. Call it intuition, if you like.'

'You maintain that its meaning is unknown to you?'

'I don't ask why, why, all the time,' Graham replied. 'Some things just are.'

'Things like your faith?'

'If you like. We should all listen to our inner selves, Mel. Instinct is a valuable resource. It is one of God's whispers. And out here is where you hear it best,' said Graham. He turned to Mel and added, 'You should come here on your own one night and listen too. Then you might learn what you wish to know.'

Mel shuddered. This time, though, it was not caused by his illness. Graham's whims were uncannily accurate but his reasoning was elusive. Mel had already decided to come on deck one dark night to listen in his native form. Listen to the messages in the air that were imperceptible to humans, that would tell him what he needed to know. For Graham, life *did* come with a musical score. That score comprised God's whispers. And now, Graham was trying to convert Mel, to attribute Mel's innate abilities to whispers from an indistinct deity. If so, there was a danger that Graham might put Mel on a pedestal that he neither wanted nor deserved.

Graham broke the silence. 'It is beautiful. As if the rest of the world has disappeared and we are on the ark.'

A voice behind them responded, 'Give the greenhouse effect a few more years to develop and you never know. We could all be latter day Noahs.'

Graham and Mel had been so absorbed that neither of them had heard Alan approaching. But Graham did not seem to mind. In fact, he raised a smile at Alan's witticism. Mel could not remember Graham smiling before.

'It's nice out here, contemplating the navel,' Alan

continued. 'Apart from the mangey mosquitoes, that is. Still, all creatures great and small, eh, Graham? These light nights, no one sleeps much. The walkway's getting like the M25.'

'M25?'

'It's a circular motorway — a stationary and overcrowded one,' Alan replied. 'Anyway, you all right now?' he asked Mel.

'I am quite good. I think that I will go to bed very soon, though. I tire myself easily.'

'I can well imagine. But you pulled through. Every dog has its nine lives.' Alan paused, then said, 'Don't worry. Just a saying.'

'Sort of,' Graham added.

The next evening, when the parties of children had finished touring the artefacts of Stone Age man, Bronze Age woman and Middle Age Vikings, Mel went to cabin G5. He wanted to express his gratitude to Mike for his part in Mel's treatment. At least, that was the pretext for the visit.

At first, no one answered Mel's knock but eventually the door opened a little and Mike peered out. 'Oh,' he said. 'Mel. How are you feeling? Come in. Quickly.' After he had shut the door again, he apologized. 'I have to be careful. You've probably been told I've got a hot computer in here.'

'Hot? Is it consuming too much electrical power?'

Mike grinned. 'No. Hot means nicked.' Then he added, 'And nicked means ...'

'I have learned all about nicking,' Mel interrupted. 'I owe my life to the art of nicking, and now I am sustained by the nicking of food. I have also learned a little of hacking,' he said. 'I have come to thank you.'

'No need. Besides, Peter and the others did the hard work afterwards. I crack systems for fun anyway. They probably told you — if there's a programme, any programme, with a password, I want to get into it. Just because it's there.'

'Could you explain your system to me?'

'Sure,' Mike said eagerly. 'You know much about computers?'

Mel smiled. 'Yes, but this one is not a familiar type. I believe that you have networked it to the ship's computer.'

'That's right,' Mike answered. 'Come on. Sit down, I'll show you.'

Mel settled in front of the VDU for the first of several lessons. He was a willing learner, making up for lost time. He was keen to ascertain how much of the ship's operation could be monitored discreetly from Mike's terminal.

Jogging health freaks, insomniacs and the merely restless occupied the *Queen*'s promenades, walkways and decks. It was neither dark nor light. In Cell Block G, Charlton had come to recognize Gail's footsteps and quiet knock at the door. He was confident enough not to check the identity of the caller. Besides, he was expecting her. He simply opened the door to admit both Gail and Alien.

'Hello,' said Mel cheerily from the chair.

'You're still up,' Gail observed. ' Good sign.'

'Yes,' he replied. 'I begin to be well again.' He stroked Alien who, tail wagging, had crossed the room to sit by Mel's legs.

There was an uncomfortable silence in which Charlton looked at Gail and Gail looked at Charlton.

'Yes?' Mel prompted.

'Go on, then,' Gail muttered to Charlton.

Charlton sighed. 'It's your idea,' he grumbled.

'Do you have something to say to me that is difficult?'

'Yes,' Gail answered. 'Charlton?'

'Oh, all right,' he muttered. 'I'll do it.' Charlton took a deep breath. 'Difficult, yes. You'll probably laugh, but I ... we .... We're curious about where you come from.'

'Oh?' Mel did not expand.

'Where are you from, Mel?'

'It is a long way off. You have not heard of it, probably.'

'Which country, then?' Having started, Charlton was determined to press for an answer.

'Why do you have such curiosity tonight?'

'Because of things you said when you were delirious.'

Mel looked down at Alien for a moment, then asked, 'What sayings?'

'Things that seemed ... I don't know ... not right for a human being. As if you counted yourself as a race apart. There's the business with distemper, as well.'

Mel closed his eyes and leaned back in the chair. 'This conversation is difficult for me, too, Charlton. Can you be specific about your suspicions?'

'Go on,' Gail urged.

'I'm convinced that you're not human.'

Mel opened his eyes again and looked at Gail. 'Do you concur with this view?' he asked her.

Gail shuffled uneasily, then nodded. 'I think so.'

'You believe me to be an alien.' The dog at Mel's feet glanced up at him but, when Mel paid him no heed, he settled down again. 'What do the others believe?'

'I don't know,' Charlton replied. 'I've only talked to Gail about it. I doubt if the others suspect anything.'

Mel's expression suggested that he was relieved by Charlton's response. 'I advise that you both sit on the bed for a while,' he said. 'I have words to say to both of you.'

Olav is all the rage in Trondheim. Olav, after putting in his oar for the good old USA and stopping off for a bit of rape and pillage (or, as sensitive Cueball puts it, raiding and pillaging) in England, got religion and died. His successor, another Olav, was just as sold on Christianity, built a church, monastery and fortress, then died in battle against the daft King Canute. Lo and behold, a spring sprung from this Olav's tomb (let's hope it was only water) so he was made patron saint of Norway and yet another chapel was built. This one, over Olav's tomb, was enlarged, extended and given an en suite chamber or two. The whole caboodle is now Nidaros Cathedral with the slimy green spires. Norway's proudest gem. Half built by Gothics, half by Norman. The real St Olav's well is outside. Just down the road in the market-place, the unsaintly Olav stands erect in stony pose, reduced to the role of giant sundial.

There's only one thing more common than Olavs, and Norwegians, in Trondheim: mosquitoes, gnats, fleas, or whatever the little flying, nipping nasties are. No coincidence that Trondheim makes Nit Home Rd. The evening air is thick with airborne thugs that cock a snook at insect repellant; in fact, they treat it like the elixir of life. You can bathe in it, dissolve your socks in it and still the dreaded red blotches come up unfailingly around the ankles and in the most uncomfortable, out-of-the-way, private places. Very irritating. Suddenly, three hundred children begin scratching more ardently than Alien (I guess it's all right to write this now that the cat (?) is out of the bag and Gail is in the dog-house).

Hell is a nice place. Better than its reputation. Around Hell it seems that Stone and Bronze Age man (and woman) had little to do but indulge in graffiti all day. The rocks are plastered with elks, long boats, seals, Gustav og Sigfrid (not sure this one was genuine Stone Age screed), interestingly rude men, and unidentifiable shapes. Some might have been jellyfish or maybe Hell's bells. The long boats had a ridiculous number of erect oars — at least I think they were only oars. Anyway, viewed upside-down, the boats looked like centipedes.

Tomorrow: one last day in Trondheim; two more meals of herring, several more erect Olavs, no doubt; millions more insects. Then it's shiver me timbers again. Out to sea, me hearties. Coast hugging, insects bugging, kids skuldugging.

'Mel?'

A muffled voice from the bottom bunk replied, 'Mm. Yes?'

'You're not asleep, are you?'

'Not really.'

'I can't sleep, either,' Charlton said in a hushed voice.

'Perhaps you are troubled by the explanation of my origins and my purpose on Earth.'

'Maybe,' replied Charlton. 'But not really.'

Mel was surprised. 'You are not perturbed by my story?'

'Not much. I trust you. Anyway there are worse things than dying, believe me. But,' he added before Mel could comment, 'I do wonder why you don't just get them to sail for home right now.'

'The basis for such behaviour is difficult to envisage. Will they turn the ship around because an alien on board has seen the future?'

'Put like that,' Charlton said, 'it does sound improbable.'

'Besides, I have to use minimum interference. The affairs of the Earth must not be unduly disturbed because other problems might ensue.' Mel sat up in his bunk. 'I must keep to the original plan but avert the crisis by the smallest possible action.'

Charlton came down the ladder and plonked into the chair by the bed. 'It's not that that's keeping me awake.'

'No. It is the effect that makes you unconcerned about the fate of this ship.'

Charlton nodded. 'You've told *your* long story. You've recovered from your disease. It's time I told you *mine* — about someone who didn't recover.' There was enough light in the room for Charlton to see Mel's outline, but he preferred to look away. He gazed out of the window, gathering strength. 'I haven't told anyone else. I … er … It was my mum.'

'The one who did not recover?' Mel queried softly. In the dark, even his human eyes could pick out Charlton nodding. 'What disease? What did she die of?' Mel was trying to make it easier for him.

'Motor neurone disease. But the disease didn't kill her.' Charlton sighed. 'It's not an easy disease to live with. Muscle wasting. If she got a cold, her nose just streamed. She couldn't do anything about it. No control. Her speech was difficult to follow — not much more than moans. When she got cramp, she just had to put up with it. She couldn't even eat or go to the loo on her own.' He ran out of words for a while.

'Is there a cure?'

This time, Charlton shook his head. 'No. It's slow and undignified. But,' he said, 'you know the worst thing? She couldn't scratch an itch but she could *think*. That's all she could do. Think. It would be easier if it destroyed the capacity to think.'

'I understand what you are saying.'

'I am sick of stagnation. I want to control my being. I am sick of dependence. I want nature's judgement. I am sick of torment. I want to die.'

Mel did not intrude on Charlton's quiet sobbing. He just waited.

'She didn't want to exist like that. She had no pride left in her life. Constantly, she tried to tell me. Beg me. It was a struggle to understand. But I knew. Knew what she wanted. I couldn't sleep, couldn't live with her like that. But I resisted. She pleaded and pleaded — as best she could — for weeks. She even asked the doctor to give her something ... you know ... but he wouldn't. She wanted out. Wanted the right to end the torture.'

'Deliverance,' whispered Mel.

'Yeah. And in the end I gave in.'

'You ...?'

'Yes. It wasn't the disease. It was me. A pillow. I smothered her with a pillow.' He cried without restraint. 'It should have felt like a release, but it was ugly. Ugly.' Charlton sniffed and wiped his nose with his pyjama sleeve. 'There are times,' he said, 'when you want to just leave the world for a while and come back when everyone's forgotten you and what you've done. Trouble is, even that wouldn't work. There's one person who still wouldn't forget. Me. I can't forget what I've done.'

'Nor should you, Charlton,' said Mel. 'You were right. There is not shame here. You gave her what she wanted.'

Charlton rubbed his eyes. 'The law didn't see it that way.'

'What do you mean?'

'I walked straight into a police station and told them what I'd done. On nights like this, I can still hear the chairman of the juvenile court, "You intended to kill. You didn't suffer a temporary loss of self-control. You made a calculated, rational decision to kill. In law, that can only be murder. And in considering murder, the courts have no provision for recognizing the quality of life taken. We'd be on a very slippery slope if we put values on life. Is it worse to kill a prince or a pauper? British justice has no defence for so-called mercy killings".'

Mel sounded indignant. 'He was wrong. It is quality of life that matters, not its quantity.'

Charlton shook his head. 'Not here. They would only accept a murder plea. "Physical provocation might have precipitated a charge of manslaughter but mitigating circumstances do not",' Charlton quoted. 'I am a murderer.'

'That is crazy!' Mel said heatedly, then realized that he was in danger of waking the whole block. 'I am sorry, Charlton,' he said more quietly, 'but it does not seem like justice to me. You humans are not logical. As I understand it, you plan for the removal of life from the young with ... what do you say? ... contraceptives and abortion. Now you inform me that you deny the terminally ill the right to an easier death. It is involuntary euthanasia for the baby in the womb, but voluntary euthanasia for the old people is not allowed. This,' he said emphatically, 'is not right.'

'But British law is right,' Charlton replied quietly, yet with cynicism.

'If a ... what do you call it? A baby in here.' He tapped his stomach.

'Foetus?'

'That is it. If a foetus is suffering a severe disability, it can be killed legitimately. Yes?' Seeing Charlton nod, he continued, 'If an old person near the end of life has the same disease, that person cannot be put out of misery?'

'I know,' Charlton replied. 'I've lived with these thoughts for months. But there's something else.' He paused before continuing. 'Who benefited by her death?'

'Your mother herself, of course,' Mel answered.

'Who else?'

'I do not know.'

'Who had to look after her? Whose burden was removed?'

'No, Charlton. That is not a worthy thought,' said Mel.

'You did it for her. Even if your chores were made a little easier, that is what she would have wanted. She would not wish to be a burden to you. Anyway,' he added, 'has your life really profited by your action? It has not, I estimate. You have tortured yourself. That was not your mother's objective. She wanted an *end* to torture. You were brave enough, and loved her enough, to offer it.'

'That's what Mr Beever said.'

'He knows of this incident?'

'He's got a file on it, yes.'

'He has more sense than your law. Your motives were not selfish, Charlton. You know it yourself, I believe. There is no need for guilt. You must convince yourself. You have to be strong enough now to take responsibility *and* credit for your actions. Sometimes,' Mel said, 'it is as difficult to accept praise as it is to acknowledge blame. Regret will continue to tear you apart.'

'But I do regret it,' Charlton replied. 'How can I not?'

'Because *she* would not regret.'

'But I regret lots of things. The disease, the fact that the whole thing happened at all, that I was the last person she saw. I'm sorry that I took away the pillow and looked at her face.' Charlton swallowed uncomfortably. 'I thought she'd be at peace but she just looked frightened. I wish, when I was ... doing it, she could have told me that she wasn't scared, that she hadn't changed her mind, that she still loved me. I wish I could have held her hand — as well as the pillow. I know she wouldn't have felt anything but she might have known, somehow.' He paused for a while. 'Lots of other things too. I regret that she couldn't be buried for ages. That was my fault, because she was a murder victim. I particularly regretted ... in fact, I hated the persecution afterwards.'

'Prosecution, do you mean?' Mel queried.

'No. Persecution. The police had to put me in a place of safety. An organization called CFM — Christian Family Movement — hounded me. They believe that only God can give and take life. They regarded me as murderer *and* blasphemer. They're a powerful lot now. In government and the legal system. That's how come the law's so tough in cases like mine. We live in an age when the moral majority has found its voice and has its wilful way. Something slightly out of the ordinary and ... censored, locked up, or whatever.'

'But surely someone tried to help?'

'Yes. I came across several social workers and probation officers who did their best. Besides, they had to write a million social inquiry and medical reports on me.' Charlton shook his head, a twisted smile on his face. 'You know what they found? Nothing. No warped mind, just an ordinary kid. "We have assessed him," they said, "and we still don't know why he did it. He's normal." They'd have been happier if I'd been out of my head. Then they could have put it down to irrational behaviour. Easier to pin a label on it. You see, they hadn't lived with the disease. They didn't understand how someone ordinary is driven to an extraordinary act.'

'An act of kindness,' Mel reinforced.

'Mm. But the juvenile court put me in a home — which was anything but a home. I couldn't be placed in a real home — with another family — for fear of CFM reprisals. I couldn't handle special schools or the various forms of so-called "care." There's so little of it anyway — those in care

are not a high priority. So ... what was left? A Young Offenders' Institution. That's home for me. A retreat from the real world — like this ship.'

'Where I come from, we retreat to sanctuaries to rest, grieve and contemplate.'

Charlton hardly felt rested. The conversation had stressed him. Yet, whilst his confession had not brought absolution, there was at least the kind of deliverance that comes from sharing.

'Look,' said Mel, nodding towards the port-hole. 'It is dawn. Not so much a brick wall dawn as before, perhaps.'

'Perhaps,' Charlton agreed. 'You know, I've never told a friend before.'

'We have swapped secrets. That is good.'

'You won't ...'

Mel interrupted, 'No. We must both ... how do you say? ... respect the privacy of each other.'

Outside, it was too early for the sounds of Trondheim waking but a couple of fishing smacks chugged out of the harbour, past the moored *Queen*, and into Trondheimsfjord. Behind them, the early birds followed raucously and optimistically.

Grey Areas, Black Holes and Green Lights

While the OBTUSE kids were rearranging Trondheim, the British Prime Minister was announcing a rearrangement of her Cabinet. At last, the outcome of the latest game of ministerial musical chairs could be reported in the newspapers. Cabinet members had known for a long time who would perch on which chairs, and who would be unseated. The game was rigged. Sternhell was looking particularly pleased with himself. He no longer had to keep quiet about his departure from the Department for Education.

Helping to clear out Sternhell's office, his Parliamentary Private Secretary came across two files on the OBTUSE Experiment. 'These will be left for the incoming Education Secretary,' he surmised.

'No,' Sternhell replied. 'The first file — yes. The smaller one — no. I'll be taking it — the one marked "private and personal." It is ... more appropriate for me to retain that one.'

'That,' the PPS suggested, 'is not standard practice.'

'I don't care what you consider to be standard practice,' Sternhell retorted. 'The OBTUSE Experiment was my personal initiative and I will keep a personal record of its ... success.' He held out his hand. 'I'll have it now.'

Disgruntled, the PPS gave up the records unwillingly, like an inept athlete passing on the baton. The file tumbled from his hand before Sternhell had grabbed it. The ex-Minister for Education swore irritably at his secretary. 'You get on! I'll clear up this mess.'

There was not much of a mess. Only two sheets of paper had gone adrift. They were the first two entries in his alphabetical list of teachers. Beever and Brown. Checking that his PPS was not prying, Sternhell glanced down the papers before he slipped them back into the file. The first contained a long list of unacceptable political activities. Clearly, Beever could not adjust to the democratic decision that only one party was fit to govern. He also seemed to believe that ineffective opposition led naturally to extremism and corruption in the government of the day — a licence to get away with anything. Such views, Sternhell believed, were dangerous. Mr Brown's details recommended him as a solid teacher, but expressed doubts about his discretion. His first court case for assault on one of his charges was irksome but escaped the media's attention. No one could keep under wraps a second offence of beating pupils — not even Sternhell and a strong hold on the press. Brown became an embarrassment. Beever and Brown. Opposite, but equally insufferable.

Sternhell tucked the file securely under his arm as he made his way along the corridor to a new office and a new portfolio.

As the *Queen* sailed away from Trondheim, the Munkholmen ferry was preparing to slip anchor, its crew waving to the young Brits on deck. The long slog from Trondheim to Hammerfest had begun. Soon, the OBTUSE experiment was conducted out of Trondheimsfjord, back into the North Sea.

When the *Queen* turned her bow north-east, no one noticed on her starboard side the world's northernmost oak tree, as old as the Black Death in Trondheim.

For Mel, the plague of distemper continued to abate. His light-headedness ceased to disorientate him. He no longer felt in imminent danger of passing out. In fact, he was experiencing luxuriousness. It was the serenity that accompanies a return to health and vitality. He spent much of the day in Mike's cabin, getting to grips with human computer technology. He also decided that he had the strength to make use of the last dark night to exploit his full faculties. Come the early hours, he would sneak out onto Deck 2 to probe the ship's radar and, if it was still there, the mysterious drone that he had sensed before.

In Form G, small groups of kids had been assembled for debate. Some of the light-hearted discussions were degenerating into infectious temper. In particular, Graham squared up to Peter's inflamed passions. The pairing of Graham and Peter was not a match made in heaven. But Mr Beever insisted. He knew how to banish detachment. He knew that religion was the only topic of debate that could cause Peter to burst a blood vessel.

'I don't have to prove it,' Graham was arguing. 'There *will* be a new world. God has promised it — to the righteous. There will be a heavenly kingdom on Earth. He will wipe away every tear. There will be an end to death and crying and sickness. Hatreds and prejudices will cease to exist and everyone will be a true friend to everyone else. The lion and the lamb together.'

Peter could hold it in no longer. 'You've got to be joking!

If there was no conflict, man would invent it.'

'Yeah,' Toni put in. 'You're right. *Men* would.'

Peter ignored her. 'Don't you see? We have to have conflict — and danger. If there's no hills to climb, there's no point. We live to overcome the odds. No conflict means no ambition, no driving force. Your heaven on Earth is not worth having. Paradise is only for fools. It means stagnation. Besides,' he added, 'the digestive system of the lion is not ideally suited to nut cutlets.'

'All this will change,' Graham protested. 'Maybe at the moment man can only see his way forward with a weapon in his hand ...'

'I'm not just talking about war. I'm talking about *challenge*. Remember Shangri-la? Where's the challenge there? Where are the disasters to cope with?' Peter asked rhetorically. ' Besides, I reckon God Himself loves a disaster.'

'What?' Graham exclaimed. 'That's ludicrous.'

'Really? Disasters make good business practice.'

'What's that supposed to mean?' asked Graham.

'There's nothing like a disaster to put bums on pews.'

'Naturally,' Graham responded, 'people turn to the church in times of hardship.'

'Exactly! And He knows it too. "Churches a bit empty. Let's have another shocker. A cyclone or an earthquake. Or ... let's see ... There's a shipful of kids. I'll scuttle that. The churches will be packed. TV coverage too! My disciples, the CFM, will milk it for all its worth." Grieve publicly, gloat privately.'

Miraculously, Graham kept his temper. 'You confuse real church with the Christian Family Movement. I grant you that lot *would* exploit suffering. But God's into recruitment, not indoctrination or blackmail. God's compassion is everywhere.'

'Yeah? In Africa, with all those starving kids? If that's compassion, I'd hate to feel His wrath,' Peter replied heatedly, sincerely.

'Man can only expect to get what he deserves,' Graham said. 'It is still true, though, that God moves in mysterious ways. Faith must be tested sometimes. But He will not suffer you to be tempted above that ye are able.'

Peter sighed. 'Well, I think that God should stand down and let Father Christmas have a go at the top job. Perhaps God would get a different perspective if he came down off his cloud and took on Santa's parcel delivery service for a while. Maybe a bit of good cheer would rub off on Him. We could all do with a bit more ho ho ho.'

'If that's a plea for love and tolerance, I'm with you,' Graham replied. 'But remember Peter, it doesn't apply to God. It applies to us: the CFM, me *and* you. In fact, tolerance may not suffice. *You* must accept, and love, people like *me*. Hate followed by repentance is no longer good enough.'

Across the other side of the form-room, Mr Beever engaged Alan Splinter. 'It's time, the teacher said, 'us political animals got together.'

'Yes?' Alan replied guardedly, putting down one of the British newspapers that had been brought on board from Trondheim. 'That won't be much of a debate, will it?'

Mr Beever lowered his voice, 'No, but it might cast some light on OBTUSE. You see, I read your … acerbic essay. Enjoyed it, in a way. But there were implications that we might think about.'

'Toss some ideas overboard and see which float?'

'Yes. It was your notion of all the embarrassing people being swept under the carpet that got to me.'

'In what way?' Alan asked.

'I wondered if you were applying it to all this.' Mr Beever waved his arms about, indicating the whole classroom, the entire ship.

'No question about it,' Alan said confidently.

'Want to talk about it?' Mr Beever asked.

'Why not? Let's *not* sweep the sleeping dog under the carpet,' Alan smirked. 'This whole trip is a cover, I reckon. Unsettled! Disruptive, or embarrassing in some way, is more like it. What's the official lingo? Emotionally or behaviourally disturbed kids. Anyway, we're nothing but a drain on time and resources. Best not to have the likes of us reprobates around for a bit. So ...'

'So?'

'Not nice for a government to admit to sending troublesome kids away. Not politically sound. So they call us unsettled. Besides,' he added, 'you don't get a very satisfying acronym if you say disruptive rather than unsettled. Thinking about it, they could have called us scum, not schoolchildren, and they'd still have had their neat OBTUSE abbreviation. Overseas Boat Trip for Unsettled Scum in Education, maybe. They spoiled the ship for a ha'porth of tar, there.'

Mr Beever smiled. 'An appropriate proverb.'

'Not really,' replied Alan. 'It actually referred to sheep, mispronounced "ship", and the practice of smearing them with tar to prevent disease.'

'Really? You're joking! Sounds far-fetched.'

'Believe me,' Alan said. 'I know idioms like the back of my hand.'

Mr Beever grinned. 'I've noticed. Anyway, we've strayed off the topic.' He pulled his chair closer to Alan's. 'I happen to agree with you. We all know how education copes — or rather, doesn't cope — with so-called problem kids. We can't afford the special attention they need. We take them out of the classroom instead. Look the other way. Hope they'll grow out of it or, if not, get to sixteen pretty quickly. Then they're out. We let them loose on society — and society loose on them. We just want them out of the system for a bit, to minimize the knock-on effects in the classroom. And that's what OBTUSE is: giving the system a break.'

Alan tried his luck. 'While they're at it, they've removed subversive, unpalatable or plain useless teachers, as well. I think they've even given us a captain who's hopeless.'

Mr Beever did not take offence. He just nodded thoughtfully. 'Mm.'

'You've got the wrong politics, Gabby's got the wrong attitude, Peter's too clever, Toni's too poor, Graham's got the wrong religion. Need I go on?'

Mr Beever put his hand on Alan's shoulder. 'No, I shouldn't. I think we've said enough for the moment.' He tapped the newspaper that Alan had been reading. 'What do you make of the news?'

'What? The moves towards privatization of schools, more press control, or the latest sightings of Elvis Presley in Barnet?'

'None of those. Sternhell taking over at the MoD. The new Defence Secretary.'

'I've no idea,' Alan responded. 'Education guru now calls the shots, eh? I'll tell you one thing though,' he said seriously, 'bet it's all part of some grand design.'

'You have a suspicious mind, young man,' Trevor Beever replied. 'And maybe you're right. Time will tell, no doubt.' He stood up and, to bring their conversation to an end, he said, 'We'll talk again sometime.'

'Okay.'

On his way back to his desk, Mr Beever noticed Gabby reading a juicy magazine instead of joining in her group's discussion. He went over to her and said, 'So you finally smuggled one on board. Put it away, Gabby, before you lose it.'

'How do I know when I'm going to lose it, Guv?'

'I meant, before I take it off you.'

As usual, Gabby was in defiant mood. 'No one's going to force me to be fucking celibate.'

'Gabby ...' Mr Beever warned.

'What are you going to do? Send me to that bulging bag of bones with a voice far too high to be a real man.'

Alan was right. Gabby's attitude would not be to everyone's taste. 'Sending you to the Head would be like throwing a match into a powder keg. I'd do better sending you to the library. To get a decent bit of literature. You'd enjoy it. Really.'

'Well ... One thing you're right about. The pictures may be interesting but the stories are crap,' she snorted. 'I could write better.'

'My point exactly. So get writing.'

'Don't you ever give up?'

'About as often as you listen,' the teacher taunted.

'Oh, I listen,' Gabby replied, 'but only when someone's saying something worth hearing.'

Mr Beever's last port of call was at Jolly Roger's desk. He was struggling over an assignment. 'Tricky, is it?' Mr Beever sympathized.

'You ain't kidding.'

'You aren't kidding,' Mr Beever corrected. 'I'll have to spend some time with you on this. See what we can do about it.'

'What's the point?'

'The point is that this is the sort of thing you'll face in your last curriculum test.'

'So?'

Mr Beever saw regret, not innocence, in Roger's face. Roger knew that the assessment at sixteen was not the type of test that would reveal his strengths. His assessment report would be lousy. And that, these days, meant compulsory community service, or possibly national service. Any concept of a leisure industry had long since been abandoned as too expensive, so Roger was faced with one of the devious schemes that the Government had concocted to restrict the unemployment figures to a politically acceptable level. Mr Beever guessed that he was well aware of his future — and that he did not relish it.

'So, you never know, Roger. If we work on it, it might just click for you.'

'Yeah ... Well ... Thanks.'

For each other's benefit, they both tried to look buoyant.

The *Queen of the Fjords* was in no great hurry. Four leisurely days of bobbing and weaving, one dark night and then midnight sun, some transient ports of call, and a few detours for sight-seeing. By the first evening, she had snaked slowly through the narrow twisting Stokksund Sound, its wall of rock riddled with caves, and cruised across the stretch of open sea to Rørvik. Just before bed-time, she sailed all around Torghatten so her passengers could see the mountain with a hole right through.

The sparkling blue sea of the morning had faded to dirty-grey in the evening. By one-thirty in the morning, it had become oily black and soulless. The *Queen* was headed towards the distant snowy Seven Sisters. On deck, the air was noticeably colder than it had been in Trondheim. The temperature had driven indoors all of the night owls but one. Mel walked right around Deck 2 to check that he was alone, then stopped at the stern where the lighting was dim and he was well out of sight of the bridge. He took a few deep breaths, glanced around one last time, gripped the rail and let loose his human veneer. Immediately, the dark night was transformed. Tranquillity replaced by frenzy. It even took Mel by surprise. On the port side, high in the northern sky, bursts of particles were arriving from the sun. Showers of radiation in the ultraviolet region blinded Mel's own eyes. The hues shifted constantly as particles of different energy bombarded the Earth's upper atmospheres. Some even threatened to cross into the spectral region that was visible to humans.

Mel turned his face from the sky. He could not afford the distraction. Even from the stern, he could feel the ship's radar echoing faultlessly from obstacles in its path. No failure yet. With his hands on the rail he tried to sense the vibrations of any distant objects. The *Queen*'s own throbbing obliterated much but, behind it all, there was something. A low frequency drone, distinct from the *Queen*'s engine. He had hoped that, outside, he would be able to see its origin but there was too much background from the activity in the heavens. Yet he still detected a glow, a heat source, under the waves and further out to sea. The vibrations that he felt emanated from an underwater, warm body. And it was just as disconcerting as it had been before.

Suddenly he sensed footsteps. They came from above. Someone was walking to the aft of the Sun Deck. Quickly, Mel cloaked himself in his human disguise. Simultaneously, his senses were cloaked and the night lost its life and lustre. The eery darkness and silence returned.

But not quite silence. Above him, the person was sobbing quietly. Mel's first instinct was to slip away quietly without intruding on someone else's solitude and grief but, when he thought that he recognized her cry, he decided to go up to the Sun Deck. His eyes were still adjusting to the low level of stimulation after the dazzle of his own vision. Even so, the silhouette of the figure at the end of the Sun Deck confirmed his suspicions. As he approached her, he coughed to avoid startling her.

She turned, trying to wipe away all traces of her tears. When she saw that it was Mel, she seemed to relax somewhat.

'Oh,' she said, 'It's you.'

'Can I help?' asked Mel.

'No.' Gail turned back to the sea and sighed, perhaps regretting her hasty response. Quietly, she added, 'Not unless you can make the world go away.'

Mel joined her at the rail. 'Yes. I can do that.'

'What?'

'We have the technology to make this world go away. It is only a small world, after all. But,' Mel said, 'it would be a pity. It is a beautiful place. Look at the mountains all around us. Even in the dark, as mere outlines, they are imposing.'

'Dark?' Gail looked at Mel briefly, 'This is not dark.'

'My eyes, you understand,' Mel explained. 'I am used to a much wider reception.'

'No. This isn't dark. The sky's slightly lighter than the sea. And look,' she pointed, 'you can make out the horizon. And the mountains, as you said. There's even a bit of moon. It's never really dark when there's a bit of moon.'

'There are some lights over there, as well,' Mel commented.

'Another boat or an oil rig, I think.' She let out a long sigh as if she had made up her mind, reluctantly, to prolong a difficult conversation. 'If all the ship's lights went out and we had an eclipse, then you'd see darkness. Real darkness. Nothing but black. No mountains, no sea. Not even your own hand in front of your face. Horrible.' Gail paused and shivered. Mel said nothing. 'You'd lose all sense of dimension. Like ... being in a black hole. You could be locked in a cupboard with walls hemming you in. Or like here lost in immense black space. I don't know which is worse. But I know what it's like.' She could not help but weep again.

Mel put his hand on her shoulder. 'Do not worry, Gail. The lights will not go out tonight. And tomorrow we will leave behind the night. It will be lightness all of the time.'

Strangely, Gail found solace in the contact that he had

made with her. Even though he was male. She didn't shrug him off. 'Thanks,' she said.

'Thanks for what?'

'I don't know. For being here.'

'Can I stay a while? There is something in this world that you should see. It would be a privilege to see it with you.'

Gail looked at him puzzled. 'What do you mean?'

'I think that you should be reassured by some of the delights of your Earth. Tonight is a very special night, I am sure.'

'What ...?'

Mel stopped her talking by putting his finger to her lips. 'It will happen over there.' He pointed to the ship's port side, just to the north of the Seven Sisters. 'High in the sky at first.'

'I can't see anything.'

'Continue watching.'

In the calm that followed, the silence between them seemed natural and comforting. A good five minutes passed before Mel said in a quiet voice, 'Look. It is beginning.'

Suddenly, the dark sky was torn by a narrow band of green light. It extended from the horizon to somewhere high above their heads, dwarfing even the mountains. Spellbound, Gail could only mutter, 'Wow!' The spectral finger flowed faintly at first but then, gradually, the colour brightened and spread. The blackness was drawn aside to reveal more streaks of colour, filling the night sky. Red, yellow and blue. A display like some vast theatre stage splashed with coloured lights.

Gail held on to Mel and whispered reverently, 'What is it? What's happening?'

'Do not be alarmed ...'

'I'm not,' she interrupted. 'It's ... breath-taking. Magnificent. Look at it!'

He smiled. 'I told you that this world is full of wonder. This,' he said, waving towards the ghostly curtain of light that had spread, shimmering, across the sky, 'is what you call northern lights.'

The folds of the curtain shifted restlessly, as if stirred by an unearthly breeze. The striped pattern changed incessantly.

'How did you know ...?' asked Gail.

'I saw the first signs of it earlier, before you arrived here.'

'But how does it happen?' Gail could not tear her eyes away from the waves of colour that ebbed and flowed majestically. 'Don't they say it's an omen of some great evil?'

For a moment Mel looked askance at her. 'How can such a thing bring evil? No, it is natural as well as beautiful. Your sun has emitted great numbers of charged particles that have hurtled for several days towards Earth, attracted to this place by the planet's magnetic field. They cause ionization in the atmosphere ...'

'Okay,' Gail said as the hues began to fade. 'I get the general idea.' She felt disappointed that such a grand mystical experience could be given a mundane explanation by science. 'You scientific types have explained another supernatural mystery. There's a little less romance left in the world.'

'But there is one more cheerful face, and less superstition. The beauty of the effect is not lessened by knowing its origin.

In fact, the more we understand our environment, the more it is that we are in harmony with it.'

'I guess so.' Gail disentangled herself from him. The moment had passed. 'I haven't talked to anyone this much in an age,' she admitted. 'I'm glad you joined me. I wasn't having a good night, but ... it's different now. I've never seen anything that comes close to this. It's like a miracle.'

Mel smiled at her. 'Look,' he said, 'the colours no longer contrast. It has shades of green only.'

'Yes. Still gorgeous, though.' Wisps of green zigzagged across the sky like luminous clouds blown by a haphazard wind. 'But soon I guess it'll all be back to normal.' Gail's voice betrayed sadness again.

'Yes. But not quite.'

'How do you mean?' she asked.

'You are a little different, I think.'

'Yeah. Perhaps tonight I can sleep.'

They stood in silence for a while longer, watching the tints of green twinkle from horizon to zenith, and slowly fade.

It was Mel who eventually broke the spell. 'You should know, Gail, that my illness was not your fault.'

'But I caused it,' she replied. 'By bringing Alien. I feel awful about it.'

'You could not have anticipated the outcome. You should not fault yourself.'

'You don't hold it against me?'

'Pardon?'

'You don't blame me?'

'No,' he answered. 'Not at all.'

'Thanks,' she said again, with relief. 'I wouldn't want to hurt ... anyone.'

'You have not. I have health again.' Mel glanced up at the sky, almost entirely dark, and then turned to Gail. 'Before we go in,' he said, 'I have a question for you, Gail.'

'Yes?'

'Earlier, I saw something else. I need to know what it is.'

'What sort of thing? On the boat, or out there?'

'It was about two kilometres away. Over there.' He indicated the open sea behind the Seven Sisters mountain range.

'Can you see that far?'

Mel did not answer directly. 'Certain things are possible for me,' he said, esoterically. 'I heard its noise also. A drone. I could detect that the object was not on the surface.'

'What?'

'It is under the water. Quite a way under. I do not have the experience to know what it is. It has a warm body, though.'

Gail was perplexed. 'I don't know what you've seen.' She hesitated, then added, 'Hang on. Bet I do know. You've seen a whale coming up then diving again. And they make some pretty extraordinary noises. Lots of whales around here. Well, not as many as there used to be, but we're all keeping our eyes open for signs of humpback whales. That's what it'll be. You're the first to spot one. Congratulations!'

Mel considered her suggestion, then responded. 'No. It is human made. I am sure. Made of metal, I estimate.'

'How do you know?'

Mel shrugged. 'Intuition, if you like. God's whispers, Graham calls it.'

'You haven't caught religion, have you?'

'Be patient with me, Gail. Is there anything metallic that swims underwater?' he asked.

'Yes. Sure,' Gail answered. 'A submarine.'

'An underwater boat?'

'Yes.'

'That will be it,' Mel said. 'But why is it there?'

'Remember you're in Norway,' Gail began, but then thought better of it. 'Look, you may not know our politics, but the Norwegian coast is supposed to be riddled with Russian subs. Keeping an eye on military bases and the like. Even *glasnost* and revolution haven't put an end to that.'

'I do not understand all that you say,' Mel responded, 'but I am sure that your deductions are correct.' To himself, he murmured, 'Why did this submarine monitor us at Trondheim? And why is it tracking us now?'

'What?'

'Ah, Gail,' he said, as if he had not expected her to hear his questions. 'There is no need to worry. I am ... how did you say it? ... keeping my eyes open — for anything unusual. That is my purpose here. Anyway,' he added, 'it is cold and I am tiring. Shall we go back?'

Less than an hour after it had begun, there remained no trace of the aurora. The night was the same as it always was: dark, unknowable and scary. The whole episode might almost never have happened. But Gail would never forget that spectacle, and darkness would never be quite as loathsome again.

As they strolled back to their cabins, Gail asked him, 'By the way, could you really zap a whole planet?'

'Zap?'

'Er ... destroy. Make it go away.'

'Oh, I understand,' Mel replied. 'Yes and no. It is possible to do it, but a long time has passed since my people renounced such abilities. Possession of such techniques did not bring much joy ... or credit.'

Gail smiled. 'I'm glad about that.'

'Here, you still measure the strength of a nation in terms of military might. That is sad,' Mel said. 'For us, love comes first. Force is the *last* resort. On Earth, it is cherished and used too lightly. But here we are,' he whispered. 'Your cabin. We must not perturb Gabby.'

Gail smiled. 'Frightened she'll swear at you if we wake her up?' she whispered in return.

'No. My words were not correct. I am concerned not to *disturb* her.'

'Concerned? You must care for our Gabby.'

Mel looked at her with curiosity. 'What a strange comment,' he said, still in a hushed voice. 'I like all humans. You and Gabby and the rest. That is why I am here.'

Gail watched him retreating along the corridor before she opened the cabin door and tip-toed inside.

In the morning, two hours after passing by the Seven Sisters, the wayfarers crowded on deck. Sixty-six degrees and thirty-three minutes North. A fabled, proud position. All eyes looked past the small jetty, the lonely fishermen's cottages and the patch of meadow, to the Horseman. A rounded mountain with a pillar of rock for a summit.

'Magic, ain't it?' Roger whispered.

'I wish it was,' Gabby scoffed. 'We could make it disappear and inject a bit of life. There's not even a dotted line!' she cried theatrically. 'All this way and it's just a con.'

Mr Beever smiled at her. 'The Horseman itself marks the spot. That's your monument to the Arctic Circle.'

'That's a con, as well. It doesn't look anything like a horse, and nothing like a man.'

Gabby strode down the open promenade, to where Alan was talking animatedly to a small group of Cell Block G inmates. 'What I'm saying is, you've got a choice. A quiet party. Eager Beever undisturbed *and* booze. Or, noise, sir joining in and hence no hard stuff.'

'Well, I could use a spin on a dance floor,' Gabby put in. 'You can't call it a party without music.'

'And you can't have music in a ship without waking up Beever. His cabin's only round the corner.'

'So who's going to slip the ear-muffs on Eager Beever when he's asleep?' Gabby quipped.

'Look,' Toni said, 'what you need here is a bit of female logic. We *can* have noise, Beever and the booze. We make a punch.'

Peter interrupted her. 'Are you saying that sir won't suss out alcohol because it looks like fruit juice?'

'Let me finish,' she snorted. 'We make two punches. One for Beever — and clean-living Graham, no doubt — without the goods. The other has a drop of the hard stuff for the rest of us.' Toni had silenced her critics. Not one dissenting voice was raised. 'All we have to do,' she concluded, 'is get our Trevor to drink from the right trough. We'll have to make sure he's served all night. Won't you?' she said to Alan and Peter.

'Okay,' Alan conceded. 'We'll *all* have to keep an eye on him in turns. Are we agreed? Eager Beever to get a special invitation? And we bring in a few kids from other Blocks so Mel can blend in. Yes?'

The others murmured assent and nodded.

'Well,' Alan said, 'no time like the present, I guess. I'll go and see if I can get the green light from Beever straight away. Are you coming as well, Peter?' he asked.

Peter was taken aback. He had yet to come to terms with his recent rehabilitation. 'Sure,' he replied eagerly.

They edged their way along the crowded gallery and found Mr Beever exchanging pleasantries with Roger.

'Ah,' the teacher greeted them. 'Have you seen it? Over there. The … something-or-other … glacier.'

'Svartisen,' Peter informed them. 'Norway's second best glacier.'

'Yes. That's it,' Mr Beever said. 'We're going to take a detour up the fjord to get a closer look. Good stuff!'

'Anyway,' Alan put in, 'we've come to talk about raising the temperature a bit, not lowering it. We're a delegation.'

'Oh, yes.' Mr Beever eyed them suspiciously.

'Remember the non-existent Kristiansund disco? Well … we thought we might make up for it. In a small way, you understand,' said Alan. He went on to describe what Cell Block G had in mind.

'When do you envisage this event?' Mr Beever asked.

'Tomorrow night?'

'Mm.' Mr Beever appeared to be studying the glacier but, in fact, was pondering on Alan's words. 'I'm pleased you've been open about it,' he said eventually. 'You could have just done it behind my back.'

Peter grinned. 'Talk about making a virtue out of necessity! We wanted music, you're not deaf. *Ipso facto* ... you're informed and invited.'

'Honest, as well. You're playing on my soft spot,' said Mr Beever. 'There are two conditions, though.'

'Yes?'

'Keep it within reason. Not too much noise. No hanky panky. No burning effigies of Cueball. That sort of thing. Limit it to ... er ... forty. Okay?'

'Sure,' they agreed without hesitation, eager to trounce any opposition. 'You'll be there to ... chaperon us, anyway. What's the second condition?'

'Charlton,' Mr Beever answered. 'Put him in charge of the music. Bring him into it.'

'It's a deal,' Alan replied instantaneously.

Alan and Peter returned in triumph to the others. 'All systems go,' they announced. 'We have lift-off.'

The land of the midnight sun beckoned. As a mark of respect to that tranquil lifestyle, the *Queen* seemed to proceed at a slower pace with reduced engine clatter. The air was crisp and cold, the water calm and clear. The *Queen of the Fjords* made a brief stop at Bodø. Hardly a bustling metropolis, the town stood against a backdrop of mountains. The people of Bodø had last witnessed a dark night four weeks ago. Their next sunset would take place in a week's time. 'All that light and bugger all to do,' Gabby lamented. 'What a waste!'

After leaving Bodø, the ship took a left turn and headed across the placid bay to Lofoten Wall. Sixty miles of indelible granite and volcanic rock. Scattered fishing villages clung tenaciously to the side of the mountains. Each village was little more than a few huts on stilts but they were doubled in size by perfect reflections in still harbour waters. Late in the evening, the *Queen* entered Svolvaer, the chief fishing port of the Lofotens. But for a quirk of the solar system, it would have been dark. Instead, a bright orange sun peered over a distant mountain and cast a narrow band of light across the dormant bay where fishing smacks rocked gently. On the headland, rows of large triangular frames stood like skeletons, the racks where cod were hung to dry. Beyond, the village was built on fingers of land that poked, this way and that, into the sea.

While the galleries were still crowded with kids watching the weird and wonderful world go by, Mel crept away. He wanted to be down below before the *Queen* cut all engines and turned off her radar. Alone in Charlton's cabin, Mel — the real Mel, not his human disguise — placed his hand on the port-hole. The ship's radar was still functioning, scanning the sea-bed and foreland. Further out, the shadowy submarine was still shadowing the *Queen*. The humanoid Mel sat on the bed heavily. Two days — just two days — from Hammerfest. He felt healthy enough to continue his mission, but he was troubled. The submarine and several legacies of the disease haunted him. How would his own people react to his infection? How would Gail and Charlton cope with their knowledge of him? Should he risk telling Mike his true role? Was there enough time to prepare himself for his task? Who was in that submarine and what was *its* mission? He sighed. He could answer only one of his own questions. He stood up and said to himself, 'It is time to confide in Mike. He and I have work to do.'

The ship's departure from Svolvaer was delayed until the next morning so that she could be navigated through Trollfjord in true daylight. Ice had sliced the bleak channel, just a hundred metres wide, between sheer black rock-faces. The towering and timeless cliffs loomed over the *Queen of the Fjords* and her passengers, making them feel puny, vulnerable and ephemeral.

'Nothing like this in Birmingham!' Toni uttered, genuinely affected.

Water from the snow on the mountain tops crashed spectacularly, noisily down the walls.

'Wow! This is what the edge of the world must be like,' said Peter.

Reverently, Graham whispered, 'Let him go for a scapegoat into the wilderness.'

Roger simply whistled in awe.

For Gail it was all too much. She could not abide the mountains enclosing her, bearing down on her. She ran inside to her cabin.

When the ship emerged from the channel, there was a communal sigh of relief from the kids, as if they had just watched the gloriously gory climax of a horror film. Heart-stopping, almost unwatchable, yet unmissable. Thankful yet regretful for its ending. Out of Trollfjord, the world was lighter and warmer. The straits between the islands seemed spacious and luxurious in comparison. The *Queen* executed a protracted curve towards the Norwegian mainland, passing the town of Harstad on her starboard side.

'Look,' Gabby cried. 'Life!'

The buildings of Harstad were new and large. No fisherman's huts. Two destroyers were in dock, and a half-built oil platform stood proudly off-shore.

Toni was looking at the white mountains behind the town. 'Still can't get used to all this snow in summer,' she said.

To the fore, the view was obscured by sea mist. Above it poked a perfectly pyramidal mountain.

'Bad weather ahoy!' Gabby exaggerated.

Before they sailed into the mist, the ship wheeled round, prow to the north east.

'What do you reckon to this party?' Gabby asked Toni.

Toni shrugged. ' Okay. Not mega, but okay.'

'A bit tame with Eager Beever around.'

'Better than nothing.'

'And is Charlton doing the disco?'

'Yeah. He said he would, as long as he can just play the tapes and doesn't have to talk!'

'Thank God for that!'

'I wonder,' Toni contemplated, 'when Beever will tuck us up in bed.'

Gabby snorted. 'Yeah. Who needs sleep, these nights?'

'You never know,' said Toni. 'He might be all right about it. After all, he is letting us have it. Bet he hasn't told Cueball or Brown.'

'Probably not,' Gabby replied. 'But I know *why* he agreed to let us have the party.'

'Oh?'

'Still trying to impress us,' Gabby griped. 'You know, he keeps hinting that I should write the story of this trip. Why? I've figured it out. Because he fancies himself as one of the good guys in the story. He thinks being on our side will put him in a good light. He wants to be our hero! What a pillock.'

Mike and Mel were huddled over a keyboard. Peter, Alan and Roger were clearing the form-room for the midnight sun thrash (the change of name having been dictated by a shortage of moon). Toni and Gabby were preparing two different versions of the same punch. Trevor Beever sat in the staff room, looking out of the starboard window at the mist which hung over the sea, perhaps a couple of hundred metres from the ship. He was wondering about the party, how much trouble it was going to get him into, whether he cared, and why he was allowing it to happen. In moments of self-ridicule, he told himself that he was as bad as the kids: disruptive. Overseas Boat Trip for Uncooperative Staff in Education. Yet his motives were not particularly abstruse. He was partaking in an unofficial party as a form of protest against the on-board regime. It was his gesture. If the party in power could have a hidden agenda for this boat trip, then the boat trip could have a hidden party.

Everything was ready. Most of the light bulbs in the form-room had been removed to provide the requisite atmosphere. Half of the room had been transformed into a dance floor. A cassette player relayed Charlton's tapes to a wider audience than normal. On Mr Beever's table there were two bowls of punch, one large and one small, polystyrene cups, and as many titbits as the members of Form G could muster. A smattering of inmates had already collected and Roger acted as bouncer, ensuring that Mr Beever's quota of party-goers was not noticeably exceeded.

When Cell Block G's governor arrived, Alan sprang into action. 'Sorry about the laser display, dry ice and uv lights. Suppliers let us down. And the DJ's not exactly rapping yet, but you never know. Still, we can offer you a drink — of sorts. A punch without punch. Okay?'

'Yes. Thanks, Alan,' he said, surprised to be pampered when he'd anticipated being treated like a damper. He looked around the darkened room with satisfaction. His conditions had been adhered to. The noise level was acceptable, at least for the time being, and Charlton lurked behind the cassette recorder. He was hardly the life and soul of the party but he *was* participating. In a corner of the room, Gail was talking earnestly with a boy, not from G Block. When Alan returned with the cocktail of fruit juices, Mr Beever asked him, 'Who's that with Gail?'

'Oh, he's from some other group. Name of Mel. He's all right.'

'Ah, yes. I remember now. I've seen him before with Peter. Seems he's familiar with Gail, as well,' commented Mr Beever.

'Familiarity breeds children,' Alan joked.

'I think our Gail is blessed with more sense than most when it comes to that sort of thing.' In fact, Mr Beever was surprised to see her mixing at all with a boy.

Gabby and Toni led the dancing and soon the party was

in full swing. Toni even persuaded Mr Beever to take to the floor for a couple of tunes. 'That'll do me,' he said to her after a while. 'Want a drink?'

'Yeah, okay,' she said, then quickly added, 'I'll get them. An oldie like you'll need to sit down.'

'Not that old,' he objected. Even so, Toni went to get the drinks.

He circulated like a genial, correct host. The evening was going off better than he thought it would. Several of the kids seemed to cast off their inhibitions, despite his presence. Even Charlton had been seen, a drink in one hand and a cassette in the other, smiling and laughing. After a couple of dances with Gabby, who was in particularly jolly mood, Trevor Beever decided to take a breath of fresh air. Really, he wanted to reconnoitre the immediate vicinity to check that the reverberations of the party were reasonably localized. The coast seemed clear, so he slipped back into the form-room and, before he was surrounded by kids unusually eager to earn creep points, poured himself a drink.

Just as he did so, Mel also arrived at the drinks table, carrying two polystyrene cups. He smiled at the teacher but did not say anything.

'Hello,' Mr Beever prompted. 'You're Peter's mate, Mel. Yes?'

'That is true,' Mel replied.

Mr Beever took a gulp of his punch, then looked in surprise at the remainder in his cup. 'I smell a rat!' he murmured.

'Really?' Mel sniffed the air. 'Your olefactory response

must be excellent.'

The teacher's eyes flicked from the drink to the boy. He hadn't decided which was odder, the punch or Mel's reply, before Alan dragged him away. 'I ... er ... wanted to discuss something,' Alan said, striving hurriedly to invent a story. 'You know you call us Cell Block G inmates? Well,' he lowered his voice histrionically, 'if we really were prisoners, OBTUSE would be called "ghosting".'

'Ghosting?'

'Yes. Did you know?' Alan explained, 'Disruptive or particularly awkward prisoners are segregated from everyone else these days and moved from prison to prison. It's called ghosting — an extra punishment. So they can never settle. We're the Overseas Boat Trip for Unsettled Sinners in Education.'

'Very droll, Alan. With an element of truth again. But right now,' he said with an air of seriousness, 'I'm more interested in discussing this drink.' He tapped his cup and looked sternly at Alan.

'The punch?' Alan rolled his drink around his cup and smelled it. 'A playful, fruity bouquet, but inherently dull. Not a good year. Fermentation failed.'

Mr Beever's expression did not reflect Alan's flippancy. 'It's not as dull as you make out, young man. And innocence does not become you.'

'How do you mean?' Alan was beginning to struggle.

Mr Beever took another swig of his drink, emptying the cup. He licked his lips, as if his suspicions had been confirmed. He handed the cup to Alan and said, 'You were eager enough to get me a drink earlier. Time for another. And this time,' he said, 'I want the genuine article.' At last his face betrayed a smile.

Retiring from the dance floor for a while, Toni and Charlton poured themselves a drink then joined Mel and Gail.

'You look ... pretty mega now,' Toni said to Mel. 'I remember you when you were just a squirming blob on a pillow.'

Mel smiled. 'Thank you for your assistance, Toni.'

'Nothing to it. A piece of cake.'

Mel's mouth opened to ask a question but nothing came out. He was bemused by the language.

She laughed. 'I mean, it was easy. Forget it. What's a pin-prick between friends? A doctor would have charged a bundle for that but I do it at discount.' She took a drink of punch, then addressed them all. 'Hey, why are elephant's feet corrugated?'

'What is corrugated?' Mel asked.

'Something that goes up and down.' She traced the shape in the air.

'I was not aware that elephants' feet are like that.'

'They're not,' Toni replied.

'Well,' Mel rejoined, 'Why did you ask ...?'

Charlton interrupted, 'It's a joke, Mel. To make it work, you have to accept what's not true.'

'Oh. How strange. I will try.'

'So, why are elephants' feet corrugated?' Charlton prompted Toni.

'To give the ants half a chance!'

'But,' Mel objected, 'that would not succeed. As the foot

came down, the pressure of air would...' Toni's glare stopped his train of thought. 'Oh,' he said, 'I understand. I have to suspend belief in physics in addition to biology.'

Toni shook her head in despair. 'I'm off,' she said.

Charlton went to attend to the next cassette. The party continued unabated but Gail was not in the mood for music and jokes, and Mel felt his body reacting in a peculiar way to the punch. He was grateful when Gail suggested that they should wander away from the celebrations. They slipped out unnoticed and went to Gail's room. With the midnight sun shining in through its port-hole, cabin G1 seemed like a confessional. Gail, her hand resting on Alien's neck, felt that she could talk to Mel as she had never spoken to anyone else. Maybe it was because he did not present a threat. He was male, but he was not human. And, in a matter of days he would be gone. She could safely confide in a ghost.

'I'm sure my dad got me on this trip,' she began. 'To keep Gabby company, he'd say. But it wasn't that. I know it wasn't. He was trying to sort himself out, I think, and I was too embarrassing to have around, and Gabby too talkative.'

'I am not sure that I understand,' said Mel.

'It's difficult to explain,' she replied. She could not bring herself to look at him. She kept her eyes on Alien as she sighed then drew a deep breath. 'Dad used to ... do things to me. Things I can't tell you about.' She pushed her hair out of her face. 'Ever since I was ... very young.'

'You mean,' Mel asked, 'things that a father should not do?'

Gail nodded. 'Horrible things.'

'And what about Gabby?'

'Gabby is stronger than me.'

'I mean, did you not talk to her about it?'

'At first I didn't know what was going on. I didn't under-stand. But I felt ashamed. Too ignorant and too ashamed to talk about it. Anyway, Dad told me never to tell *anyone*. Not Gabby, not Mum. He said he'd ... punish me if I told anyone.'

'Punish?'

'As a taster, he'd lock me in this cupboard. Just for a bit. But a bit was enough. I hated that black hole. If I told anyone, he told me he'd lock me in for days. Can you imagine it?' Gail paused. 'I was terrified. I did whatever he said.'

'And this has been occurring for several years?'

Gail looked horrified. 'No, I couldn't have coped with that,' she replied. 'It stopped some years ago. I guess, when I got older and wiser. Knew what it was all about. The risk was too great for him then. He tried to control himself. He did. But ... he'd get angry and beat me. Not like before. Not ...' she hesitated. 'Anyway, the beatings were bad enough. They were his frustrations, I suppose. In controlling ... other things, he got mad.' She sighed again. 'It was then that Mum and Gabby guessed what had been going on and ... Well, here I am. Being here is like protection for me — and Dad. He's trying to keep a lid on it — for the sake of his career. The school reported my bruises, of course. Social workers paid visits. But, be-cause of his standing, it was all very discreet. He was scared stiff that Gabby would blurt it out, though. So, here we are. While Mum and Dad try to sort it out at home.' She patted Alien. 'I don't know what'll happen when we get back.'

'Maybe he will have cured himself,' Mel suggested.

'But I can never trust him again anyway.' She looked at Mel and said. 'When ... if this boat gets back, I'm not going home. I'm powerless when I'm with him, so I'm not going back to him. I can't love him. I can't even respect him.'

'What will you do?'

She shook her head. 'I don't know, Mel. I don't know.'

At last, Gabby had the promised date with Mike. It was a short date. She could not dance for long with someone who did not know how to immerse himself in partying. He did shuffle about, but his mind was elsewhere. Charlton, though, was a different kettle of fish. After a slow start, he began to come alive, much to Gabby's surprise. A few friends, a few drinks, an end to sickness, and ... Charlton was rejuvenated. He could leap tall buildings after all. On the floor, his movement and sense of rhythm made the others look like statues.

Gabby, thoroughly out-danced by Charlton, retired to the sidelines. She'd had enough to drink but was having some more anyway. In a break from dancing, she was swapping stories of misdemeanours with Peter.

'Hope you don't brush your teeth with Colgate,' he said.

'Uh?'

'Take a look in the shop tomorrow. There's none left.'

'So what?'

'You haven't heard about Cueball and the Colgate Crew?'

'No,' Gabby replied. 'Tell all.'

'Somehow, the entire Colgate stock disappeared last night. This morning the whole lot turned up. Squeezed lovingly into Cueball's desk, apparently. One hell of a sticky mess.'

Gabby laughed. 'Great! Should help him brush up on his books.' She took another gulp. 'Anyway, I never did ask what a clever clogs like you did to deserve this trip, Pete.'

'Deserve? Nothing!'

'Oh, come on! The qualification for this trip is being a misfit. And no one gets expelled from three different schools for nothing.'

'Well, that's *exactly* what I got expelled for. Doing nothing,' Peter said. 'It started a long time ago. I used to get sent to the Head for not working at the deadly boring stuff. She said, "If you're not going to work, you might as well not be here." So I went.' Peter smiled as if at a fond recollection. 'I bunked off most of the time. But I always went in for the tests. And came out top,' he added. 'So, what was the problem? I got expelled for doing nothing — persistently.'

'Good for you! What were you doing instead of school?'

Peter shrugged, obviously unwilling to answer the question. 'This and that.'

'Seeing a bit of life?'

Alan who had joined them, put in, 'Life begins at fourteen, eh? Usually behind the bike sheds.'

Peter shrugged again. 'Not really.'

'Knowing you, you were probably in a dusty corner in some library or other,' Alan said.

Peter could not help but smile. 'I hate school, but I like learning,' he confessed. 'And I like books.'

'You skipped school so you could work in a library!' Gabby hiccuped. 'You're weird!' she exclaimed. She took another drink, then said, 'And there's another thing. How did you get that scar?' She pointed to his cheek. 'Not by reading in a library. There's got to be life in someone with a scar.'

With a glint in his eye, Peter replied, 'Well, I hate to disappoint you but ...'

'Surely not!'

'Haven't you ever cut yourself on a piece of paper?' he asked.

'Yeah, but it didn't leave me scarred for life.'

'Imagine a great big book falling off the top shelf. Some of its sharp pages hit me right here.' He touched his cheek. 'Sliced out a great chunk.'

Alan was smiling. 'I think that means he's not going to tell us what really happened,' he said to Gabby. 'Believe me, I can read him like a closed book.'

'Mm. I reckon there's a good scandal there somewhere, though,' Gabby speculated.

'Talking of scandals,' Alan ventured to ask, 'have you noticed your sister, Gabby?'

'No,' she replied, glancing around the room. 'Why scandal?'

'Well, have you seen Mel?'

'I don't think ... Not our Gail.'

'You never know. They've got quite friendly. From little acorns do grow big fish.'

Gabby still shook her head in disbelief. 'No,' she said. 'No bike sheds on this tub.' Then dismissing the idea, she added, 'Anyway, Al, have *you* seen Chaz?'

'Yeah,' replied Alan. 'A dark sea horse, it seems.'

'He sure can shake his stuff — when he wants to.'

Peter was more guarded in his answer. 'Mm. Quite a revelation is our Charlton. Very volatile. God knows what he'll get up to next.'

'He's no problem. Just that whatever was eating him up seems to have had enough,' Gabby reassured him. 'But I haven't had enough. Let's have another tipple.'

Mr Beever remained on duty to the bitter end, trying to exert a calming influence without ruining the occasion. He was wondering how he could wrap it all up when he noticed, with relief, that the more popular of the two punchbowls was empty. The drink had been finished in time to stop Gabby sinking under the table that held it. He had never known a party to extend long beyond the last drink, and this one was no exception. Slowly, the kids drifted away till only the diehards of the Splinter Group were left. He stopped to share a joke or two, then said, 'Well, I'll let you off clearing up. Go on. You can do it in the morning.'

'It is the morning,' Gabby retorted.

'You know what I mean,' the teacher replied. 'Time for bed. Console yourselves that there's the big disco — a legal one — on the return trip. Cueball hasn't cancelled it.'

'Yet,' Gabby added.

'Well, that's one reason for calling it a day now. Less aggro now, the more likely he'll not play up later.'

Trying to keep the peace, Peter said, 'Okay. And ... er ... thanks. Thanks for ... '

'Yes, yes,' Mr Beever said. 'And thank you for the punch. I won't ask where it came from. Go on, now. Off to your rooms.'

Gabby's route from the table to the door was circuitous and her walk erratic. She hiccuped again, tripped over a chair and nearly keeled over. By the time Mr Beever had ushered her out, all but Charlton had dispersed. Charlton was still collecting together his tapes and cassette player.

Mr Beever nudged him and said, 'Why don't you escort Gabby back to her quarters? I'm not sure she'll make it on her own.'

Charlton, more cheerful now than at any time on the trip, agreed happily.

Deprived of bike sheds to creep around, Cueball was patrolling the ship — on the look-out for mischief makers. He was determined to ensure that the incident with the toothpaste would not be repeated. Yet he was not prepared for such overt bad behaviour as a couple of the opposite sex, clearly the worse for drink, dancing to some unearthly cacophony on the Sun Deck. His shriek penetrated the music. 'What's going on here? It's despicable!' He took the names of the culprits, Grobb and Ng, and demanded that they report to his office in the morning at nine o'clock sharp.

Gabby sniggered, 'Oh, good. That'll be fun.'

'Back to your rooms,' he ordered, 'with all the dignity you can muster.'

'Aye, aye, sir,' Gabby drawled.

On Top of the World

The morning was cold and damp. A strong wind had dispersed the mist but, instead, it blew low clouds briskly past the ship. It was depressingly overcast. The hundreds of thousands of sea birds nesting on the island of Fugløy could be heard but not seen. Once, when the island was inhabited, its cottages had to be anchored to the ground with cables because of the ferocity of the ocean wind. This particular day, the worst tempest was expected in Mr Uunk's room.

Gabby and Charlton formed the Plimsoll line outside his office while Trevor Beever, summoned to see the Head at ten to nine, parried the first blows inside. 'So what exactly were they up to?' he asked Mr Uunk. 'I can't imagine ...'

'They were ...' the Head cleared his throat uncomfortably as if he were about to speak the unspeakable. 'They were playing some dreadful music and dancing.'

For a moment Trevor was speechless. When he found his voice, he could only check that he'd heard correctly. 'Dancing?' he queried.

'That's right. After midnight!' Cueball broke two aspirin tablets and let them plop into the glass of water on his desk. 'If what they do these days can be defined as dancing, that's what they were doing.' He swirled his glass of aspirin as he spoke. 'It's not allowed!' he blurted.

'I know it's not. But is it such a crime? They were only dancing, weren't they? Where's the harm in it?'

'You don't fully appreciate the gravity of the situation, Mr

Beever. When I interrupted them, yes, they were dancing. But one thing leads to another in my experience. Especially when they'd both been drinking as well! Besides,' he added before Trevor could object again, 'what if they all danced on deck? It would be a riot. It's a serious matter.'

Trevor was imagining a hundred drunken couples dancing on deck — then doing what Mr Uunk seemed to believe was the inevitable consequence of dancing. He thought better of making a joke about it. The Head's sensibilities had been wounded enough. And he was yet to confront Gabby. No wonder that he was taking aspirins. Trevor felt that he ought to preserve what was left of Mr Uunk's composure. 'All I can say is, Charlton's ... highly strung — for good reason. He needs a bit of latitude.'

Mr Uunk retorted, 'I know that lad. He's the only murderer on this ship.'

The word stung Mr Beever. Technically, of course, Charlton had committed murder, but he did not deserve to be labelled a murderer. Trevor tried to keep his own composure. 'Charlton's a good lad. You know the circumstances of this so-called murder. He's still trying to come to terms with it. And he's beginning to succeed. I'll not have you forcing him back into his shell. Last night, like Gabby, he'd had a drink or two, I imagine. He was allowing himself to feel happy for once. It sounds harmless enough to me, unlike other ways a lad like him might let it out. Don't make him regress again.'

'Mm.' Mr Uunk considered the situation, and gulped down the solution that had finally finished fizzing. 'I'll bear your comments in mind,' he said. 'Now, you've already told me about Gail Grobb and her dog. It seems that problems run in that family. It's Gabrielle Grobb this time.'

'Yes, Gabby. But before you judge her, you should know that I let all my lot have a little get-together last night ...'

'Don't tell me *you* supplied the drink!'

"Course not. I guess they smuggled it on board. I didn't find out till late on. But about Gabby — I got her wrong myself. I nearly missed it. But I'm sure now. Her written project work is ... super. The ideas expressed in most kids' work are those of their last teacher. But not Gabby. She doesn't just join in the chorus. She's an original voice. Not everyone would like her style — or some of the words she uses — but there's a certain panache. Some of the best stuff she throws away — to try to annoy me or prove she doesn't care. But I'm making progress ... *She's* making progress. She's on her way to making a success of her life — as long as no one yanks her back now.'

'Her behaviour,' Cueball commented, 'is a different matter. It can't be condoned. And some skill at writing doesn't make up for it — or for insulting me this morning.'

'This morning?'

'Yes. When I walked past her and Charlton Ng.'

'Ah, well. That's Gabby for you. Original voice. Unique style.'

'Is that all you can say?'

Trevor thought about it for a moment. 'I don't know. There'd certainly be something wrong with her if she didn't insult us all regularly. What did she say that was so awful?'

Mr Uunk shook his head as if stunned. 'I can't repeat it. But mark my words, Miss Grobb, well known for her disrespect, was disrespectful in the extreme. Now,' he said sternly, 'let's get them in here.'

The two defendants were told to stand in front of the Head's desk. Charlton stood as stiffly as a soldier. Gabby fidgeted constantly. During the first few sentences of Cueball's lecture on alcohol, Gabby was clearly not paying attention. Her eyes flitted around the room and she sniffed the air repeatedly. Losing patience almost immediately, Mr Uunk snapped, 'Miss Grobb, is anything bothering you?'

'Yes,' she said with affected grace. 'I'm sorry but I couldn't help noticing a strong smell of toothpaste in here.'

Mr Beever put his head in his hands, in the vain hope that it would be a sign to Gabby to behave. Keeping his head down also had the advantage of concealing his amusement.

'You don't seem to realize the trouble you're in,' Mr Uunk cried. 'You've come here expressly to issue insults.'

Behind the Head, Trevor put his finger to his lips to quieten Gabby. 'Look,' he said stepping forward into the fray, 'if I'm to know what's going on with this insults business, someone's got to tell me what was said. Gabby,' he asked quickly before Mr Uunk could object, 'what did you say to Mr Uunk this morning?'

'I simply commented that only a complete dickhead would make such a song and dance about a song and a dance.'

'Ah.'

'Ah, indeed,' the Head uttered. 'Now you understand my viewpoint.'

Trevor understood that some people do not have the stomach for the truth, and that Mr Uunk's sensibilities were not having an easy ride that morning. 'Not necessarily,' he replied. 'Gabby was just drawing your attention to the triviality of their ... prank.'

Cueball seemed to be on the point of exploding. 'Dancing! In full view of ...'

'In full view of what?' Gabby growled. 'The mist?'

'In full view of ... anyone who was watching. And besides,' he continued to rant, 'everyone in this room knows what this ... modern dancing is all about. We all know what it leads to.'

'Oh,' Gabby exclaimed. '*That's* what it's all about. We're guilty of creating a situation in which we might have done something wrong — but didn't.'

Eager Beever said nothing. He was savouring the sight of Gabby making mincemeat out of Mr Uunk.

Charlton, though, looked bemused. 'Excuse me,' he said. 'But what are we talking about here? What does dancing lead to?'

'Well ... er ...'

Gabby curtailed Cueball's embarrassment. 'Sex!' she pronounced.

'Sex?'

'Yes,' Gabby confirmed. 'Sex.' Turning back to the Head, she asked, 'Tell me, does Charlton's response suggest to you that he was only dancing with me so he could have it away with me later?'

'That's not the sort of language I want to hear in my office, young lady.'

Gabby was not to be deterred. She was enjoying herself enormously. 'Last night I danced with at least five fellas, including him.' She pointed to Trevor Beever. 'If I'd bonked them all, I'd never have made it to this office by nine. Neither would he!'

No amount of aspirin could alleviate the effect of Gabby. 'Miss Grobb! Your language ...!'

'With all due respect, Mr Uunk, Gabby's language has been quite restrained — so far,' Trevor Beever put in. 'Look. There's no crime here. Just a boy and a girl enjoying themselves, and a young lady who speaks her mind.'

'That's it!' The Head thumped his desk in frustration. 'I'll be making a report on this incident when we return. There is crime here. In fact, there are three. Mixing with the opposite sex after midnight, making an unholy row after midnight, and the imbibing of alcohol.'

'And not realizing it was supposed to lead to torrid sex?' Gabby suggested.

'You're just making matters worse for yourself, Miss Grobb,' Cueball said, wagging his Biro threateningly at her.

'Shall we go, then? I've run out of things to say. I've only got insults left — and I know you don't like those.'

Mr Uunk shuffled the papers on his desk, then looked up. For the first time, he agreed with Gabby. 'Yes,' he said. 'You two may go. But I will discuss your punishment with Mr Beever right now.'

After they had left, Trevor tried again to plead for clemency. 'Try to remember when you were their age,' he said. 'Didn't you ...'

'Mr Beever! I am not prepared to listen ...'

'I just think there are worse things a pair like that might

do. And I'm not prepared to have their record besmirched
by some innocent act. The worst you could pin on them is
underage drinking and, by being there at the time, I condoned that, I'm afraid. Charlton has had all the hard luck he
can handle. More than enough for one lifetime.'

The Head was not to be placated. A punishment there had
to be. 'I've noted your role in this matter,' he said. 'A lack
of responsibility and authority. There'll be a report on you
too. Mr Brown has already warned me about your attitude.
And, in his view, your form was at boiling point. Obviously,
he was right. These things must be put down sharply — to
keep a lid on any further nasty business. And let me tell you,
Mr Beever, I'll hold you personally responsible for the future
conduct of these pupils. Now, let's work out how to penalize
them. Our options are limited. But you've been opinionated
so far — do you have any suggestions?'

'If you insist on punishments, yes, I have some advice.'
He suggested that Gabby and Charlton between them should
have to produce an illustrated travelogue on Hammerfest and
the journey back to England.

'That,' Mr Uunk complained, 'smacks of punishing a
masochist by giving him a good beating.'

Coming from anyone else, the comment would have been
humorous. But Mr Uunk cracked whips, not jokes. Trevor
tried to respond without a smile.

'You can consider it appropriate retribution. I would find
it palatable — I'll certainly not administer a stiffer, and less
just, penalty. More important, Gabby and Charlton *would*
regard it as a harsh punishment.' It was more a white lie than
a complete white-wash of the truth.

'Well ...' The Head hesitated. 'I guess a compromise has some merit. However, they can make the account cover the whole trip. Such is the seriousness with which I view this incident. And let me tell you, Mr Beever, any more excesses from your lot and ...' His voice trailed away, implying unimaginable vengeance.

'Yes, yes,' Trevor replied, eager to get away from the Head and his threats. On the way out of the office, Trevor felt the urge to stop, sniff the air and say, 'Gabby was right. There *is* a smell of toothpaste in here,' but he curbed the impulse. It was one of those times when prudence required that he play the part of a toothless lion.

Mel paced the cabin like a caged animal. 'The iceberg is out there somewhere,' he said, clearly tense.

'Not according to this, it isn't,'Mike replied.

Mike's room was an internal cabin. It had no outside view but, between them, Mike and Mel *had* hacked out a window on the world. Mike's microcomputer was so intimately net-worked to the ship's computer that they could monitor its echo sounder.

'Mel,' Mike asked, 'what if the radar doesn't malfunc-tion? What if the captain simply makes a dog's dinner ...?'

'A dog's dinner?' Mel queried.

'Sorry — a mistake. You can't do anything about human error, can you?'

'Mel had already picked up several mannerisms. He shrugged. 'I will have to.' Then he said, 'Let us have another attempt to access the computer in the submarine.'

Mike inhaled noisily. 'Well, okay. But you'll be lucky.'

'Yes,' Mel replied. 'I hope so.'

Despite the wind and the temperature, most of Beever's bunch were on the Sun Deck for their morning break. 'Look,' Toni cried. 'Another one.'

'One what?' Gabby asked.

'A glacier. Just about every mountain's got its glacier here.'

'Yeah,' Alan said. 'The whole area's snowed under with them.'

It was not a clear day but the cloud had lifted enough for the tourists to take in most of the coastal scenery.

Gabby complained, 'Snowed under with midges as well. Bloody things.' She waved her hand in front of her face in a futile attempt to scatter them.

'Never mind the tiddlers,' Alan said, 'I want to know about the whoppers. You haven't told us about you and Cueball. Drunk and disorderly, and all that. Did he survive the encounter?'

'He really is a berk. The madder he gets, the more pathetic he is.'

Alan grinned. 'So you didn't get six of the best and half a dozen of the other?'

'No,' Gabby replied. 'Eager Beever got our sentences reduced. I have to write about this whole damn trip and Chaz has to do some sketches to go with it.'

'Hardly the ultimate sacrifice,' Toni commented.

'Bad enough,' Gabby grumbled. 'But I bet it was Beever's idea, this punishment. I told you, didn't I? He wants me to write it because he thinks he'll come over as our idol. The one who saves us from the big baddies. As if we needed him! He doesn't con me, though. He'll be a bit player trying to smarm his way into the big scenes.'

'You're going to write it, then?'

'I don't know yet,' Gabby answered. 'I might. I might not.'

A small flock of birds flew elegantly over the ship towards the mainland. 'What are they?' Toni asked, with her hand to her forehead as a shield against the Arctic sun.

'Eider ducks,' Peter replied. 'Some folk up here make a living from collecting eider down.'

'Talking of coming home to roost,' Alan put in, 'have you noticed Mel?'

'How do you mean?' Gabby queried.

Gail shuffled uneasily.

'Well, we're a few hours short of Hammerfest and he's hardly dashing round saying fond farewells. In fact, he's looking more and more on edge. After what he's been through, he should be feeling on top of the world. But he's more like a dying duck in a thunderstorm.' Seeing only blank faces in response, Alan turned to Gail. 'Do you know what he's up to, Gail?'

'Er ... Not really,' she replied. 'Just that he might not leave us at Hammerfest, after all.'

'What?' Gabby exclaimed. 'He's hitched a lift all the way up to the back of beyond, just to go back again!'

Gail stared out to sea, avoiding her companions' looks of curiosity. 'I guess he changed his mind,' she mumbled.

'Ah, you mean we're such good company?' Alan probed. 'Or at least, he likes the company of certain of us.'

Gail understood the insinuation and did not deny it. It was a more convenient explanation of Mel's behaviour than the truth.

'Time to go inside,' Gabby said, rescuing her sister. But she knew that Gail had clammed up to conceal something — just like she always had done. And experience told Gabby that no amount of prising would open her up.

The *Queen* negotiated a stretch of choppy, open sea. Sailing into the sound that led directly to the sheltered bay of Hammerfest, her passage was unimpeded.

Below, Mel was mournful. Shaking his head, he muttered, 'I have miscalculated.'

'Well,' Mike consoled him, 'is there any reason why it should've happened on the way to Hammerfest? Perhaps when we leave ...?'

'I made an assumption. An event near Hammerfest does not necessarily mean before reaching Hammerfest.'

'So it buys you three more days. Safely docked. That's good.'

'Yes. It is good,' Mel replied. 'I wish, though, that my task was concluded. I thought that it would be finished by now.' He kept his main concern to himself. He did not know how he could justify his continuing presence to the rest of his friends. After all, they expected him to disembark at Hammerfest.

'Stop grieving,' Mike urged. 'Come and help here. I need all the help I can get if I'm going to hack into a submarine system.'

'You are right,' Mel said. 'Despite your connections to

several government defence computers, this task is uneasy. We have not even one idea which country controls this submarine. Gail guessed that it is Russian. A guess, though, is too speculative.'

'So,' Mike asked, sitting back in his chair, having been blocked from entering yet another military system, 'what do we do?'

Mel sat beside him. 'What about communication? This vessel must receive and transmit messages. Can we intercept its communications?'

'Now, that's not a bad idea.' Mike sat upright again. 'If it's in this vicinity, it'll probably use the same satellite facilities as our ship. Let's have a shot at it,' he said eagerly. 'And hope the whole thing's not a red herring.'

Mel looked bewildered. 'I am not sure, but I estimate that you do not intend to fire guns, nor mistake the submarine for a small fish. Am I correct?'

'You are! You'll get the hang of English yet.' Mike paused. 'Sorry. I mean, get used to it. Oh, never mind. Let's get down to work.'

Hammerfest. 70° 39' 48". Anagram of theme farms. It throbs with life and energy. For example, there's the Meridian Stone — a monument to dead scientists who measured the exact size and shape of the Earth from Hammerfest. There's lamp-posts too. First town in Europe to get electric street-lights. We got to see exciting outcrops of schist (at least, I think that the guide said schist). There are reindeer everywhere, but no Santa Claus. A few tame Lapps were brought out to show us. What they lacked in stature, they made up for in colour. When the tourists aren't around, do they really wear that bright embroidery? The real Lapps were off following the reindeer herds. Most peaceful folk in the world, we were told. Of course, it helps that they live in a land that's so barren that no one else wants it. Who's going to fight over a pile of schist? We had an excursion into the tundra. What's there? Bugger all. What a waste of the one long day from 17th May to 28th July.

Stones, lamps, Lapps and reindeer. What else thrilled us? A church, with one entire wall made of stained glass, and the Findus frozen fillet factory, fed by the Arctic Fishing Fleet. Fascinating. Hammerfest, the fish restaurant at the end of the universe. Guess what we'll be eating all the way home.

Well, okay, there have been a few skirmishes in Hammerfest. But the object of desire was the naval trade tour — the sheltered port — not the land. For example, the Germans in World War Two put paid to the buildings that escaped the regular avalanches and an earlier great fire (a spark from Trondheim, no doubt). Once they'd given the tundra the once over, the Germans didn't stay for long. After they'd gone, the best little winter harbour for miles around was rebuilt. It seems they could only get hold of sickly yellow and red paint.

And today came an announcement. Pity to come all this way and not pop up the coast to North Cape itself. Well, indeed, we wouldn't want to miss a chance to circumnavigate another rock, would we? We will be visiting a souvenir shop, a cave, a post office (so we have the thrill of sending letters home, franked at North Cape), and two monuments to dead kings. We might even see the spot where a German battleship was sunk. Such were the conditions in the sea that only 36 survived from a crew of 1,970. Still, look on the bright side, Cueball isn't coming with us on this jolly jaunt. He's staying in Hammerfest. Perhaps he knows something we don't. Maybe it's even more boring than it sounds. Let's hope the driver forgets to pick him up on the way back.

The natives were getting restless. Hammerfest had come and was about to go, and Mel had not made a move. Suspicions were rife. Yet Mel's cover was not blown by pressure from his young companions. It finally succumbed to curiosity from a different quarter.

In an idle moment, Trevor Beever was thinking back to Charlton's caper with Gabby after the party. Why, he wondered, did they choose to dance on deck, with all its risks, rather than the security of a cabin? They wouldn't have gone to Gabby's cabin because of Gail. Yet there was always Charlton's cabin, even if Gail's dog was in it. Perhaps the deck offered a certain magic, with its shady space and fresh air, but Trevor felt that there was something else afoot. He was sure that Charlton harboured another secret in Cell G9.

As usual, music issued from Charlton's cabin. Mr Beever tapped on the door and, in reply, Charlton's voice, rather chirpier than it once was, called, 'Yes?' If Mr Beever was right, Charlton must be convinced that his room was free of clues. He went in.

Charlton looked up from his sketch, clearly surprised. 'Oh! Hello.' He turned off the cassettes and glanced rapidly around the room.

'That's good,' Mr Beever said, looking at the drawing of Hammerfest's front, with the mountain rising impressively behind. He pointed to the bunk and said, 'May I sit down?'

'Sure,' replied Charlton.

'Good place for inspiration, Hammerfest?'

'Nice contrasts. Dark mountains, light days. Young town, old traditions. Good reflections too. But ... er ...' Charlton pushed his pad aside. 'You haven't come about that, have you? I'm sorry about ...'

The teacher interrupted. 'You've nothing to be sorry about — not unless there's something *else* I should have been told.'

'How do you mean?'

'I mean, is there more than a dog I should know about?'

Charlton sniffed and looked away. 'I'm not very good at lying.'

Above Mr Beever's head, the bunk let out a rattle as the *Queen* started her engines. He ignored the noise and asked, 'Are you going to tell me about it?'

'I'm not sure you'd believe ...' His voice trailed away.

'Just tell me this. Do I have something serious brewing?'

'It's ... er ... in hand.'

There was another knock at the door and Mel burst in without waiting for an answer. 'Success! We have hacked into the sub ...' He stopped when the door swung back, revealing Mr Beever on the bunk.

'Now,' the teacher said, 'I *do* smell a rat.'

Charlton shrugged at Mel and said, 'Best come in. We have a little explaining to do. This,' he admitted, 'is Mel. He's ... er ... he came on board at Bergen. Sort of, hitching a lift.'

'Hitching a lift? Where to?'

'To ... er ...' Charlton could hardly say Hammerfest. Mel would not still be on board if that were true. 'To North Cape,' he ventured.

'I agree,' Trevor Beever announced. 'You're not good at lying.' He turned to Mel and said, 'Your accent is hardly Norwegian. And hitch-hikers don't generally involve them-selves into hacking into ... Were you going to say sub-marine?'

The boys sighed simultaneously. 'Mr Beever. I think we could have a useful discussion,' said Mel.

'Yes, I think so too.'

'Perhaps we should go somewhere private. Do you mind if we leave you, Charlton?' asked Mel.

His cell-mate shrugged. 'Fine.'

Mr Beever led Mel towards his own cabin. Out in the corridor, they passed Alan and Peter, both of whom had just been thrashed by Roger at snooker. 'Ah!' Peter exclaimed.

'Ah, indeed,' Mr Beever responded. 'More mischief in Cell Block G.' He marched along the corridor with Mel, like a captured prisoner, behind him.

Peter and Alan darted into Cabin G9. 'Looks like Eager Beever's just had a maximum break,' Alan said.

'Yeah,' Charlton said sadly.

'Well,' Peter added, 'It's his own fault. Mel's, that is. If he'd gone ashore straight away he'd be all right. He lingered too long on board. All for the love of Gail, I suspect.'

'No,' Charlton replied. 'It wasn't that.'

'So, what was it?'

It hardly seemed worth pretending any more. They had as

much right to know as did Charlton. 'Well, it's ... er ... You know that humans can't catch distemper? Well ...'

'Don't tell me,' Peter interrupted. 'You're going to tell us Mel's not human.'

Charlton simply nodded.

Peter and Alan smiled at each other, then looked at Charlton. 'You know,' Alan said to Peter, 'I do believe he's serious.'

'I am,' Charlton muttered. 'He's an alien.'

'Like Gail's pet python?' Alan asked with a grin.

'No. Not like that.'

'How do you know?' Peter asked, not entirely playfully.

'Lots of reasons. Things he said. And he's admitted it. Ask Gail, or Mike.'

'So he's convinced the three ... of you.' Peter thought better of calling them the most unbalanced trio in the Splinter Group. It would have been heartless.

'Well, nothing on earth would convince me,' Alan remarked.

Peter smiled. 'Perhaps he will — when Eager Beever's finished with him. You must admit, it would explain the distemper episode.'

'True,' Alan replied. 'But proposing he's a Yorkshire terrier would as well. He doesn't look like either to me.'

'He has a human disguise,' Charlton explained.

'Human disguise. Dog's disease. Now he's in a dog-fight with sir. Not a very well organized alien, is he?'

'But he doesn't seem the type to work a con on Charlton or Gail,' Peter observed. 'And there's something else, apart from the lack of antibodies. He once quoted me a time to ...

I think it was three decimal places. Weird. Said he had a good sense of time. I thought he was still a bit delirious at the time. But ... I don't know. There is something funny about him.'

Even from cabin G9, the characteristic whirring of the motors that wound the thick ropes around the capstans could be heard. The pitch of the ship's engines also shifted. Signs of imminent departure.

'If being weird is proof of being an alien, this ship is over-run with them,' Alan said. 'Come on. Let's go up and wave goodbye to Hammerfest.'

'It's cold and drizzling,' Peter objected.

'No need to pour cold water over a dead duck,' Alan retorted. 'Let's go. Then, when Beever's done with Mel, maybe we can make sense of it all.'

Mr Beever's cabin was bigger than the others, and almost as untidy. Books, pads of paper, journals, pupil's work, files, and Norwegian guides were scattered everywhere. There was a portable music centre and head-phones in one corner. The bed had been made, but not with much conviction. Originally, the cabin had been designed as a family room. There were two pairs of bunk beds, but the second had become a repository for books. The port-hole overlooked Hammerfest harbour.

'Sit down,' Mr Beever said, waving Mel towards the easy chair. 'Let's have this useful discussion.'

'I have to be honest with you,' Mel began, rather uncom-fortably. 'It is difficult, however, for me to express myself adequately. It is also uneasy to know where to start.'

'Your English is fine — almost. To start with, why don't you tell me where you come from?'

Mel considered it for a moment. He decided that he could not lessen the shock of what he had to say, so he might as well get straight to the point. 'I am an alien,' he said unflinchingly.

Mr Beever interpreted Mel's hesitation as his inability to find the exact words. 'Sure,' he replied. 'We all feel a little strange here. Away from home.'

Mel smiled endearingly. 'No. I selected my words very carefully.'

'You mean ...'

'Yes.'

'This is a joke, right?' Mr Beever asked incredulously.

This time, Mel did not smile. 'I understand that jokes require a belief in the impossible. I ask only that you believe what seems merely improbable.'

'This is ...' It was Trevor Beever who was struggling to find the right words. 'Nonsense. That's what it is. You look honest enough, but I can't ... I'm not that gullible.'

Mel sympathized. 'I know that it must be difficult for you, so I will prove it to you. Unfortunately, I do not have much time. Forgive my haste and the shock that it will cause.' He stood up.

'What ...?'

'I survive in your atmosphere courtesy of this body ...'

'Mr Beever interrupted, 'I'm not sure if I should laugh or cry.'

'Just listen and watch. I will not revert to my natural form entirely.' He rolled up one shirt sleeve. 'I will try to restrict it to this limb. Watch.' Mel breathed in deeply and closed his eyes. He had never before attempted a partial reversion.

After a moment, the teacher's gasp told him that he had succeeded. 'Your arm! It's ... My God. The colours!'

Mel opened his eyes and smiled. 'Do not be alarmed.'

'I'm not,' Mr Beever said, his eyes transfixed on Mel's hand and arm. 'It's ... radiant. Beautiful. And your hand — it's webbed.' He reached out and touched the alien hand. 'The membrane's like a butterfly's wing.'

'You have seen enough.'

Mr Beever was not sure whether Mel's response was a statement or a question. 'I'd love to see more, but that's not what you mean.'

'No.'

'It's ... incredible. But I've seen it with my own eyes so I have to believe it.' Mr Beever said. He was convinced that he was sharing his cabin with something wonderful — however ridiculous and implausible it might seem.

Mel relaxed. The layers of muscle, fat and pale skin obliterated all trace of his nature.

'That hand,' Trevor said, still in awe. 'It ... You must feel very bland to be like us.'

Mel shrugged. He did not wish to lie by denying it. 'My hand — as you call it — is like it is because of the many different nerves within it. It is very sensitive. With it, I feel more than humans. And, in my own form, I see more than humans also.'

'You're very lucky. And I feel privileged to have seen ... what I've just seen.'

'My extra senses allow me access to certain information. I

have knowledge that you do not share — yet. You must be told, because it explains why I am here, and I will need your help.'

'Sit down,' Mr Beever said. 'You'd better tell me. What are you here for? In fiction, it's usually to take over the world. But you're different, right?'

Mel did not return to his chair. He went to the window and bent forward to watch the activity on the quay. 'We have not a wish for any home but our own,' he answered. 'I am not here to save your world, either. My mission is not so grand.'

'But there is a problem?' asked Mr Beever.

'Yes. We are just a few of your hours away from disaster.' The *Queen*'s engines surged. The water churned by her propellers thrust against the quayside and slowly she wheeled around. 'Somewhere between here and North Cape, or on the return journey to Hammerfest, this ship will be holed by an iceberg and sink,' Mel said without turning away from the port-hole.

Mr Beever stood up. 'What?' he cried.

Outside, the *Queen* began to draw clear of the dock. Mel faced Mr Beever. 'I am sorry, but it is true. It is why I am here. Will you help me, or at least not hinder me, in my task of preventing this incident?'

'I ... er ... I'm still having trouble taking all this in.'

'It is real,' Mel assured him 'I am real and the danger is real.'

'Are you sure? How do you know?'

'Believe me, I know.'

'How many others know about this?'

'Charlton, Gail and Mike. By now, though, I assume that many in your class know something of the truth,' Mel replied.

'You mean, Peter and Alan?'

'It is my own fault,' Mel admitted. 'Still, we are obliged to be as discreet as possible.'

'Well, at least we ought to go and see the captain ...'

Mel interrupted him. 'That would not be wise. We are in the vicinity now. A change of course is as likely to cause the collision as it is to avoid it.'

'We could tell him to look out for icebergs. Are there any around here anyway?' Mr Beever had so many questions that they tumbled out in any order.

'Not normally. We meet a stray one, it seems.'

'Don't we have echo-sounders to prevent that sort of thing?'

'That is why I need Mike. From his cabin, we are monitoring the sonar equipment. I assume that it will fail. When it does so, I hope to correct it.'

'Letting the captain know won't hurt.'

'We can position other children on deck to keep watch.'

'Why are you so keen to keep the captain out of it?'

'Will he act on the advice of a clairvoyant alien? I would have to reveal myself to him, also. I trust you because the children report well on you. Letting the captain know *will* hurt. If my true origin becomes widely known, the authorities will come for me. I will be placed in isolation and examined. I am an alien, Mr Eager Beever. I am unique. A curiosity and an opportunity for experimentation.'

Trevor nodded slowly. He was so intent on his immediate

fate and that of his charges that he had not contemplated the reactions of the world outside the *Queen of the Fjords*. Too easily, his mind turned to those science fiction films in which aliens were captured and met unspeakable ends at the hands of humans. Out there, a mixture of ignorance, curiosity and fear could easily result in the situation that Mel had envisaged. And that was an intolerable thought. A being as wonderful as Mel could not be reduced to the role of laboratory specimen. Trevor could never bring himself to pin a butterfly into a collection, so he certainly could not allow Mel to be held, studied or dissected. Once Mel had completed his mission, humans must open their cupped hands and let him fly away. That was the right of any creature.

'If I am quarantined,' Mel continued, 'I will not be of any further use to you. I feel more secure now that we have left Hammerfest.' He glanced through the window at the increasing expanse of clear water between the *Queen* and the trawlers moored in Hammerfest harbour. 'But if knowledge escaped, I am sure that other ships or helicopters would be sent for me.' Mel looked at Trevor. 'Believe me,' he said with determination, 'I will not fail. I live here by two rules. I must cause minimum interference on Earth and I must not be captured. Human development does not need the distraction of an alien visitor at this time. So,' Mel concluded, 'what is best for me is also best for you. All of you.'

'What do you want me to do?'

'You are better at the words than I am. Would you speak to Peter and the others in ... I think that you label them the Splinter Group?'

'You want me to explain the situation and stress the need for secrecy?'

'Yes. I will need Mike, though, for computing work in his cabin.'

'That reminds me,' Mr Beever said. 'What was it about a submarine anyway?'

'For many days, a submarine has undergone a parallel course. It has been monitoring us.'

'How do you know?'

Mel put up his hand. 'Remember? Under this, I have many sensors.'

'So, you and Mike have hacked into its computer?'

'We have attempted to do so but we failed. As an alternative, Mike has accessed its communication system. It is interesting that, when it does communicate, its language is English.'

'It's British or American, then,' Mr Beever deduced. 'What message did it send — or receive?'

'It reported its own position, and ours.'

'To whom?'

Mel shrugged. 'That is all we know.'

'Is it relevant?'

'As I said,' Mel replied, 'I have not yet learned more. I should return and continue working with Mike. Also, I must check the functioning of the radar. Perhaps you will speak to the others now.'

Trevor nodded. 'I guess so.' He sighed. 'I've explained some difficult concepts in my time ... I've felt foolish on many occasions, but this ... It's hardly credible. I'm still in shock, I think. They'll laugh me off the boat.'

Mel smiled. 'I think not. They are now very suspicious of me. They smell a rat, too. Charlton and Gail will aid you.'

The dark Arctic Ocean buffeted the *Queen*'s hull as she laboured north. The rugged coastline was scored with great grey clefts. In places, vast numbers of puffins with their garish and grotesque beaks, and quarrelsome guillemots with their ridiculous red dangling legs, dotted the sky. Repeatedly, they flew from their nests in the cliffs to the sea and back. Thousands of young puffins groaned loudly for food. Their droppings gave the rock the appearance of being streaked with chalk. Beyond the cliffs, the tundra stretched endlessly and desolately. A land of treeless moors and stone-strewn desert. It was a miracle that such a place could sustain human life at all.

Once more, the *Queen of the Fjords* was alive with vibrations. On deck, the salt-coated fittings rattled, the entire ship moaned and shuddered every time she dipped into a trough, only to meet the next crest. She seemed to bow respectively before each tyrant wave, her only reward being a callous blow.

Gabby, oblivious to the conditions, leaned over the aft rail and said, 'Still no whales. Have you seen one?'

Gail shook her head in reply. 'No.'

'That's thanks to the Norwegians,' Gabby complained. 'Anyway, you probably wouldn't tell me even if you had seen one.'

'Oh, don't go on,' Gail groaned. 'You wouldn't have believed me about Mel anyway. Like you wouldn't have believed about Dad.'

Gabby shrugged. 'You never know — because you never try. My own sister cavorting with an alien on the *Titanic* and she doesn't even mention it.'

The rhythmic pitching of the ship was taking its toll on Gail. She did not relish a long conversation. 'We weren't cavorting. And he didn't want it put about.'

'He doesn't even look like an alien.'

'He's taken human shape.'

'So what's he really like?' Gabby asked. 'Green and slimy? Or cute and cuddly like ET?'

'How should I know?' Gail responded tersely.

'He might have revealed all to you.'

'No. His appearance doesn't matter. He's just nice, that's all.'

'No curiosity!' cried Gabby. 'I'd love to find out. Never seen a green slimy one from outer space.'

'Gabby. Just let it be.'

'Okay. But I reckon we're wasting our time out here. Not even an incompetent driver can hit an iceberg in broad daylight. "One fine day in the middle of the night" and all that. We don't get anything but broad daylight here.'

'The weather's not so fine, though.'

'No. I'll give you that. It's beginning to close in. But it's getting less rough as well. Still, could test a few stomachs yet though, eh, Gail?'

'I'm about to fail, I think,' she replied.

Graham sat alone in the form-room. His hands and arms were laid out on his desk like a dog's front paws. His eyes were lightly closed. He sat upright but seemed relaxed. When

Peter entered the classroom to collect G Block's communal binoculars, Graham's eyes flickered open unwillingly. 'Enjoying yourself, Graham?' Peter asked with irony.

'Yes — and no.'

'What are you doing? Meditating?'

'You might call it that. I'm praying.'

'Praying that there *is* a God, or praying that He'll save us?'

Graham did not rise to the bait. 'Neither. Better it is to die than to beg. If He sees fit to deliver us, it will be His own volition and not at my request. So I simply pray for forgiveness.'

'Have you done anything wrong?'

'We all have. I pray for exoneration for us all, not just me.'

'Even a heathen like me?' Peter jibed.

Graham was deadly serious. 'Of course. I have no right to judge anyone. Love thy neighbour as thyself. I pray; someone else will judge.'

'You could do something helpful,' Peter rejoined.

'There are times when the *only* thing worth doing is praying. This is one of them. I'm helping in the only way I know. I believe my efforts here are just as helpful as anyone else's. Possibly more so. I believe my efforts are essential.'

'It's hardly hard labour — sitting here calmly looking after our souls instead of doing something positive about our mortal coils.'

'As I said,' Graham answered, 'my task is more important. Souls need looking after. They last longer than a lifetime. Besides,' he added, 'if you don't pray, how do you know how hard it is? Half-hearted prayer is easy, but useless. I find honest prayer very difficult. I may look peaceful outwardly. But inside, honesty hurts.'

'And because it hurts, it must be doing some good?'

A trace of a smile appeared on Graham's face. 'We all have our burdens here,' he said. ' Come unto me all ye that labour and are heavy laden, and I will give you rest. It's important that I'm convinced of the power of prayer. Luckily, I don't have to persuade you — however much I'd like to.'

There were three puzzled faces in cabin G5. 'What do you mean, it's gone?' asked Mr Beever.

'Gone. Not there anymore,' Mike replied. 'Last time we looked, it was bleeping away nicely. Now it's gone.'

'A whole submarine can't just vanish.'

'No,' Mel replied. 'It is unquestionable that it is no longer scintillating the screen, but it is perplexing.'

'Perhaps it's just sailed away,' Mike suggested. 'If a submarine can be said to sail.'

'Yes,' Mr Beever agreed. 'I hope you're right.'

'It may have moved away,' Mel conceded, 'but something tells me that it is still out there.' He paused, then muttered, 'God's whispers, perhaps.'

'What?'

'As you frequently say to me, Mike, "Never mind".' Mel concentrated on the VDU. 'Look,' he said pointing to different blips on the screen, 'Here — and here.'

'Rocks. Island.'

'Yes,' said Mel. 'Rocks behind which a submarine could conceal itself.'

'Are you saying that they know we're monitoring them?' Mr Beever asked.

'I cannot estimate,' Mel replied. 'Let us resume our vigilance for other objects.'

Peter rejoined the others at the pointed end of the ship. 'Here we are,' he said. 'An extra pair of eyes,' he indicated the binoculars. He leaned against the rail and used them to peer out to sea. 'Mm. I can see the fog bank much better now.'

'Let's have a look,' Toni said. In a department store in Kristiansund, she had considered pinching either a pair of binoculars or a portable CD player. She'd opted for the latter. Binoculars might be appropriate for Norway but she would have little use for them at home in Birmingham. She put them to her eyes and gazed beyond the fore. 'I see what you mean,' she said. 'Clouds, a few islands, and that's your lot.'

'I reckon it's Mel who's got his head in the clouds,' Alan said. 'There's no icebergs around here.'

'Not normally,' Peter replied. 'But years ago, just north of here, a Soviet liner was holed by an iceberg. Called the *Maxim Gorky*, it was. The ship, that is.'

'That was probably in bleak midwinter,' Alan commented hopefully.

'June, actually. I read about it before coming on this trip,' Peter replied. 'But, even though Gorky wrote a play called *The Lower Depths*, the passengers survived. Does that reassure you?'

'Oh yeah. The clouds have really lifted from me now. I suppose it happened on a hot sunny day.'

'No. In freezing fog.'

'So what's that ahead?'

Peter smiled wryly and checked with the binoculars. 'Yeah. You're right. Looks like freezing fog to me!'

'In that case, your reassurance cuts no ice with me,' Alan rejoined.

'Well, okay,' Peter said, 'I admit I was skating on thin ice there.'

'Oh, shut up, you two,' Toni complained. 'It's no joke.'

'She's right,' Peter conceded. 'This conversation should be put on ice.'

Toni groaned. 'How long can you two keep this up?'

'What you've heard,' Alan boasted, 'is just the tip of the iceberg.'

Roger and Charlton made their way to the dining room, whispering to each other.

'You scared?' Roger asked.

Charlton shrugged. 'Don't know. I don't think so. Every beat of the heart is one closer to its last, no matter how much time has passed. There's no point being scared about it. Are you?'

'A bit, I guess,' Jolly Roger answered. 'But it's exciting, like thieving. Exciting *because* of the risk, like.'

'It's different though. You've no control over the risk, here. It's out of your hands.'

'Yeah. I never done nothing like this before. Mel don't need me. Except for food — but even that ain't a buzz any more. Mel's having the buzz.'

'He doesn't *look* thrilled. He's suffering, I'd say. The responsibility is getting to him.'

'I don't know why he don't just turn the boat round.'

'Because,' Charlton explained in a whisper, 'the iceberg might be behind us.'

They had arrived at the counter and Roger asked for five packed lunches.

'Five?' the lady queried. 'There's only two of you!'

Roger would have preferred to pocket three extra lunches while she wasn't watching but instead he produced Mr Beever's note. 'Our teacher and two other boys need them. See! All above-board.'

The lady looked at the boys. 'Above-board, eh. Is that a joke?'

'No,' Roger replied, as if reacting to an accusation.

'Is this letter genuine, or did you forge it?'

'What do you mean, forge?' Roger cried. 'I don't do nothing like that.' He was affronted by the slur on his honesty. He had never stooped to deceit in furtherance of his banditry. Fraud was outside his code of practice.

The serving lady was taken aback by how much her charge had wounded him. 'Oh, all right,' she said. 'But you'd be surprised how much food disappears from here. Probably some of your colleagues to blame.'

On the way back to Mike's cabin, Charlton nudged Roger. 'Bit funny, you kicking up a fuss like that.'

'Well,' Roger replied, 'It ain't nice to be accused of something what you haven't done.'

'But you have been known to nick food,' Charlton said quietly.

'Yeah. She could've blamed me for that. No complaints. But not forging stuff. That's something else.'

Charlton nodded thoughtfully. 'I know what you mean. It's not nice to be accused of a crime that you regard with contempt. Like being dragged through the mud for no good reason.'

'Yeah. You got it.'

'It's happened to me, too,' Charlton said. 'I committed a crime,' he confessed, 'but, you know, it wasn't as bad as they made out. I'm beginning to see that I'm not such an ogre.'

'That's right,' Jolly Roger agreed without even knowing, or wanting to know, Charlton's crime. 'It ain't us, it's them.'

Cabin G5 had the tense atmosphere of a gambling den. The chief players had given it their best shot, and could only wait to see if their method would come up trumps. Reverential onlookers crammed into the room, admiring the champions' dexterity, praying for good fortune. The stakes could hardly be higher.

Mike stopped eating his sandwich and pointed to the screen. 'What's that?'

'It is land,' Mel replied.

'So why are we headed straight for it?' Mike asked agitatedly.

'Wait,' Mel said, trying to be calm. 'We will turn.'

'Maybe it's North Cape. Then we'd obviously head straight for it,' Mr Beever ventured.

'Too small an island,' Mike responded. Then he asked Mel, 'Are you sure it's an iceberg we're looking for, not a rock?'

'Have not a fear. The captain can observe this scan,' Mel said. 'He will steer around the rocks.'

'We're talking about my future here, you know,' Mike voiced. 'I have a vested interest. I want to preserve it.'

'We're all in the same boat,' Trevor said. Then reacting to his unintentional pun, he cursed himself under his breath. 'All a bit on edge.'

'Look,' Mel said. 'We are turning.'

Mike watched the scan intently for a few moments, then sighed. On the grey VDU, the small flashing speck of green light had moved off the vertical. The rock was no longer an obstacle in their path. 'Thank God for that.' Mike picked up his sandwich again but could not bring himself to eat any more. The tension had taken away his appetite.

'I understand our course now,' Mel said. 'We head for this narrow channel behind North Cape,' he pointed to the screen. 'We will sail through it and then cruise to North Cape. There is not danger here. We must be vigilant in the open sea. There is time now to relax, Mike.'

'Relax?' Alan queried as he poked his head around the door of the cabin. 'There's a pea-souper out there that really takes the biscuit.'

'Pardon?' Mel said.

'You can't see the wood to bark up the right tree. Thick fog.'

Gabby's voice boomed down corridor G. 'Rear search party also reporting in. We could be going round in circles for all we know. God knows how the driver sees where he's going now.'

'He does not,' replied Mel. 'His radar sees for him.'

'Well, he hasn't got much faith in it,' Gabby retorted.

'He's not exactly burning it. His speed is somewhere between dead stop and dead slow.'

In the cabin, Mike looked at Mel and said, 'Did you say we could relax?'

There was no time for Mr Beever to relax. The ship's Tannoy announced an immediate meeting of all staff. His eyebrows rose significantly, as the kids turned to him, questioning. 'Don't ask me,' he said. 'I've no idea. But you'd better carry on here while I go and find out.' He left, parting the gathering throng of the members of Group A in the corridor, and mumbling to himself, 'Whatever next?'

The captain of the *Queen of the Fjords* challenged the tradition of old sea dogs. No peaked cap. No bright eyes and bushy black beard. Not jolly at all. He'd never have survived the audition for a fish fingers commercial. His face was neither weather-beaten nor lived in. His eyes betrayed an old man lost. He was out of his depth. His expression was too passive and too innocent to command respect. And his voice, when he addressed the staff, had neither the authority nor the assurance to inspire confidence. 'You can hardly have failed to notice the … er … adverse conditions. Came all of a sudden,' he whined. 'I should tell you that there's no great danger but we have been advised to head directly back to Hammerfest. Honningsvåg can't take us. The fishing fleet has berthed there for the duration of the weather. So we'll have to call off the North Cape trip, I'm afraid. The trip's … er … I don't know … disappointing anyway, I'd say. A bare slate headland, the usual souvenirs and junk food.'

'There must be other ports around here,' one of the teachers prompted.

'A few. Small ones. We can't put in at those either. I checked as much as I could. They're clogged with local trawlers sheltering. It's difficult but, as I said, there's nothing to worry abut. Not really. It just looks bad. We navigate by radar in these conditions. Besides, we're ... er ... only a few hours from Hammerfest. And now,' he concluded, 'I should return to the bridge. I think it best if I take personal charge of the ship as soon as possible.'

Trevor turned to his nearest colleague and commented, 'How come I'm not delighted at that prospect?'

'He seems calm and on top of the situation to me,' she retorted.

'He's in about as much control as our beloved first mate, Mr Brown.'

'Mr Brown is an excellent teacher,' she responded tersely.

Trevor's level of stress had worn thin his patience. 'Yes,' he said, 'And the *Titanic* was unsinkable.' Then he left the staff room. His concerns had not been assuaged. In fact, he felt even more anxious after the meeting. The *Queen* was still on course for disaster.

The Devil in the Deep Blue Sea

After the briefing, Trevor Beever went out on deck to experience the weather first-hand. The *Queen* was enveloped; a ship in a frosted bottle. The suffocating fog billowed like smoke. It chilled the throat and lungs. And the heart. The air was too laden to propagate external sounds. Trevor felt insulated. The rest of the world was dormant, silent. The only noises that reached his ears were the muffled booming and groaning of the ark itself and the breaking of waves on nearby, but unseen, rocks. The ship had emerged from the strait that separated the island of Magerøy from the mainland and sailed by Honningsvåg — a port under curfew. She had begun to wheel to the west. Unseen, she would slip past the legendary North Cape, its walls of rock obliterated by a wall of cloud, before turning her prow southwest towards Hammerfest.

Making his way along the gallery, Trevor noticed another figure. It looked like Charlton. 'Hello?' His greeting was also a question.

'Hi,' Charlton replied.

Trevor reached out with fumbling hands in mock blindness. 'Is that you, Charlton?'

'Mm,' he said, 'Alan wasn't joking about the peasouper.'

'Filthy weather.'

'Maybe,' Charlton replied. 'I rather like it.'

'I'd have thought you'd want to see clearly. Detail is everything.'

'Not all the time. In this,' Charlton waved at the nothingness, 'you can use your imagination. Reminds me of ... a blank piece of paper. What else could be more infuriating and inviting?'

'Well, it makes me feel ... like a monk,' Trevor said. 'Cloistered. But,' he added, 'it's hardly a place of safety. Doesn't make me feel secure.'

'Roger says the threat makes it more exciting. I think I know what he means.'

'The attraction of a menacing atmosphere.'

They both stared hypnotically at the curtain of cloud that brushed the sides of the *Queen* as she laboured forward. Then Trevor turned to Charlton and said, 'How are you now? Okay?'

'Yeah. I'm okay.' He paused, then explained, 'You heard about Mel getting sick? It brought back memories. I talked to him about ... it all. It helped.'

'That's good,' Mr Beever said. 'I'm pleased. Really. You can concentrate on the future — not keep looking over your shoulder.' Trevor hoped that there was a future for Charlton to look forward to. He deserved one. 'I guess I'd best be getting back to see how Mel's getting on.'

'I'll join you soon,' Charlton replied.

'Want to soak up a bit more of the sinister atmosphere?'

'Right.'

With some trepidation, Trevor Beever made his way back to Mike's cabin. For the first time in his life, Trevor was unsure of his rank. Until now, his responsibilities had always been clear-cut. He was in charge of the class. If it went badly, it was his fault. If it went well, it was an achievement that would allow him to feel proud. For good or for bad, he was in control — even on those days when the children seemed to control him. After all, he was their servant as well as their master. But what was his role on board a ship sailing towards catastrophe? Servant or master? He certainly wasn't the captain. He couldn't steer them safely around the obstacles. Even with his kids in Group A, he felt redundant. He had been side-lined by a superior youngster disguised as a mere human. That superior had already recruited and regimented Trevor's troop. All of the Splinter Group seemed to have something to offer, or had already assisted Mel in some way. But there did not seem to be a part for Trevor Beever.

The high density of children in one place — Mike's cabin — threatened to tilt the ship. 'Budge up!' Alan cried. 'Here comes another.'

'Who is it?' someone else called.

'It's the boss.'

Gabby's unmistakable, unfettered voice answered, 'Mel and Mike are boss in here.'

'Thanks, Gabby,' Trevor retorted. 'You really know how to make a chap feel welcome.'

Protocol, if it ever existed in Gabby's presence, was utterly suppressed in the face of adversity. 'Don't like being knocked off the top perch, eh?'

Diplomatically, Mel said, 'I need you all.'

'Pity you didn't get a bigger cabin, then,' Alan responded whilst moving aside to let Mr Beever in. 'This is no Tardis.'

'What ...?' Mel began.

Mike interrupted. 'Never mind about that. Look!'

On the VDU, one blip had suddenly become two.

'That,' said Mel pointing to the response that remained stationary, 'is a rock. And this must be ...'

Mike interrupted again, 'Our friendly neighbourhood sub!'

The two blips continued to separate.

'Where's it going?' Roger asked.

'There is not enough evidence here on which to base an answer. If it travels as before, it will take a parallel course but maintain a considerable distance from us.'

All eyes watched the innocuous, but strangely ominous, flashing speck. It could have been a warning light.

'Shouldn't we monitor its communications?' asked Mike.

'No,' Mel answered. 'We must be vigilant with the radar near here. If the submarine communicates, its messages will be written into your capture programme. We should examine its contents every few minutes but return to the radar as soon as possible.'

'How do you know it's not our mega-unfriendly neighbourhood iceberg?' Toni queried.

'Icebergs don't hide behind rocks,' Mike replied.

'Look at its path,' Mel added. 'It curves to assume a parallel course.'

'It's a dirigible iceberg!' Alan could not bring himself to treat their situation seriously. It reeked of theatre. Aliens, icebergs and submarines. It could even be a farce. He stayed for the entertainment and because he had one nagging doubt.

He couldn't verbalize the doubt. It was just something about the OBTUSE experiment. Right from the start he knew that there was something fishy about it.

'What are you talking about? A dirigible's an airship.'

'That's the noun. I'm talking adjectives here,' Alan answered. 'It means steerable. A steerable iceberg.'

Charlton appeared at the door and shook his head when he saw the crush.

'Someone call the Guinness Book of Records!' Alan said jovially. 'Five on the bed, two sitting, three standing. It's the full complement.'

'No,' Peter responded. 'No Graham yet.'

'Thank God for that,' Gabby cried unkindly. 'He'd sink us for sure.'

'He's saving our souls,' Peter commented dryly. 'Praying.'

'That is good,' Mel replied. 'We need the help of all types, and Graham is far sighted. His God makes him wise. Graham and God offer much assistance. I am gratified that he prays.'

Mel's words put an end to further scorn.

Mike was the first to break the silence. 'Let's access my capture file.'

'Yes,' Mel agreed. 'It is a good time.'

Mike aborted the monitoring mode and clicked on the folder that he had called 'Dump'. The computer whirred for a few seconds then displayed its contents on screen. No message had been sent by the submarine, but two words had been captured in the input column. 'Begin operation.' Nothing more.

'Don't like the sound of that,' Toni said.

'Hardly worth getting worked up about,' Trevor Beever replied, trying to take the sting out of the situation. 'It could mean anything.'

'Yeah, like, "Put the kettle on, lads".'

'What do you make of it, Mel?'

'How do I interpret this command? I cannot interpret it at all. Something is beginning. That is all. It is not a precise instruction. Let us return to the radar,' he prompted Mike.

The dichromatic representation of their world was unchanged. To the left of the screen, a mass of bright green indicated the mainland. The middle of the screen was mainly grey with dots of green where islands were strewn across their course. The submarine was still lurking, now on the far right. A small isolated pulse of colour on a dull backdrop of open sea. Nothing substantial was moving at the whim of the tide.

'Are you sure you jumped the right boat?' Alan asked Mel.

'He means, "Are you on the right ship?",' Mike translated for Mel's benefit. 'But he's not serious.'

'I really wish that I had avoided involving you all,' Mel addressed the entire congregation. 'It cannot be easy for you to believe … all this.'

Pointing suddenly to the VDU, Peter declared, 'That helps, though.'

A warning had begun to flash across the screen. 'Radar malfunction.'

For a moment, they were spellbound by the message. Then Toni exclaimed, 'Oh hell!'

'It begins,' Mel affirmed. His note suggested both nervousness and a degree of relief. It was as if a hidden, stalking enemy had finally revealed itself. At least, Mel knew what he was up against. The radar picture flickered and the green blips shifted, ebbing and flowing across the screen unreliably.

After studying the VDU for a while, Mel announced, 'I do not understand. The picture is unstable and useless for guiding the ship but the radar appears still to be good. The picture is accurate but imprecise because it travels across the screen.'

'Can you check the radar from here?' Gabby asked him.

'Not in your presence,' he replied. 'I may go ... But before I do, let us examine your capture programme again, Mike.'

'Okay.'

When the computer responded, it revealed two more words. To the right of 'Begin operation,' in the output column, was written 'Radar malfunction.'

'What ...?' Mike ran out of words.

Mr Beever completed his question for him, 'What does it mean?' He looked to Mel for an answer.

Mel had come to the obvious conclusion but was loathe to enunciate it. The expectation of his audience, though, was impossible to resist. He shook his head and resigned himself to be the bearer of bad news. 'It means .. that the message about the radar problem was transmitted from the submarine. It did not originate from this ship's system. The radar appears to be faulty only because of external interference.'

There was a short silence, then Gabby asked heatedly,

'Why? Why should they do that?'

Peter answered her. 'Because they want to cripple our navigation. Why else?'

Mel rubbed at his itching left arm. 'The people in the submarine have hacked into the ship's system also.'

'But why?' Mike asked impatiently.

'Because the buggers want us to crash,' Gabby speculated.

'No,' Mr Beever said. 'It's a mistake. It must be.'

'We *are* being swept under the carpet,' Alan whispered, suddenly convinced of the seriousness of their situation.

'It is getting difficult,' Mel muttered, mainly to himself, as he aborted the programme. 'It is getting complicated.' While he waited for the computer to log onto the radar again, he examined his other arm.

'Goose pimples,' Mike explained. 'That's what's bothering you.'

'Goose pimples? What causes them?'

'They come when we feel cold ... or scared.'

'I wouldn't describe it as cold in here,' Toni said. 'It's a sweat shop.'

Mel did not reply but Alan came to his rescue. 'Don't put him off. Don't let's cook our goose before it lays the golden egg. He's got to get us out of this.'

'I am not sure that I can,' Mel said, clearly troubled. 'There are complications that you ...'

'What do you mean?' Gabby screeched.

'It is difficult ...' Mel paused. 'Let me assume that this,' he indicated the screen that once again flashed its unnerving message, 'is not deliberate. On the basis that it is a mistake, I can continue.' He hesitated again, but this time it was thought, not uncertainty that occupied him. He spoke to Mike. 'The submarine has a link to the ship's computer. If we could ...'

'Tie the ends together,' Mike interrupted. 'Of course! It should be possible. Given time.'

'It is a network. We must join one part to another.'

'Then we overwrite the sub's messages,' Mike suggested.

'Exactly so,' Mel confirmed. 'We also assure the submarine that we are not an enemy vessel. But we do not have much time. Think, Mike, how *you* hacked into the system. Perhaps these other humans behaved similarly. If they have logged on, they must have a user name. We need that name. We need to discover their entry connections. You will know how.'

'But they're deeper in than us. It won't be easy.' Mike felt like a spectator at a tennis match. He could see both players. The submarine and the *Queen*. He could watch their exchanges. But he could not influence the game. He had not learned how to make an input. He just monitored the output. A read-only user. Now, Mel was asking him to hack further, to complete in minutes a job that could take days. He had to put into the system a message that contradicted the message from the submarine. Then the computer would query his priority over the user from the submarine and, in the process, reveal that user's identity. Then he would have a user name to search. And the search should provide a gateway to the submarine.

'I know you don't want to involve the captain,' Trevor

Beever said to Mel, 'but this might be an appropriate juncture ...'

'What are you going to tell him?' Alan interjected. 'Once upon a time there was a submarine, a stolen computer and an alien? And a ship that fell victim to inhospitable hacking during inhospitable weather?'

'He'll err on the side of caution anyway,' Peter added. 'We can't shed any more light on it, so you could only tell him to be careful. I dare say he'll be doing that anyway.'

'Do you agree, Mel?' Trevor asked.

'Yes. Let us keep the secret between ourselves for as long as possible,' he replied.

'Here,' Mike said, drawing Mel's attention to the VDU. 'A brick wall that we've seen before.'

The message on the screen read, 'Access request. Status of user: *Read Only; Read and Write; Priority.*'

'But you've already got access to the ship's computer,' Toni said.

'Yeah. We went in through the easiest door. Read only. Now we step up a gear or two. *Read and Write*, or *Priority?*'

'Do not make it too difficult,' Mel replied. '*Read and Write* is sufficient.'

Mike clicked on the appropriate window. The computer requested a user name and Mike entered, 'Anon.' Then the dreaded response appeared. 'Password.'

'Well,' Mike said, 'I hope you've got something up your sleeve, Mel, because this is where I failed before. My usual capture programme wouldn't work on this higher grade system. More locks on the door. We've got ten random guesses then it shuts us out for ten minutes.'

'The ten-minute intervals are useful for checking the submarine's communications and the radar,' Mel replied, making the best of a bad job.

'And for us to take a breather,' Trevor added. 'To take a gander at the weather.'

Mel forced a grin. 'Is this the language that I had to learn exhaustively?' he asked in a pretence of exasperation. 'In which the things up my sleeve are the pimples of a cooked goose, and someone wishes to escort a male goose on deck!'

'If they told you that you'd exhausted all the possibilities of the English language,' Alan responded, 'they were leading you up the garden path on a wild goose chase.'

'Come on,' Mike said, his tone betraying impatience with his colleagues. 'There's a job to do, you know.'

'There is a chance that I can help with the job depending on the mechanism of recognition of passwords. Put in A as your first guess, Mike.'

Mike looked bemused but obeyed him anyway. Mel concentrated hard. The programme responded, 'User authorization failure. Enter password.' Mel did not seem displeased. 'Now try B,' he said.

'What ...?'

'Just try it, then I will explain.'

'Okay. Here we go.'

The result was the same. 'Good,' Mel said. 'The time from depressing the key to rejection was the same in each case.'

'So?'

'When we enter a correct letter, the comparison between our entry and the encoded password may take a little longer.'

'But it's so fast at rejecting any false password. Less than a second, I reckon,' Mike replied. 'If there's a difference between good and bad guesses, there'll be next to nothing in it. You'll never tell the difference.'

'I can measure time more accurately and precisely than humans do,' answered Mel. 'Let us continue for a while.'

The letters from A to G were all rejected with the same delay. After the eighth guess, though, Mel perked up. 'That took a little longer,' he said.

'I didn't notice any difference,' someone remarked sceptically.

'You would not be able to. It has to be measured in milliseconds.'

'You reckon H is the first letter of the password, then?' Mike asked.

'It is quite possible.'

'Well, the second should be easy,' Peter interjected. 'Must be a vowel.'

'Or a Y,' Alan added. 'As in hysteria.'

Mike entered HA. 'Okay,' Mel said. 'Next.'

'Our last try for a bit.'

Almost immediately, Mel said, 'It rejected HE more slowly than it rejected HA.'

'It's HE something, then. Could be anything still.'

'Hernia?' Peter suggested.

'He-man,' Gabby added.

'There is a long way to go,' Mel replied. 'Let us use this delay to check your other programmes, Mike.'

The radar malfunction warning still flashed across the screen. And the submarine had received another message.

'Input: Continue one hour. If no result, execute second mode.'

'Sounds terrific,' Alan said with irony.

'I think that we had better gain access within an hour,' Mel said. 'We must draw up a list of the most likely letters to follow HE.'

Trevor Beever took advantage of the break to walk to Deck 2. Members of the crew had positioned themselves every few metres towards the fore and strained their eyes to see even a few metres ahead. One of them, on noticing Trevor, explained, 'Bad weather watch.' He tried to make his comment sound as uneventful as a greeting but did not quite succeed. His unconcerned tone was faked.

'Routine in weather like this, is it?' Trevor asked.

'When it's as thick as this, yes. We always up the look-out. Purely precautionary. We're heading out to more open seas, as well, away from the islands. For greater safety.'

'I understand,' Trevor replied.

The near absence of external sounds had become total. No birds screeching, no breakers crashing. Nothing. Just eerie silence. The fog was dense, grey and foreboding.

The first batch of ten three-letter codes had all been rejected with the same time interval. Mel's eyes did light up, though, when they tried HEN in the second batch. 'That must have compared well with the password,' he said. 'It took longer to reject it.'

'Is it part of the first word or is it the first word, though?' Mike replied cautiously. 'There's lots of possi-bilities yet.'

'Like hendecagon,' Peter said.

'Actually,' Mr Beever tried to inject some authority, 'there aren't many words beginning with HEN.'

'Could be a name,' Mike said, 'Like Henry.'

'Or Henrietta,' Toni added.

'What is the best suggestion for the next letter?' Mel asked.

No one was confident enough to offer a firm favourite. 'Okay then. We've got to get moving,' Mike said. 'So let's try R for Henry, then start from the beginning of the alphabet. But it'll lock us out after four more tries.'

Mel did not detect a further increase in rejection time up to HENC and so they suffered another ten-minute delay.

'This is getting boring,' Gabby moaned.

'Hacking is like fishing,' Mike answered. 'Mostly dull with the adversaries trying to outwit each other. But it's worth waiting for the big bite when it comes.'

'We don't have all day,' Alan reminded them. 'Twenty-odd minutes since the hour's warning and we've only got three letters.'

'Thirty-odd minutes before we're back in there.'

'It strikes me that we're short on better ideas,' Mr Beever put in, 'so let's not get on each other's nerves.'

The submarine had neither transmitted nor received any more esoteric messages, and the radar warning flashed over a blank screen. Apparently, the radar had been shut down as a distraction. Trevor wondered how far out into open sea they had strayed. Were they into iceberg tracks? Was the captain still sure of their position? How far away was Hammerfest — and safety? Also the effect of seeing Mel in his natural shape was waning. Even so, Trevor could not question the wisdom of handing the reins to Mel. He himself was clueless. It was right that the young had taken control.

'Right,' Mike said, looking at his watch, 'Here we go again.' He requested access again and entered HEND as his password. 'That is ... interesting,' Mel said thoughtfully. 'Let me compare it with HENC.'

'What, waste a go?' Mike queried.

'Yes. I need a closer comparison.'

Mike shrugged. 'Okay, you're the boss.'

The test confirmed it. HEND seemed a closer match with the password than did HENC.

'It *is* hendecagon,' Peter exclaimed.

'What is a hendecagon anyway?' Gabby asked.

'An eleven-sided figure,' he replied.

Mel shrugged. 'Try it.'

The computer rejected the response. 'Damn,' Peter cried.

'Are there any other words beginning HEND?' Mel asked, mainly directing his question at Mr Beever.

'I don't think so,' the teacher answered. 'Hard to be sure, but there's nothing obvious I can think of. You're good with words, Gabby and Peter,' he said. 'Any ideas?'

Gabby shrugged. 'Don't look at me,' she said.

'I'm sure there are some,' Peter mused. 'But they're pretty obscure. I could go to the library for a dictionary.'

'There's no time for that,' Mike replied. 'And we need you here.'

For once, Peter allowed himself to feel warm inside. Yes, he was needed, but he thought that this time he was also wanted.

'Besides,' Mike continued, 'there's a good chance it's not in a dictionary. It might be a name. Any suggestions?' he prompted.

No one responded.

Systematically, they went through the alphabet for the letter that followed HEND. The first and second batches were rejected with equal speed.

'We *must* get it in this session,' Mike said in irritation. 'There's only five minutes left.'

The response to HENDR excited Mel. 'That is it,' he said decisively. 'HENDR.'

'Hendrix,' Charlton said excitedly. 'It's Hendrix. The old guitar player.'

'Very old,' Alan added. 'He's dead.'

'Just try it,' Gabby called. 'Don't debate guitar styles now.'

After a moment, Mel disappointed them. 'It did not take longer to discount it than HENDR.'

'Our hour's up,' Alan uttered.

Suddenly Roger, who hadn't spoken before, said, 'Could try Hendry.'

'Hendry?'

'Yes. He's …'

Before the explanation came, Mike had entered it and Mel responded animatedly, 'Yes. That is better than Hendrix. Hendry is the first word, I estimate.' He sounded relieved.

'What's the second?'

All eyes turned to Roger. He gulped. 'Search me.'

'Another name, perhaps,' Mike urged. 'Or maybe a number.'

Roger's face lit up. 'Yeah. Why not? A number. 147.'

'What?' someone questioned.

'He's a snooker player,' Roger explained. 'The best when he was young. Maximum break is 147. Know what I mean?'

'Get on with it, then,' Gabby yelled.

'Okay,' Mike said. 'Let's go for Hendry, underscore, 147.'

The VDU reported, 'User authorization failure. Enter password.'

'Bollocks!' Gabby shouted. 'Seemed a good idea.'

'Just a sec,' Mike said. 'Let's not give up yet. I'll try ...' He typed as he talked, 'Replace underscore with dollar sign.'

They were all quiet for a few seconds then, jointly, let out a cheer. The screen read, 'Welcome user Anon.'

'We did it.'

'Nice one, Mike — and Mel.'

Trevor added, 'Nice one, Roger.' He said it with feeling.

'Yeah,' Roger replied. He looked stunned, as if he'd pulled off the crime of the century. Amongst the best detective minds that could be mustered under one roof, Jolly Roger had successfully walked off with the crown jewels. The incredulity in his face slowly turned to pride. 'Yeah,' he repeated.

Toni put an end to the celebrations. 'Now what?' she asked.

Mike typed, 'Radar function,' and hit return. The computer replied with, 'Programme already in use by Blue Devil. Priority user. No overrule allowed. Okay? Y/N'

'Okay, indeed!' Mike clicked on the Y box and waited for the programme to abort. 'Now for the Blue Devil.'

'I hope Graham's still praying,' Alan said. 'Caught, as we are, between the Blue Devil and the deep sea.'

'Before you contact this user,' Mel said, 'Let us take note of any new communications. The one hour has elapsed. I wonder if they have received further orders.'

'All right,' Mike replied.

A short exchange between the submarine and its base had taken place. Mike's programme had captured it. In silence, the kids read the screen.

'Output: No result after one hour.'

'Input: Begin second mode.'

'Output: Confirm live ammunition to be used.'

'Input: Confirmed.'

Aghast, none of them dared to say anything for a while. Then Peter whispered. 'We've blundered into some military manoeuvre, you know.'

Alan denied it. 'It's not that. We're being disappeared. We really are. Like the police death squads in Guatemala. But being British, they're not torturing us first. That's the only difference.'

'No. The new Dark Ages aren't that dark, are they, Alan?' Mr Beever asked. He shook his head in disbelief.

'You can read it as plainly as I can,' he replied, pointing towards the VDU. 'Live ammunition.'

Suddenly, Mel rose from his chair. He looked beaten, drained of hope. 'I ... have a problem,' he muttered. In despair, he edged his way to the door and left the cabin.

Nonplussed, they watched him go — the rat deserting the sinking ship.

'I think it's us that have a problem,' said Peter.

'How could he ...?' Gabby blurted out.

Only Trevor Beever, Charlton and Gail did not stare through the doorway with accusing eyes. Tearfully, Gail looked around her mates. 'It's not his fault,' she cried. 'He's not ... There's a reason.' She jumped off the bunk and dashed after Mel.

The real Mel stood at the aft and looked skywards, even though he could see barely ten metres. Out there somewhere was his world, his home. Comfortable and familiar. A place where he would be amongst his own people, his own language and his own customs. A place where hundreds of lives did not depend on his decisions and actions. A place where he was neither hero nor villain. Even closer was the craft that had brought him to Earth.

He cast his thoughts through and beyond the fog, then waited for a reply. It was not a long wait. 'You were right,' the Elder's thoughts responded, 'to halt your intervention. You have done well, Melvyn, but can do no more. Prepare yourself for your journey home.'

'But I still want to help them.'

'You know our criteria.'

'These children helped me when I needed it. You know what'll happen if I leave now.'

'A purposeful act of aggression will be perpetrated and later disguised as an accident — a collision with a stray iceberg. Unbeknown to us till now. We have been misled.'

'Excuse me, but you're trying to avoid saying that I'll condemn them. They'll die.'

'It's disappointing, I know, but we have no right to interfere ...'

'They're my friends.'

'You cannot involve yourself in acts of hostility.'

Mel changed tack. 'The disease I carry,' he enquired, 'Is it a problem?'

'This is a dangerous line of thought, Melvyn.'

'I repeat. I don't have long in this form. Is it serious?'

'It is a small problem. We have already begun relearning old skills. In time, we can copy the vaccine. Everyone will need it before you are released from quarantine.'

'That does not sound very practical,' Mel responded.

'It is not insurmountable.'

'It would cause fewer problems if ...'

The Elder's thoughts interrupted him. She said, 'You have only seconds now before you must revert or return. You must think of yourself.'

'No. Myself *and* my friends.'

'They are humans, Melvyn. Do not overestimate them.'

'Neither do I underestimate them.'

'Do you understand the implications of what you are contemplating?'

'Yes,' said Mel firmly.

'Assume humanoid form or return now. Have you decided?'

He let out his last gasp of air. 'I am reverting, so I may breathe again.'

As he cloaked himself, he caught the final words transmitted by Elder Posthumus. 'I cannot applaud your actions,' she said, 'but I will be watching. I wish you good luck and goodbye, Melvyn Ten Noever de Brauw.' He had lost the capability to reply. He could not even offer his thanks. Even at this distance, she could have forced him back. She hadn't, though, and Mel took heart. He felt that the Elder sympathized with him really but her position forbade her transmitting the thought. Mel derived some measure of reassurance from her refusal to recall him involuntarily. He needed that unspoken blessing if he was to carry through his intentions with conviction. He needed to feel that he was right.

Gail burst into the classroom. 'Did Mel come in?' she asked Graham.

'No.'

'Well, did he come past here?'

'I don't know,' Graham replied.

'He puts a lot of store in you,' she said urgently. 'Do you know where he is?'

'Is it serious?'

'Yes. Very.'

'Then he'll be on deck. Leave him be, Gail. He'll be listening to God's whispers.'

'On deck, you say. I must see him,' she replied, heading for the door. 'God or no God.'

Gail stopped short of the faint glow on the observation deck. She knew that she must be seeing Mel in his true shape but she had no wish to intrude on his privacy. She had no desire to confront him as he really was. It was not for any human to see. Mel was not a diversion for human curiosity. She would not be reduced to gawping as if at an exhibit in a zoo. The humanoid Mel was good enough for Gail. She kept her distance and acted instead as his minder.

In a short while, Mel resumed his familiar shape. He clung to the rail as if he were trying to get his breath back after exhausting himself. Gail approached him cautiously. 'Mel?' she called.

'Ah, Gail.' He looked tired and pale but seemed pleased to see her. 'I am sorry that I had to leave.'

'They think you're running scared. Think you've deserted them. You haven't, have you, Mel?'

Mel smiled limply and shook his head. 'No.'

'Can you come back to Mike's and help out?'

'No. Mike and the others will cope now. You will be surprised how well they can fend for themselves when they have to. I trust them to continue. They are very resourceful.'

'What about you? What're you going to do?'

'I had a hope that you would not ask,' Mel answered. 'My role is out here now, not in the cabin of Mike. I do not know exactly what I must do, though. Perhaps you can help.'

'If I can,' Gail replied. Really, she felt like putting her arm around him or at least touching his shoulder. She thought it might comfort him. It would be like stroking Alien when he was alarmed. Yet Alien and Mel were worlds apart and she did nothing but clutch the rail by his side.

'It's out there,' he said nodding to the west. 'The submarine prepares to fire at us.'

'What? Now?'

'Soon.'

'Are you scared?'

'Yes,' he said. 'I have never witnessed any form of hostility before. We do not have such events. I have always been taught that it is a great evil. Now I must try to defend us against this weapon that I do not understand or know. I also fear the responsibility. Imagine, Gail, if you were protecting the lives of three hundred children.' He hesitated but did not have the time to allow her to reply. 'I am going to rest my true hand on this rail for a while, Gail. Do not look if you do not wish to do so.'

'Do you mind if I see it?'

'No.'

'Why are you doing it anyway?'

'I can sense vibrations a little better with my own hand. To monitor fully the activity in the seawater I would have to … become myself fully. Then I could not survive for long. This,' he glanced down at his membranous hand, 'will suffice for major changes.'

'What major changes?'

'I do not know. The release of a missile. I will detect its vibrations.'

'I see.'

'What sort of missile could be directed at us surreptitiously, Gail? One that would put a hole in the ship below water level.'

'You mean a torpedo.'

'Torpedo,' Mel repeated. 'How do they work?'

'Work? I don't know. They fire underwater. I think

they're guided by heat or something. A heat-seeking missile. Or maybe the sub's computer directs it at us.'

'Ah,' Mel replied. 'Then they have an electronic guidance system. That is all that I need to know. They have a weakness.'

'Weakness?'

'Electronic systems can fail, or be confused.' He did not seem to want to expand on his plan.

'I'll take your word for it,' she said.

Whilst she did not wish to see Mel as he really was, she was fascinated by the thin and colourful hand that seemed almost to hover above the rail. It was easy to imagine how such a delicate and fine hand could feel the faintest tremble. She could trust such a hand. Unlike a human hand, it could never be used to inflict injury.

'What'll you do if a torpedo's fired?' she asked him.

'I will revert to my proper form. Then I can generate electromagnetic interference.'

'What?'

'Bombard it with radiation that will confuse its control mechanism.'

'Do you still want me here?' Gail asked.

He looked at her and smiled. 'I would rather not take this action alone. You are a help to me. I hope that you will stay.'

'But I'm not doing anything. You're doing it all.'

'You are here. That is good in itself. Besides, you have instructed me on the topic of torpedoes,' Mel replied.

'I suppose so.' This time she did overcome her reticence. Fear overcame reticence. She linked her arm with his. 'All right?'

'Very all right,' Mel answered. 'Until I must revert.'

Gail shivered, perhaps because of the cold and damp. More likely, it was caused by her fear — or by Mel's words. There was an implication of finality about them. 'Do you think the captain has the remotest idea where he is in this muck?'

'If he were relying on his eyes, no. But satellite signals will pinpoint our position. He should also have radio contact with land-based stations.'

'So if ...' She paused. 'If this ship went down, he'd radio for help pretty sharpish.'

'Pretty sharpish?' Mel queried.

'Quickly.'

'Yes, but the conditions would not favour an easy rescue. The ship also goes down rather quickly, I estimate. No lifeboats were launched. That is why ... *all* lives are at risk.'

Gail looked down towards the murky sea. 'How long would you last in there?' she asked.

Mel seemed taken aback. 'Who? Me?'

'No. Anyone. Humans only last a few seconds in *very* cold water. I wouldn't want to last long in there.'

'Do not think about it, Gail. The water is not so cold, and I do not anticipate failure.'

'I know. I just can't help ... thinking.'

'Think more of what you will do when this ship returns you to your home.'

'I've no idea ...'

Mel put up his human hand to silence her. His face showed concentration on something out to sea. 'It will work out, Gail. I am sure. But now you must stand back ... It is better that you do not watch.'

'Torpedo? Now?' She trembled and disengaged herself from him although she would have preferred to cling tighter.

He nodded. 'Turn away.'

She wanted to wish him good luck but the words would not come. In the moment before she obeyed him, she saw determination and utter sorrow in his eyes. Why sorrow? Without turning round to face him again, she asked, 'Mel? What are you going to do?' There was no reply, but she still dared not look over her shoulder. 'Don't do anything ...' Further along the deck , she saw Charlton hurrying towards her. 'Charlton!' she called.

'What's going on?' he asked urgently.

'It's Mel. He's ...' She saw Charlton look around then stare at her blankly. Then she knew. She span round, looked for herself, and cried, 'He's gone!'

'There's no one here,' Charlton confirmed.

'He ... He must have ...' She gulped. 'He's gone overboard, Charlton! He's ...'

Her words were lost in the loudest explosion that she'd ever heard. They both let out a cry and were thrown violently against the rail. Water, rock and shrapnel flew around them. In the turmoil, Gail yelled out over the sea, 'It's hit! Mel!'

There was, of course, no response.

There was a stunned silence in Cabin G5. First, Mel had rushed out of the room followed shortly by Gail. Once the door had swung slowly shut by itself, all eyes turned to

Charlton as if he should be able to explain the mystery. He shuffled uneasily. 'Don't look at me,' he said. 'But I'll tell you this. Mel's no coward. He'll have a plan.'

'He didn't look like a lad with a plan,' Gabby replied. 'More like someone doing a bunk.'

'Well, it's no use arguing about recriminations,' said Mr Beever, the voice of pragmatism. 'Wingeing and whining won't help. Let's get on with the job. Mike?'

'Er ... yeah. Sure.' Mike shook his head, still in disbelief, and turned back to the keyboard. 'Let's see ... We need to set up a line of communication to the sub, to the Blue Devil.'

'That's right,' Alan agreed. 'We know they're going to pass this whole thing off as a freak accident with an iceberg. Let's scuttle *their* plan. Tell them we've recorded these communications, dumped them into a computer at home. Logged them into a Fleet Street computer, or something. Then they can't use the iceberg story. The truth will out. We'll have 'em by the short and floppies.'

'But I haven't logged this into any other system,' Mike protested.

'Bluff!' Alan replied. 'It's called bluff.'

'Or get it sent pronto to someone you know back home,' added Peter.

'No time,' Mike replied. 'Let's bluff.' He tapped into the keyboard a request for access to another user by intermail. The screen prompted him for the destination. He typed 'Blue Devil.' He then clicked on the box labelled 'From'. He asked the others, 'What shall we call ourselves?'

'They must be told it's us if the plan's going to work,'

Peter replied. 'Put "The ship you're attacking" or "*Queen of the Fjords*".'

'All right.' He named the ship and then pressed return. The computer asked for the message to be transmitted. 'Well?' he enquired. 'Any great ideas?'

'Just tell them we're friendly first,' Mr Beever said. He still hung onto the belief that the whole thing was some gigantic mistake.

Mike typed, 'We are a friendly vessel. Do not attack.' He struck the return key to transmit the message.

They waited impatiently for a minute but no reply was sent. 'How do we know they got the message?' Toni asked.

'No error reported,' Mike answered. 'They got it.'

'If this *is* a military manoeuvre gone wrong,' Peter argued, 'Won't they be trained to ignore this sort of thing as enemy propaganda?'

His words rang true but Alan said, 'Trust me. This is no practice run. This is for real. Bluff, Mike. Hurry. Tell them we've got all their communications from ...' He paused. 'London. Guess it's coming from London.'

'No.' Mr Beever overruled him. 'First, tell them the *Queen*'s just a shipful of children. Even if Alan's right, the captain of this sub may not know what we are. He may be just following orders. Maybe he reckons this is an expendable tub. I don't know.'

Mike prepared to send another intermail message. He typed, 'We are a school trip, not a military exercise. Repeat: do not attack. There are over 300 children on board.'

'Yeah,' Peter agreed. 'Three hundred cuddly ones.'

Another minute passed. The second message suffered exactly the same fate as the first.

'Let's just check ...' Mike left the intermail programme and opened yet again the submarine's communication file. Two further entries had been stored. 'Output: Received following messages from ship. Advice needed.' Then Mike's intermail memoranda were duplicated. The response that they elicited was terse and discouraging. The advice read simply, 'Input: False info. Ignore and continue manoeuvre.'

'I don't believe this!'

'The buggers!' Gabby swore venomously.

'I'm going to warn Mel,' Charlton said, and dashed out of the cabin.

'Now what?' Mike asked.

'Now they fire,' Toni replied despondently.

'Over to Alan's idea,' Trevor Beever conceded.

'Okay. No messing. No time. Name names,' Alan said heatedly. 'OBTUSE was Sternhell's idea. Bet he's behind all this. That's why he got shifted to the MoD — so he could complete the job. Tell them we've got Sternhell's message to use live ammunition. That'll scupper them.'

Cursing himself each time he made a typing error in haste, Mike keyed in feverishly, 'We have hacked into your communications network. All messages between you and London have been monitored, captured and deposited in a document in several computers in England. It includes orders to fire on a ship that identified itself as a school trip.' On Alan's prompting, he continued, 'Tell Sternhell that he is incriminated. We have identified him in the document. If we go down, he goes down with us. This was no iceberg and everyone will know it. The game is up.'

Mike hesitated before transmitting the message to the Blue Devil. His finger hovered over the 'return' key. 'Are you sure?' he asked.

Everyone nodded, even Mr Beever. 'Get on with it,' Gabby said. 'Throw the switch!'

Mike's finger hit the key.

Within thirty seconds, they had their reply. 'To: *Queen of the Fjords*. From: Blue Devil. Message: countdown to firing of missile one irreversible. Further firing suspended pending review of your memo.'

'Irreversible?'

'Bloody hell!'

'Prepare yourselves ...' Trevor Beever never finished his sentence. The *Queen* was rocked by a massive stomach-churning blast.

'Out! Out!' Mr Beever ushered them out of the cabin. 'Deck 2. Remember your safety code. Get up to Deck 2, while I clear Block G. Get going!'

The gallery was chaotic. A seething mass of bewildered children and crew. 'What was that? Never heard nothing like that before.' Somewhere a siren wailed. Life jackets were being issued from the white boxes on deck. 'Which cord is it we're supposed to pull?' The crew were calling for calm amongst the shambles. 'Is it sinking?' One lifeboat slid down the side of the *Queen* and splashed heavily into the sea below, others were being prepared for lowering. 'I can't swim! I can't swim!'

The captain joined in the mêlée, through the loudspeakers. 'There is no need for alarm,' he said, tinnily but reassuringly. He seemed to be addressing and informing his own crew as much as the passengers. 'There has been some sort of detonation near the ship but no damage has been incurred. We are safe. I repeat. The *Queen* has been checked and is undamaged. Cease evacuation measures. Effect immediate roll call.' A sort of order slowly returned. Confusion replaced panic.

At the aft, Charlton and Gail looked at each other. They both had the same question. 'Well?' Gail said. Implicitly Charlton knew what she was asking. Should they raise the alarm? Does Mel wish to be rescued? Isn't it cleaner if he just disappears? Maybe he can't return home because of distemper. Would he prefer this way out? Was it a suicide mission all along? Charlton had had to make a similar decision a year ago. But distemper and motor neurone disease were not the same. Mel's case was not hopeless. It *could* be managed. Charlton could not abandon and condemn him, even if Mel wanted out. He still had a life to be proud of. For one thing, he had deflected the missile to a nearby rock. He had saved them.

Charlton nodded. 'Where's the nearest crewman?'

'Never mind that,' Gail said and yelled at the top of her voice, 'Help! Man overboard!'

Two deck-hands rushed to them. 'It was when the ship rocked,' she explained hastily. 'He was here by the rail. He just tipped up and over. Hurry!' she pleaded.

One of the crew radioed the captain. The other said, 'Okay. We've got a lifeboat down. We'll send it for him.

But,' he said looking helplessly out to sea, 'in this weather ...'
He shrugged.

The *Queen* went round in circles. Two lifeboats systematically criss-crossed the circle, searching for Mel in negligible
visibility. As the rescue attempt progressed, Mr Beever,
eager to quash talk of Mel's desertion, gathered together the
Splinter group. He asked Gail to explain what Mel had done.
'So,' Trevor said when she had finished, 'he went overboard
to stop this missile. He risked everything for us. And I mean
everything — he risked his life. We have Mel to thank for still
being here.'

'The lad done brilliant,' Roger enthused.

'Brilliantly, Roger,' the teacher corrected. 'The lad done
brilliantly. You all done brilliantly.'

'Yeah. You got it.'

'The Lutine Bell can rest easy tonight,' Peter remarked.

Their smiles faded as they thought of Mel. In silence, each
of them contemplated the debt they owed him.

The silence was broken by Graham muttering to himself,
'Praise be to God.'

Unfortunately, Peter was close enough to hear him.
'God?' he exclaimed. 'What's He got to do with it? Don't talk
of God when Mel's out there. Praise be to Mel!'

'Come on, boys,' Mr Beever said. 'Let's not have bickering. Not now.'

'Okay. No bickering,' Graham replied. 'But,' he said to
Peter, 'let me tell you a story instead. It'll only take a minute.'
He drew Peter unwillingly aside. 'There was a priest,' he
began, 'whose church was in a land prone to flooding. One

Sunday, during his sermon, the flood-water burst into his church. The congregation ran out, saying to him, "Come on, before we all drown!" But the priest wouldn't budge. "No," he said. "This is God's place. I have the faith." Well,' Graham continued, 'the water carried on rising up to the pulpit. A boat came by and the people shouted to the priest, "We've come to rescue you!" But again the priest refused to leave. "I have faith. No harm will come to me here." But the flood continued to rise till it was up to the priest's shoulders. Another boat came by. "Come on, before it's too late," they shouted. "No," the priest said. "I have faith in God. I will be all right." The water rose further and further till only the tower was left above the water. The priest stood on the tower and a helicopter came by. They dropped a rope down for him but he shouted, "I have faith. I will stay here, in God's house." Well, the water continued to rise and of course the priest drowned.' Graham knew that the story had captivated Peter because it had taken an unexpected turn. "The priest went up to the pearly gates, somewhat peeved, as you can imagine, and called for Saint Peter. "What went wrong?" the priest asked him. "I had faith. I didn't waiver, but here I am. What went wrong?" Saint Peter was amazed. "I don't know," he said. "It doesn't sound right at all. Let me go and check the records." Saint Peter came back with a big, open log book. He was shaking his head. "I still don't know what went wrong," he said to the priest. "You have indeed been good and faithful. So much so that, according to our records, we sent out two boats and a helicopter for you".'

Peter laughed aloud. 'Okay,' he said. 'Good one. Nice parable. You've got me. I can't prove who sent Mel to us.

And,' he added, 'I didn't know you had it in you, Graham.'

'The meek choose not to flaunt,' Graham replied.

'Yeah. Well, let's just hope Mel doesn't meet the same fate as your priest.'

Graham nodded. 'Indeed. But let not your heart be troubled. Trust in God. Mel is in God's hands. It wouldn't be the first time that a saviour had to be sacrificed for our sins.'

Mike returned to his cabin. He wanted to put into effect what he had said was already done. An appropriate document needed to be intermailed to some computers back on dry land. First, though, he needed to protect the document with a minefield of passwords. Then he would lodge a copy in his own computer at home, another with Netherstone Health Centre. If someone went looking for the document, he wanted to give them a hard time. He thought of one place that they'd never search. He planned to deposit one version of the document in the MoD computer into which he had hacked earlier.

He logged on and immediately accessed his capture programme. It had grabbed two further messages. 'Output: further communication from the Queen.' There followed Mike's revelations about hacking and Sternhell. The response was short and, to Mike, sweet. 'Input: Abort mission at once.' The radar had mysteriously repaired itself and the blip that was the submarine was heading rapidly for the edge of the screen. Mike smiled. 'Didn't even stay around to say its fond farewells,' he said to himself. It was doing a runner, with its tail between its legs. With the enthusiasm that he reserved for a new computational challenge, Mike began to construct the document in an impenetrable folder.

Mr Beever, Charlton and Gail remained together on deck, wistfully gazing into the impenetrable fog. The *Queen* still chugged slowly round and round like the engine of a train set. Getting nowhere. A crew member approached them and, in a respectfully soft voice, said, 'Not much longer, I'm afraid. Nothing to go on, you see. No radio signals. It's pointless to send up a flare. And,' he added, 'he doesn't have anything to cling to. He can't last long ...'

'We're in no great hurry, are we?' Trevor asked.

'For the sake of everyone else, the captain would rather us get to Hammerfest. He still doesn't know what caused the explosion. Very odd.'

'Well, it's over now. So we can try for a little longer, surely.'

'Yes. For a bit. Then we hand over to the authorities. The navy is better than us at this game. They'll send out a helicopter as soon as they can.'

'To look for what?' Mr Beever asked in exasperation and frustration. 'A body?'

The deck-hand did not reply. His silence confirmed Trevor's suspicions.

'We don't want his body!' Gail cried. 'We want him alive.'

'I'm sure they're doing all they can,' Trevor consoled her, 'under the circumstances.'

'But it's been ...' She looked at her watch. 'I don't know. A good half hour since ...'

The crewman added as kindly as he could, 'Any hopes of finding him were never good in this weather. As time goes by his chances get even slimmer, I'm afraid.'

Gail nodded dismally. 'I know.'

After the crewman had gone, Charlton remarked, 'Mel believed in the quality of life, you know, more than quantity. Maybe he couldn't get home and couldn't face life here. Maybe this is what he wanted.'

'You don't believe that. You're just trying to make me feel better in case he's ... you know,' replied Gail.

Charlton nodded. 'You're right. He persuaded me that life was worth living. Even if he has his problems, I'm sure we could persuade him the same.'

'Cheer up, both of you,' Mr Beever said. 'He seemed very resilient to me. Perhaps he's strong enough to withstand this ... ordeal.'

'He may have been too close to the explosion,' Charlton mumbled.

'Look on the bright side,' Trevor Beever answered. 'He may have left. His job's done. Perhaps he's on his way back home already.'

'He'd have said goodbye first,' Gail said.

'I don't know,' Mr Beever replied thoughtfully. 'Reluctant heroes often sneak away without the embarrassment of accepting praise.'

'He talked to me about learning to accept praise,' Charlton put in. 'I don't know if he'd learned the lesson himself. Perhaps not.'

'Well ...' Gail began to see a straw at which she might clutch. It was, she thought, more to do with her own need for hope than with reality. Right now, reality seemed hopeless. Just as Mel had felt by intuition that the submarine lingered in the vicinity even when a rock hid it from the probing radar, so Gail believed innately that Mel was still out there. Mr Beever and Charlton's logic could not dispel the notion that, alive or dead, he was still there, tugged this way and that by the waves, like so much flotsam. 'Well, I hope you're right,' she said. 'But something tells me ... you're wrong.'

'Perhaps we'll never know,' Mr Beever warned.

That was the worst thought of all. To spend the rest of her life wondering. Did they abandon him in the cold Norwegian Sea? Or did Mel, job done, simply evaporate? Once she had opened up with Mel because he seemed just like a harmless ghost. Now, she didn't want him exorcised from her life. She needed him.

It was the captain himself who joined them next. 'Mr Beever, isn't it?' he enquired. 'Look. I ... er ... I've just radioed the search parties. I've ... ordered them in. We can't ...'

To put him out of further misery, Trevor Beever interrupted. 'Yes. Okay. We understand,' he replied. 'For the sake of the rest.'

'Yes,' the captain affirmed. 'I'm sorry. But we must head for a place of safety.'

'Just another minute!' Gail exhorted. When the others looked at her with pity, as if her outburst were the frustration of a little girl who had just lost a favourite doll, she felt annoyed. 'I just think ...' she began to explain.

The captain interrupted. 'I'm sorry,' he repeated. He looked to Mr Beever for support. Trevor nodded sadly and the captain turned and walked away.

Two long blasts on a whistle stopped the captain in his tracks. He darted back to the rails and peered over. Obviously he saw nothing because he swore at the weather.

'What's the whistle mean?' Mr Beever shouted to him.

'It means,' he called back, 'that they've found ... something.'

'Mel?' Gail queried.

Trevor Beever put his arm around Gail. 'I think he means it could be just his body.'

There was hope, though, because the captain was yelling orders to all and sundry. 'Cut engines. Ready by the winches.' Finally, he shouted, 'And someone get the nurse up here. Just in case.'

The Queen's engines subsided. For a time, there was quiet except for the slovenly lapping of waves on the hull. They waited. Then someone called, 'There she is,' and the first lifeboat slowly emerged from the fog. One crewman was hunched anxiously over a body that lay in the bottom of the boat. The other called up from sea level, 'Found him as we were coming in. No idea how.'

'Is he alive?' the captain shouted.

The other sailor looked up the side of the ship. 'Yeah. Exhausted. Taken in a lot of water. Done what I can with him. Badly bruised as well. Bet he was too close to the explosion. Must be tough as old boots.'

Mr Beever grinned at both Charlton and Gail. In fact, he could hardly contain himself. 'You were right, Gail,' he said. 'Women's intuition strikes again.'

Gail could say nothing. Through tears of relief, she just smiled back.

The motor whirred, the capstans revolved. Painfully slowly, the lifeboat was winched up to Deck 2. The two crewmen lifted Mel out onto a waiting stretcher. The nurse knelt by his side and started checking him over straight away. 'All right,' she said. 'You can all stop gawping. He'll be okay.'

When the crowd dispersed, there was just Gail, Charlton and Mr Beever. Mel lay like a stranded fish. Seaweed clung to one of his legs. He was white, his skin shrivelled. His eyes were shut tight. He looked five years older.

'You his friends?' the nurse asked.

They nodded.

'Help me get him to the surgery, then.'

As they lifted the stretcher Mel groaned and shifted. His eyes did not open. 'It's all right,' Charlton whispered respectfully. 'You're back on the *Queen*. You'll be okay.'

Mel did not reply but another groan seemed to indicate that he had heard and understood.

On the way to the surgery, they met Alan and Peter. 'Here he is,' they chimed. 'We heard.'

'More fans?' the nurse queried. 'Quite an entourage. He must be special. Who is he?'

'He's special all right. He's ... er ...' Mr Beever looked around the kids. Mel was most like Alan in stature. 'Splinter,' he replied. 'Alan Splinter.'

'Yes,' Alan said. 'He's a special friend of mine.'

'Just get him in here,' the nurse said bossily opening the surgery door. 'Over there. Then you can go.'

As they were putting him down, Mel's eyes flickered open. He looked startled but conscious. Peter said, 'Back with us? You missed all the excitement when you went for your leisurely dip.'

'Yeah,' Alan added. 'There *is* a pool on board, you know. No need to go to extremes.'

Mr Beever smiled to himself. So much for the hero receiving too many plaudits.

'Off you go,' the nurse said. 'Let him rest.' She went off to prepare something for Mel from a cupboard in the corner.

Gail lingered to whisper in his ear, 'While you're here, you're Alan Splinter. Understand? I just hope that his medical record matches.'

Mel's speech was slurred, as if he'd had too much punch, but he managed to reply, 'It is okay, Gail. I am just human now.' There was some relief in his eyes, but mostly sadness.

Gail's face creased but she asked no more. Mel's eyes had closed again and the nurse shooed her away.

Snapshots on the Way Home

In truth, Charlton and Gail would have preferred to have Mel to themselves, but they had fallen victim to Gabby's curiosity. She accompanied her sister. They sat in Cabin G9 as Mel, under orders to rest, lay in bed. 'Just like old times,' Gabby remarked.

'Yes. That is how it began,' Mel said. 'The episode of distemper was the origin of the problem. Remember, though, that it was not your fault, Gail. You could not know.' He coughed painfully. 'My people have been uninfected by disease for many generations. If I had returned, I would have spread the distemper virus among them. That would be a tragedy. We could not stop the spreading. We have no doctors to combat such an outbreak.'

Gail was suspicious. There was something in Mel's demeanour that told her that he was not telling the whole truth. He was also labouring the point as if trying to convince himself. Besides, she thought, it couldn't be beyond the wit of an advanced race to develop a vaccine. He *could* have returned home.

Mel continued, 'Then there was another problem. I was sent here to avert a natural disaster. I had no ... what is the word? ... mandate to alter an act of aggression. In fact, it is forbidden for me to intervene in hostilities. But I disobeyed instructions because I could not return home in any event.'

Gail interpreted his motives differently. She guessed that he had broken the rules in order to help them. His punishment was exile. He was marooned on Earth against his will. That accounted for the sadness in his eyes.

'So,' Mel concluded, 'it was arranged for my transformation into human form to become irreversible. I am human!' He leaned over the edge of the bed and, in an attempt to sound pleased about his new circumstances, he patted Gail's dog, saying, 'Now there is only one Alien on board again.'

Charlton and Gail looked crestfallen. 'I'm sorry, Mel,' Charlton muttered.

'Sorry?' Gabby questioned. 'It's great. He can stay with us. Will you have special powers,' she asked Mel, 'and save the Earth from evil like Superman?'

Mel smiled. 'No. I am human. That is all.'

Yes, Gail thought to herself, he *is* being punished. A cruel punishment, even if Mel himself was putting on a brave face. She did not dwell on it, for fear of making Mel even more forlorn. She simply echoed Charlton's sentiments. 'I'm sorry. But I'm pleased you'll stay. We'll try to return the favour. Somehow.'

And so it came to pass that Gabby was struck by a mighty thought. And the mighty thought did trouble her for it concerned the extent of her contribution to her own salvation.

Mel was the mastermind, the leader who became a mere boy. Without Mel, they were sunk. Gail and Charlton nurtured him in his own hour of need. The stealth of Roger and Toni supplied Mel with his daily bread and his medicine. Mike, the resident hacker, had become ambulance driver, providing the vehicle to the fount of all medical knowledge. And thereafter Peter acted as Mel's locum.

Once the pestilence had passed, Mel and Mike led the battle against the forces of darkness. And lo, Roger saw the light that lit the way ahead and Graham prayed that the road be travelled fruitfully, no matter where it led. Twas Alan who understood the nature of the road and of the battle. From him came the wisdom that laid low the evil empire and secured triumph of good over the hounds of Sternhell.

For each in the Splinter Group there was a role. Except two. All along, Gabby had known that Eager Beever was just there for the ride. He was, she would admit, relatively harmless and possibly even well-intentioned, but he was inherently useless. He was an extra, neither good nor bad. By definition, he could not be a hero. The mighty thought that so shocked Gabby was the realization that she was the second useless person. She had been there and witnessed it all but she had not contributed to their victory. Like Beever, she was a bit player. Gabby in the same camp as Beever! Almost unbelievable! To make up for it she decided that, after all, she would act as raconteur. That would be her role in the OBTUSE experiment. She would tell it like it was. The whole lot.

The smell of toothpaste was barely perceptible. Cueball did not so much sit behind his desk as wear it like protective armour. He needed it. He was feeling vulnerable.

'Yes, yes,' he was saying. 'I have heard about the ... near-miss. All the captain's efforts to establish the cause of the explosion have come to nothing, I understand. We have to put it down to a mystery accident.'

'Accident?' Trevor smiled wryly. 'An incident, perhaps, but no accident. It was a deliberate attempt to scuttle this vessel. We know why it was done and who did it. We just don't know how many accomplices there were, that's all.'

Immediately, Mr Uunk became defensive. 'You must share your evidence with me sometime! But, let me tell you that, even if you're right, I was not involved, if that's what you're insinuating.'

'Oh,' Trevor replied, 'I know you're not likely to be in on such a crazy scheme, but you must see that you have a credibility problem. This stay of yours in Hammerfest — it does ... er ... suggest ... It would appear, to the outsider, that you were aware that something was on the cards, wouldn't it? And you can protest your innocence all you like — with justification, no doubt — but actions speak louder than words. When the story breaks, your *actions* will come under scrutiny.'

Cueball swallowed. 'But I ...' He sighed. 'I see what you mean. Despite everything, I do *appear* culpable, I must admit. But appearance is all it is.'

'Appearances. So hard to shake off, aren't they? I think you're going to need good friends sooner or later,' Trevor suggested. 'Perhaps the best thing is for you to lie rather low for the rest of this trip.'

'Mm, yes,' he replied thoughtfully, 'What exactly ... do you have in mind?'

'I don't really know,' Trevor replied, as if he didn't really know. 'Perhaps you'd make good friends if you relieved

Mr Brown of the bother of organizing the disco and handed it over to some of the more responsible of my bunch. Mr Brown has his strengths, I'm sure, but he couldn't even run the library properly. He'd be the kiss of death to a disco.'

'Yes, I suppose so.'

'And there's the reports on some of my lot. You know. Smuggling dogs, little outdoor escapades and issuing insults. I'm not suggesting that any facts are changed. I'm not into book burning. But perhaps you might re-examine your interpretation of those facts and your recommendations. It would all help in the long run, I think.'

'This is beginning to sound like blackmail, Mr Beever,' the Head objected.

'I'm sorry. It isn't meant to be. Just advice really.'

'I will ponder on it,' Cueball said in a dismissive voice, meant to put an end to Trevor's advice.

'Okay,' Trevor replied, rising from the chair. 'That's good enough for me. I know you'll consider all my points with due respect.' He left the Head's office, still wearing his wry smile like a victory salute. He felt that, by making the journey home bearable for kids, he had begun to compensate for his redundancy earlier when they, not he, had won the day.

Life on Earth was never going to be easy for Mel. For starters, he did not exist. No birth certificate, no educational history, no identity. Whilst he could get by without qualifications, Mel could hardly get by without being born. Mike was left in charge of creating a background for him. It required only a little tinkering with the births, deaths and marriages register.

'It is a strange kind of birth,' Mel said to Graham. 'Birth by manipulation of computer records.'

'Like a Virgin birth,' Charlton joked.

Graham tried to scowl but did not quite make it. 'There are comparisons, Charlton. But that isn't one of them.'

'Comparisons?' Mel queried.

'God,' Graham explained, 'is all-seeing. But He could no more talk to us feeble creatures than man could talk to ... ants. So when he saw humankind teetering towards destruction through sin, God warned us by becoming one of us. He became Jesus.'

'What's this got to do with Mel?' asked Charlton.

'Mel's people had the power to see *our* plight. They could warn us only by sending Mel amongst us. In saving us, Mel fell victim to our sins — in the shape of disease. He's been banished — sacrificed for our salvation. As an alien, Mel died.'

Charlton nodded slowly. He understood. Mel had suffered death of a sort. 'Jesus had a happy ending,' Charlton commented. 'He was resurrected.' Mel's rebirth as a human was like a man becoming an ant. The analogy did not comfort him. Charlton also thought of his mother. A woman become vegetable. Quickly he banished that particular comparison. Mel's mind was trapped inside a body that he would regard as feeble, but he still had a recognizable life. He had his own will. He could develop. He was a burden to no one.

There was a knock at the door and Mike came in. 'I've done it!' he announced. 'I've cracked the system *and* found you ... someone to be,' he said to Mel.

They all went to Mike's cabin where, on the screen, were the vital statistics of John M. Yonker.

'John!' Charlton exclaimed. 'I couldn't get used to calling you John.'

'You don't have to,' Mike said proudly. 'The middle name is Melvyn. See?'

'That's not bad,' Charlton replied. 'How old is he?'

'Sixteen last year when he died. So he'd be seventeen now.'

'If this boy is dead ...' Mel began.

'Then he no longer has a need of his identity,' Mike said. 'And I've just deleted the registration of his death. Brought him back to life — as you.'

Charlton smiled. 'Told you. Resurrection.'

'What about John Yonker's family?' Mel enquired.

'Mel Yonker from now on,' Mike corrected. 'They all died together. The whole family wiped out in a car crash. Except that now, our Mel survived.' Mike looked at Mel. 'Well?'

Mel shrugged. 'I suppose that it is well,' he replied.

'Okay. Let's sort out the details while you're here.' Mike sat down in front of the keyboard. 'Born in York. Your dad was an engineer, your mum a part-time teacher. Is that okay or do you want them changed?'

'I have no objection.'

'Oh, look,' Mike pointed at the date of birth. 'Your birthday is 25th December. That's not so good. Want it changed?'

'No,' Graham replied for Mel. 'Keep it. It's a good birthday.'

'I really do not mind,' Mel said. 'I accept it all.'

'Okay,' Mike said. 'I'll close the file.' The computer responded by asking, 'Save changes to file?' Mike clicked on YES. 'Replace existing file?' He responded YES again then said. 'There you are, Mel Yonker. Done.'

'Mel Yonker.' Mel repeated the words slowly, trying to get used to the sound. He was having to get used to his own birthrights being stripped away. He smiled the best smile he could muster. 'It's not such a bad name,' he said.

The lights of the club room twinkled quaintly. No smoke, no lasers. The revolving ball of mirrors would have graced *Come Dancing*. The stage was built for middle-aged men in suits doing Elvis Presley and Beatle covers. The PA system was designed not to compete too seriously with the hubbub. Tonight, though, things would be different. The fittings of the ballroom groaned and quivered as if they knew. The vu meters would overswing constantly into the red. The amplifiers and speakers would strain and shake to deliver a wall of sound. Distortion was not a problem. After all, the idea was not to listen to the music but to feel it through every pore.

Charlton cued the first tape, tapped the microphone, then got the proceedings underway. 'Okay?' his voice bawled through the speakers. 'Welcome to the Southbound Bash, the last chance dance. You've heard of garage music. You've done house music. It's time for boat music. Let's rock the boat!' The crash of Blind Noise put an end to conversation, obliterated thought. Nothing was possible but dance. In a dark corner, Mr Beever watched and smiled. The inane thump thump thump was perfect. The revellers deserved their rave.

Between bursts of frenetic dance, groups of children migrated to the decks where conversation was possible and the air could blow away the sweat. The fog and the land of the midnight sun were well behind them but it was hardly dark. Twilight was still prolonged. The *Queen*'s vibrations were intermingled with the pulse of the disco on the other side of the panel.

'Phew!' Mel groaned. 'This activity,' he indicated the club room, 'is it supposed to benefit us?'

'Like a plateful of prunes,' Alan replied. 'It shakes everything loose and works it out of your system. You'll feel better for it.'

'When will it end?'

'Late,' Alan answered with a grin. 'As loud and late as we want. That was the deal Eager Beever struck with Cueball. He must have really gone to town on our beloved Head.'

'Town? Which town?'

'Since you're here to stay,' Alan quipped, 'we'd better start learning you to speak proper. And talking of Mr Fix-it,' he added, 'here he comes.'

Trevor Beever joined them on the open gallery. Inevitably, the conversation soon turned to politics. 'You do realize, Alan, what a big story we have, don't you?'

'I think I can handle the concept,' he replied. 'Minister moves to make mincemeat out of miscreant minors.'

'Seriously,' the teacher said, 'it'll bring down the government.'

'Shame, eh?'

'Yeah,' Mr Beever agreed wickedly.

'By what mechanism?' Mel asked, still innocent of the ways of humans.

'The spoken word,' Alan explained, 'is nothing. Just a vibration in the air. The merest trembling of the ether. Just like the music in there.' He pointed to the disco. 'But you know all about that. Once you've heard the verbals, they've gone. Nothing. You couldn't even prove they were ever really said. But Sternhell didn't just talk. The modern way is the computer. And the recorded word is different. Permanent. We have it all on disc. Or at least Mike has. Oh, we added Sternhell's name. He didn't identify himself. But the action stopped because we identified him. He's nobbled and he knows it. He may try to locate the evidence and destroy it, but Mike says he's got that covered. It wouldn't surprise me if, somehow, sometime, the press got hold of this story. Even heavy state censorship won't stop this one. It's just too big to lie down quietly. The media won't toe the party line when the stakes are this high. Sternhell will be hounded like only the British press knows how. He's had it. Our man from the MoD will end up with more than just birdshit on his shoe,' he said with delight. 'And the next election — these governmental machinations will be played and replayed, like Beatles hits. Opposition — lots; Government — nil. Kaput.'

Mr Beever listed to Alan's account with amusement and pleasure. 'You know, when the powers-that-be are so underhand,' he said, 'it makes me proud to be on their black list.'

'I wonder about Mel Yonker. The real one. If he'd been alive,' Alan pondered, seriously for a change, 'would he have been on the black list? Would he have been on OBTUSE?'

'I do not know,' Mel answered. 'But *this* Mel Yonker is proud to be here.'

Alan smiled at him. 'Thanks, Mel.'

'Shall we partake of another plate of prunes?' Mel asked.

'Why not?' Alan replied.

They left Mr Beever looking puzzled.

'I just can't swing my pants properly,' Gabby complained, 'without alcohol inside me.'

'It's not so bad,' Toni said. 'A party that runs out of alcohol is a dead duck, but when it's dry from the start ... Well, you just get used to it. You've got to make the most of it. It's pretty mega for a school do.'

'Well, I blame Eager Beever,' Gabby retorted. 'If that prat had forced a better deal out of Cueball, it needn't have been a dry disco.'

'I doubt it. Beever's all right but he wouldn't break the law. Anyway,' she added, 'what about Charlton tonight?'

'A different breed of animal,' Gabby agreed. 'He's actually good at it. Says little, but loud. Keeps it moving.'

Having crept up behind them, Peter chimed, 'Yep. Even I have to admit it. Still punky, maybe still angry, but not self-destructive and certainly not silent. Mel's played the part of the anchor — somehow. Put Charlton back on an even keel.'

'Yes,' Gabby agreed. 'Chaz is okay.'

'How about your joint venture with him? The illustrated history of OBTUSE. Still up and running?'

'Yes, I guess it is.'

'So Eager Beever got his way in the end,' Toni taunted her.

'Not really,' Gabby argued. 'Because he couldn't force me to do it. Neither could Cueball. No one forced me. *I* decided to do it.'

'Why?' asked Peter.

'I don't know. But me and Chaz, we decided to do a proper job on the whole bloody thing. From start to finish. Must be crazy.'

'Oh, I see,' Peter said knowingly.

'What do you see?'

'I see you selling the kids' eye view of the OBTUSE scandal. You could call it "The Kids' OBTUSE Angle." Earn millions. The unexpurgated version.'

'Well ...' Gabby replied. 'It had crossed our minds — if someone would publish it.'

Inside, Charlton rapped, 'A special request, for Kylie — the best. From one Jason Court. Wasn't he an Argonaut? Wants a sixties hit. While I'm in charge, forget it!' The speakers throbbed again. The *Queen* was trampled underfoot.

When Their Ship Came In

By the time that the *Queen of the Fjords* had returned to England, Sternhell was like the cat that got the cream. In a more-or-less official raid, Mike Zlatkis's computer had been confiscated by nameless servants of the state. Believing that there would be another copy of the incriminating evidence, the families of Zlatkis's co-conspirators were interviewed. Shortly after, the folder lodged in a Milton Keynes medical centre was unearthed and deleted. That, Sternhell believed, was the extent of the boy's cunning.

The Minister's confidence was misplaced. There are more than two ways to skin a cat. On his return, Mike retrieved the copy that he had stored in an MoD computer. He stripped away its protection and mailed it to all of the major publishing houses. As a result of the ensuing scandal, a few sacrificial, and probably blameless, MoD heads rolled. But that wasn't enough. It became a political hey-day for the press and opposition. Eventually the big head rolled. The OBTUSE episode was portrayed as a one-man-gone-off-the-rails operation and not as a government conspiracy. A classic case of a man corrupted by power, Sternhell became a political liability. A cat in hot water, as Alan would have said. Inevitably, Sternhell resigned to spend more time with his family (though newspaper reports suggested that his family was anything but pleased at the prospect). Yet his forfeit was not enough to appease the masses. Sternhell was prosecuted and the whole government was tainted. The Prime Minister faced unending opposition taunts. 'Does the Prime Minister have the competence to appoint his Cabinet Ministers? Can the Right Honourable Gentleman assure the House, and the electorate, that he hasn't another Jack-the-Ripper amongst his ranks — or indeed, that he isn't one himself?' Attrition paid dividends at the next election, just as Alan had predicted. An unelectable opposition suddenly acquired respectability and inspired confidence. The new government did not resuscitate the OBTUSE experiment.

Mike never did save the world by exchanging secret details of weapon systems. He was distracted by something much more lucrative. His skills were recognized once the Sternhell saga became public knowledge. His exploits came to the attention of the Managing Director of Silkie Software Incorporated, who enticed and recruited him. Mike is still a computer buff but now he is respectable, highly prized, and rich.

What about the others? Trevor Beever. His reward for making the OBTUSE ruffians feel significant, even important, was the deputy head's job at a school for the bewildered — a centre for hopeless cases. Hardly a promotion, it was simply a shift from a dead-end job to a mission impossible. He isn't unhappy with the challenge, though. After all, he is an expert at spotting the faintest of light at the end of a tunnel.

The good, the bad and the ugly. Graham resisted two further attempts to deprogramme him before his parents gave up trying to instil in him a respect for a career, a steady girlfriend, status and, most important of all, money. Materialism left no impression on him. Yet ill feeling simply bounced off him. He prayed for his parents. He even said a little prayer for Sternhell, the ultimate in deprogrammers. Now Graham takes his message from door to door, town to town. With each doorbell he rings, each crowd he addresses in each city centre, he draws a little closer together God's Kingdom and the Earth. There was not much for Toni Junk to return to. No ladder was provided to escape from her particular hole so she remained in the underworld. Sometimes she gets by legitimately, sometimes not. She alternates her time between the outside, where the streets are paved with homeless girls, and the inside. But Toni's all right. She's a survivor. Rumours about Mr Uunk's role were legion, but those in the know — the Splinter Group — made no attempt to denounce him. Trevor Beever went so far as to state that the Head's alibi of ill-health forcing shore leave in Hammerfest seemed entirely plausible. In the absence of skeletons in Uunk's cupboard, the press soon lost interest in him. Even so, Mr Uunk could not be described as a survivor. His blood pressure got the better of him. He retired to spend more time with his roses. The vacant post of Headteacher at his school was filled by a certain, like-minded Mr Brown.

While Graham seeks to create Eden on Earth, Alan and Peter work merely to keep the garden tidy. On the verge of a brilliant career in earth science, Dr Peter Fallick heard the call of the spokesperson and chief executive of World Vigilantes, one Alan Splinter. Now, Peter tours the world gathering samples, analysing, interpreting — an expert in environmental science. And Alan's pressure group, snapping at the Achilles heels of the big multi-nationals, has brought a string of successful prosecutions against companies that put their own interests above the good of the ecosystem.

Roger was anything but jolly on community service. He was caught in a trap. His tasks, repeatedly painting out graffiti and striving ineffectually to stem the rising tide of litter on the streets, were so relentlessly dull that he had to seek excitement elsewhere. The excitement that made life bearable earned him more community service. He was desperate to escape the trap. But how? He had nothing else to do. Just a cycle of mindless chores, a few minutes of exhilaration, the due process of law, then more mindless chores. One day, unexpectedly, his fairy godmother turned up. It happened in a club. Cyclone Klotts versus some cocky counsellor. Relentlessly, Roger knocked the balls into the pockets and the counsellor into a cocked hat. After the game, a man with a flamboyant cigar, green suit and a heart in the right place requested the company of Klotts, community worker. In a matter of weeks, Roger was an apprentice player in the best snooker stable in the land. Now, Roger gorges himself on the thrill of competition. He's found his pot of gold and looks likely to be jolly ever after.

Mel Yonker did not find it easy in England. He requested a copy of his lost birth certificate and, with it, he applied for a passport. Then he left the country to start a new life. He was not the only one. Gail never did return home to stay. She remained faithful to Mel and went with him abroad. Despite Gail's age, her father was only too happy to encourage her departure, to have temptation removed. He funded their fresh start and, perhaps genuinely, wished them well. And where did they put down their roots? The land of trolls, rain, fjords, midnight sun, fog and intrigue. Mel took a shine to, and shines in, natural history. The admirers of his work point out that, when he examines what other naturalists have examined a hundred times before, he has the uncanny ability to observe and interpret afresh, unfettered by previous interpretations. With Gail as able assistant, Mel's studies, and the grants they bring in, eke out a living for them. Their relationship is unusual. Almost professional, it's also probably platonic. But what about living happily ever after, like Roger? Gail can neither re-live nor forget her past and Mel cannot come fully to terms with the human condition. Gail has a recurring dream — a nightmare really — in which Mel slinks away from her, finds a quiet and dark corner, transforms into his former self and enjoys a final sixty seconds of his own flesh and blood before succumbing to Earth's poison. It is, of course, a dream. Mel is physiologically incapable of such an act. What haunts Gail is the thought that he might wish for that release. Her fears will come to nothing. Mel's curiosity in the nature of the planet looks set to last a lifetime, yet so does the subtle sadness in his eyes.

Following a glowing report from his form teacher and a sympathetic testimonial from Mr Uunk, Charlton was rehabilitated into the community. Now, a Charlton Ng costs a thousand. Advertising agents pay even more for a commission. He lives and sketches on a house-boat. He's happy, almost famous, and not short of cash. He's also an occasional rock music critic for one of the music papers. A successful oddball. He keeps in touch with Gail and Mel, and promises to visit them one day — for a reunion of oddballs. An